THE METHOD

Duncan Ralston

SHADOW WORK PUBLISHING

SHADOW WORK
- publishing -

PRAISE FOR THE METHOD

"The story builds steadily and really picks up to a breakneck pace for the final third."

— *SCREAM THE HORROR MAGAZINE*

"*The Method* is one of those stories that subverts the reader's expectations again and again. You think you know where it's going? You're wrong. That's the mark of a great writer."

— JAMES NEWMAN, AUTHOR OF *ODD MAN OUT*

"Intense and full of action, this is definitely a fast-paced read."

— *HORROR NOVEL REVIEWS*

"The story keeps you guessing until the end, and it is NOT for the squeamish."

— ERIK THERME, AUTHOR OF *KEEP HER CLOSE*

ALSO BY DUNCAN RALSTON

Gristle & Bone (collection)

Salvage (novella)

Wildfire (novella)

Woom (novella)

The Method (novel)

Video Nasties (collection)

Ebenezer (novella)

Ghostland (novel)

In Every Dark Corner (collection)

Afterlife: Ghostland 2.0 (novel)

Ghostland: Infinite (novel)

Gross Out (novel)

Ghostland: Ghost Hunter Edition (omnibus)

Try Not to Die: At Ghostland w/ Mark Tullius (gameboook)

Puzzle House (novel)

Pedo Island Bloodbath (novel)

Helloween (novel)

CVLT (novel)

Contents

For Sherri,
Through it all.

When two people are under the influence of the most violent, most insane, most delusive, and most transient of passions, they are required to swear that they will remain in that excited, abnormal, and exhausting condition continuously until death do them part.

— GEORGE BERNARD SHAW

"I wanted the ideal animal to hunt," explained the general. "So I said, 'What are the attributes of an ideal quarry?' And the answer was, of course, 'It must have courage, cunning, and, above all, it must be able to reason.'"

"But no animal can reason," objected Rainsford.

"My dear fellow," said the general, "there is one that can."

— RICHARD CONNELL, "THE MOST DANGEROUS GAME"

CHAPTER 1

TRAP

"We're just going around in circles! There it is again!"

The edge in Linda's voice was sharp as razors, but Frank was immune, having heard it countless times before. That edge was part of the reason they were here, trudging around—*in circles*, he thought, *sure, maybe, likely* —in the middle of these godforsaken woods.

Not that he didn't accept a good share of the blame for getting the two of them to this place. His signature was on the contract right beside hers, after all.

"There what is?"

"*That*. It's the same tree we saw earlier."

"It's not the same tree," he grumbled, although he knew saying it would only piss her off more. She was always in charge of the maps because she'd always been better with directions. Frank, who would do the driving, was a creature of instinct. With no time restrictions, he would gladly go where the road took him.

"It's the *same fucking tree*," she said, on the verge of growling as she stomped up alongside him in her ergonomic walking shoes. "Look! That's the same knot that looks like a vagina with the same initials carved into it!"

Frank couldn't help but laugh, even though he knew it would aggravate her. But he saw she was right. Engraved in the tree, below what looked more like a weeping gash to him, were the initials **HK + JD**.

He was still laughing as he stepped on something hard that shifted beneath his shoe. His laugh became a yelp of surprise a split second before the pain struck his calf like a snakebite.

Except it wasn't a snake. He'd heard a sharp *click*. A rusty squawk of metal. The crunch of bone.

Frank dropped to his knees and the pain followed him down, metal grinding against bone like nails down a chalkboard.

"What the hell, Frank?" Linda turned, flashing with anger. When she saw what had happened, her eyes went wide.

The agony swelled up his calf and down into his shoe like a swarm of fire ants. Screaming, he rolled back on his buttocks, scrabbling at the metal jaws of the bear trap.

"Stop moving!" Linda dropped to her haunches beside him and groaned, her eyes preceding her head as she turned away in disgust.

It was far worse than he thought, if such a thing was possible.

He didn't want to look. He *had* to.

The thick, rusty teeth had torn into his calf. The wounds gaped on both sides of his leg, red muscle and yellow fatty tissue exposed. Blood had already soaked the rolled-down white tube sock like a nosebleed handkerchief.

In fevered glimpses it was difficult to tell if the bone beneath was broken or merely fractured. Pain and adrenaline came in waves to the drumming of his heart, his vision alternating from gray to Kodachrome bright, each wave threatening to pull him under.

Need a tetanus shot, he thought.

"Okay, everything's gonna be all right," Linda said, her eyes still wide with fear as she lied. Her trembling hands hovered over the trap. She was too worried to touch it for fear she'd make it worse. "Just breathe, honey. *Breathe*."

Even through the mind-shattering pain, he noticed she'd called him *honey*. Was it loving? Nurturing? Or simply professional, like an ER nurse or a waitress? He couldn't tell. Every phrase between them these days was a secret code the other was never meant to decipher. Every look loaded with hidden meaning.

He let out a hiss and sucked in a shivering breath. The trees seemed to close in around him, mirroring the trap they'd been caught in for hours, for *years*, circling them like carrion birds, spiraling ever closer to the pain at its center.

To the metal jaws.

To this sharp-edged metaphor of their imploding relationship.

He held his wife's gaze, forcing a smile. Jaw quivering. Teeth chattering. Tears burning his cheeks. He tasted them from the corners of his lips.

He thought, *Is this where it all ends?*

Linda reached for his sneaker. "I'm gonna take off your shoe, okay?"

"What... for?" he breathed.

"Because when I pry this thing open, I want you to yank your foot out as fast as you can, okay?"

Frank nodded, his whole body shaking as he blinked away sweat from his eyes. He lost control of his muscles during another wave of pain, and his upper body swayed toward the ground. He struggled to remain conscious, to hold himself upright.

As delicately as possible, Linda untied his shoe. She looked up to gauge his reaction, to see if she was hurting him too much with just this tender movement.

She thought, *Did I give up on him too soon?*

The shoe slipped off his heel, and she cast it aside urgently. The scattering of dead leaves where it landed made a distinct metallic clink.

Linda scowled in the direction of the sound.

Frank followed her concerned gaze and saw nothing.

She grasped the loop of rusted chain fastened to the trap.

Frank gritted his teeth in agony as she tugged on it, pulling it up from the ground. He wanted to tell her to stop, but her determined look made him think better of it. Her pulling exposed more and more rusty dirt-clodded links, previously hidden beneath leaves and roots and earth, snaking off toward the big tree with the initials carved in its bark.

"What the hell...?" she said.

Frank saw the chain tied around the base of the tree and wondered how they hadn't noticed it the first time around.

"This wasn't there before."

"Someone just put it there in the twenty minutes since we last came around?" He didn't want to start another argument, but the pain made him reckless, and so often now, they argued just for the sake of it. "That makes no sense, Linda."

"It *wasn't there*, I swear." She shook the chain in frustration, causing another searing wave to travel up his leg and settle in his groin.

"What does it *matter*?" he growled in agony.

Linda's gaze snapped toward him, and all her anger instantly evaporated. "You're right." She lowered the chain gently to the ground. "It doesn't. Let's get this thing off you, okay?"

"Okay."

Frank thought, *Is it too late to take it all back? The arguments? The complaints? The name-calling?*

She grasped the jaws, her fingers streaking with his blood. "On the count of three, okay?"

He nodded eagerly, tensing against the impending pain.

"One..." Her voice hesitant, her gaze unsure.

They both thought, *Can't we just start over?*

"...Two." More assuredly now, determination returned to her warm brown eyes.

They thought, *Can't we go back to what it was like before?*

"... Three!"

Her muscles strained as she pried open the jaws, tearing them free from the meat of his calf. Blood-slicked fingers slipping, her fingernails tore on clumps of rust and the trap clamped down harder than before, juddering against naked bone.

Frank's howl of agony sent a host of sparrows fluttering from the branches of a nearby aspen. In the silence that followed, they both heard the dogs, and Frank wondered, *Was Linda right about the chain?*

CHAPTER 2

IT'S NOT A CULT

Pain seized Linda's left calf, and she might have cried out if not for the men above and below her.

She'd climbed above the trees just fine but had suddenly found herself forty or fifty feet above the rocky ground without a foothold and nothing within reach of her straining hands.

In an extremely risky dynamic leap, she'd launched herself too far from any previous holds, the crimp she held in both hands barely deep enough for her fingers to maintain their precarious grip. Her strained leg quivered as she scoured the rock for somewhere to place the other.

With her friend Trevor belaying, she could easily have given up, called "Falling!" and just let go, hanging in space until he lowered her down. But Frank had assured her he wasn't up to the climb and that she wasn't either. As much as she wanted to prove her husband wrong, she also wanted to prove to herself how far she'd come since the Year From Hell.

The trouble was Dillon and Trevor weren't just experienced climbers, they also appeared to be in the best shape of their lives. Dillon was already nearing the top of the rock, climbing like a sexy little gecko on methamphetamines despite baby Clayton snuggled in a papoose on her back.

Trevor leisurely picked holds and glided languidly from one to the next in a semi-doped haze.

"So she cheated on me," he shouted down at Linda, oblivious to her pain. "Do you believe that?"

Linda knew he expected a reply, so she hummed in disbelief, even though she could actually believe it. She'd known Trevor far longer than Dillon had. They'd even dated briefly in college, back when his ego could have received its own honorary PhD. He'd mellowed since then apparently, but the last time the four of them had gotten together, Dillon and Trevor had gotten into a huge fight about some slight he'd committed, and Dillon had stormed off. Now that Linda and Frank were having trouble, it seemed like Trevor and Dillon were suddenly the perfect couple.

"You all right up there?" Frank called up from a good ten feet below, looking up between her legs. He probably noticed her twitching. His concern, tinged with an obvious "I told you so" edge, pissed her off, but at least he was good enough not to call attention to it.

"I'm *fine*," she grunted.

"There's a hold right there." He let go of his own hold to point to a crimp she hadn't noticed.

"That's a crozzler," Trevor said, looking down through rainbow-tinted sunglasses. "Crumbled under my foot. Careful there."

"Thanks," she said.

Frank mumbled something under his breath.

"What's that?" Linda asked, unwilling or unable to just let it go.

"I said, 'You're welcome.'"

If he had said it, he'd done so in a snarky tone. She let it go and felt the crimp for give. It seemed solid enough. Trevor must have crumbled off a layer of loose rock.

She relaxed her leg, putting more weight on the other. The cramp in her calf lessened to a dull throb, and she rotated her shoulders one at a time, relishing the crackle in her joints.

Of course, now that she was safe, the pressure on her bladder returned. She'd have to pee relatively soon. She just hoped she could make it to the top of the cliff first.

"So yeah, she cheated on me with three other guys," Trevor continued. "Not at the same time. But I deserved it, you know? I was a prick. Took her for granted," he said, pronouncing it like *granite.*

"And you forgave her?" Frank said, forgiving the mispronunciation.

"Oh yeah. We got to the root of the problem just last week. But we worked through it, didn't we, Dee?"

Instead of answering, Dillon shouted, "Rock!"

Trevor jerked his head back just in time. A large chunk of slate shot through the space he'd left. It struck the cliff face a few feet above Frank, smashing into smaller bits that rattled on his helmet and rolled off his shoulders.

"Shit!" he cried out.

"Guess who didn't want to wear a helmet," Linda mocked.

Trevor flashed down a toothy smile that would have melted her like butter in their college days. "Oh, you gotta wear a helmet, bro. One hundred and ten percent."

Frank scowled up at Linda. She gave him a big, self-satisfied grin.

If asked, she could have pinpointed the exact moment hers and Frank's relationship had become like navigating a barbed wire fence. The fact that the root of their problem wasn't entirely either of their faults had turned their marriage following their Year From Hell into a battle of wills, neither of them willing to admit their share of the blame. Both of them wore their guilt on their faces like flashing road signs.

It could be that they'd always been hurtling toward the edge of a metaphorical cliff like *Thelma and Louise.* Their favorite fictional couples had all been contentious: Maddie and David from *Moonlighting,* Sam and Dianne from *Cheers* (although Frank preferred Sam and Rebecca—*of course* he preferred the hot one over the one with brains), Buttercup and Westley from *The Princess Bride*. When she was young, Mr. and Mrs. Twit had been her favorite storybook characters. Frank, believing himself a special child merely lacking in parental nurturing, had preferred Charlie Bucket.

There'd been an element of teasing and toying to their relationship from the very beginning, of push and pull. They'd met at a college basketball game rooting for rival teams, enrolled in rival schools.

Frank had picked her up with a classic technique of pointing out how great she would look "if not for that stupid hat," in reference to the team cap she'd been wearing. In retrospect, it likely wouldn't have worked on her if she and Trevor hadn't had their huge public breakup a few weeks prior, but when she'd told Frank it was a terrible pickup line, he'd laughed and admitted to it.

"So let's trade," he'd said.

"Trade? *Caps?*"

"Yeah, why not? What's the worst that could happen?"

She'd given him a suspicious look. "Head lice?"

He'd laughed and she'd loved it immediately. It was uproarious, infectious. Not like these days, when he usually just uttered a sharp and sardonic "*ha*" rather than dare to really let go.

"I don't have lice," he'd assured her. He'd taken off his cap and held it out for her to inspect. The band had been sweaty but it appeared to be free of bugs. "What, are you afraid they'll catch us on the JumboTron and all your friends'll disown you for rooting for the bad guys?"

"Oh, come on. You're not bad guys." She'd smirked, being playful.

Frank had grinned. "*Some* of us are..."

He'd played the bad boy during those first few weeks of courting, but he just hadn't had it in him. Linda had seen the nice Canadian boy in him from the very beginning. Her breakup with Trevor, a true bad boy back then, had practically thrust polar opposite Frank Moffat into her bed.

Whether it was ironic or inevitable that she had been the one to end up filling the bad guy role after the Year From Hell, Linda wasn't sure, and she didn't want to think too deeply into it.

She reached up for a bucket hold far above her head, pushing with both feet. The tips of her fingers scrabbled against it. Straining, her cramped leg buckling, she thrust upward with all of her remaining strength and slipped her hand into the groove.

"Nice one," Frank said, without a trace of his usual sarcasm.

Trevor was pretty, but Frank was unconventionally handsome and far more intelligent. Where Trevor had provided excitement and spontaneity both in bed and elsewhere, Frank had a better sense of humor, wit, and at one point, romance as well. They were comparable when it came to their sexual appetites and prowess, although Trevor was slightly more inclined toward self-gratification.

Frank and Linda had dated for six years and had been married for three. She'd gotten sick a few months after the honeymoon.

But she wouldn't think about that. Not here, clinging to the edge of death. Not now, with Trevor above her and Frank below.

"How'd you do it?" Frank asked.

For a moment, Linda didn't know who or even what he was asking. Then she remembered Trevor's admission. Dillon cheating with multiple men. Him forgiving her. As far as Linda knew, there had been no such transgressions in hers and Frank's own relationship.

If only it was that simple, she thought.

She reached for a hold and pulled herself up.

Trevor grunted as he wedged himself into a ledge just wide enough to rest a single butt cheek. He sat with his shoulder and hip against the rock, breathing evenly, and brought out a joint from his fanny pack. He twisted the precise flame of a butane lighter around its tip, taking a luxuriant drag.

Linda noticed bruises on his legs and arms she hadn't spotted before. Climbing injuries, she supposed, or from any number of extreme sports he and Dillon participated in. But the gash on his right forearm looked nasty, like it had only recently been infected. Multiple stitches stood like black barbs around the wound.

Trevor held the smoke in for a moment. Exhaling, he said, "If I told you, I'd have to kill you."

"Ha!" Frank said. It wasn't a laugh, merely an acknowledgment that a joke had been made. Never that laugh like he used to, like she'd loved. "Seriously, though."

Despite the buildup he'd provided, Trevor seemed hesitant to tell them. Working his jaw like a man chewing on a secret, he raised his sunglasses to conceal a sudden look of anxiety, or fright. "You know what? Forget I said anything. It's not all that important."

It seemed unlike Trevor to overshare and then take it back, as if he worried about what she and Frank might think of him. That haunted look in his eyes concerned Linda, especially when she knew the weed should have mellowed him out.

"Go on and tell 'em, hon!" Dillon called down. They all looked up to see her on her hands and knees at the top of the climb. Her slim, muscular body silhouetted by the sun, she waved down cheerily.

"You guys sure you want to know?"

"It's The Method!" Dillon shouted. "Now come on, you gumbies! Catch up!" she said before laughing and disappearing behind the rock.

"'Gumbies,'" Trevor sputtered, exhaling a lungful of smoke. "Ch'yeah, right."

"What's The Method?" Frank asked. More than just a little curious, Linda noted. "Is that like meditation? Yoga, or something?"

Trevor shook his head and frowned. "Nah. It's, uh...it's

more like unconventional therapy. Cutting edge stuff." He uttered a seemingly anxious chuckle, and his expression darkened. "Wait, you two aren't...?"

"*No*," both Frank and Linda said, all too quickly.

"We're good," Frank added. "I'm just curious."

"He's just curious," Linda agreed, not about to open up about their relationship troubles on the side of a rock with Trevor, Dillon, and baby Clay.

"Good. You two were always my rock. If you guys broke up...shit, there's no hope for any of us, is there, Dee?"

"Nope!" Dillon shouted down from the edge.

Linda had never thought something Trevor would say could move her close to tears, but here she was, fighting them back. She felt Frank looking at her and knew that if he caught her eye, she wouldn't be able to stop them from falling.

"Friends of ours, though," Frank said. "Couple friends. They're having trouble. Can't seem to stop fighting. Almost like they enjoy it, but they're pretty sure neither of them does. Like it's a full-contact sport."

Trevor nodded thoughtfully, holding the smoke in his lungs. "Well, I'll give you the info. You can pass it along to them." He looked from Frank to Linda and raised his eyebrows. "Coolio?"

Linda managed a look in Frank's general direction. He nodded.

"Coolio," she said.

LINDA CAME BACK from squatting in the bushes to where the rest of them sat on the top of the rock, eating the food they'd packed, looking out over a huge expanse of brilliant green treetops of the Enchantments. She'd had to pee a lot more frequently since the surgery. Her frequent urination since the Year From Hell was one of the reasons Frank had thought coming out here wasn't such a good idea.

Dillon passed a tall boy from the cooler to Trevor. He finished his mouthful of sausage, blew foam off the rim, and drank greedily before handing it back. Dillon took a sip too, mindful of baby Clay's fuzzy little head as he breastfed, and burped.

Everyone chuckled. The atmosphere was amiable, the strange moment they'd had on the cliff face apparently behind them. Linda sat on a rock a little ways behind him, still distant. Frank smiled back at her, and she gave him a half-hearted smile in return. He wondered if she was still angry. When he'd first met Linda he'd been instantly attracted to her, but it had been her playful, spitfire attitude that had won him over. It seemed like since her recovery that attitude was a constant, and Lin was quick to anger all the time. He felt like she was always setting little situational and conversational booby traps for him, and he would only discover them once they'd already sprung on him.

Frank noticed the gash on Trevor's forearm under a tattoo of a rose dripping blood. "That's a nasty cut. All those bruises. What happened to you two?"

Trevor gave Dillon a startled look. He swallowed a mouthful of food. "Motorcycle accident."

Dillon smiled thinly. "You should see the bruise on my thigh. Cracked a few ribs too."

"You should be more careful now that you've got Clay to think about," Linda said. "I'm surprised you brought him along, actually."

Frank agreed but never would have said questioned someone's parenting aloud.

"Dee won't let him out of her sight," Trevor said, smiling at his wife and child. "Not since . . ." Again his expression darkened. ". . . not since the accident."

"*Trev*," Dillon said, as if to draw him out of his mood.

"That's why we tried The Method," Trevor said. "For my little Clayman." He took the baby's chubby foot between his thumb and forefinger and gave it a little jiggle. "And it worked. One hundred and ten percent."

"Unconventional therapy," Frank said.

Trevor smiled, all teeth. "*Exactly*."

"How does it work?"

"It's a weekend thing," Dillon said. "A private lodge in the woods. They only take two couples at a time so they can give you personal treatment."

Baby Clay clawed at her breast with a tiny hand, and she smiled down at him. In an unintended glimpse, Frank noticed three oblong bruises below her clavicle that looked almost like fingermarks.

"But what is it, exactly?" Linda wondered. "It's not religious, is it?"

Trevor and Dillon shared a knowing smile. "It's definitely not religious," he said.

"But by the end of the weekend," Dillon added, "it's like a spiritual awakening, you guys. It's..." She nodded ecstatically. "...*pretty intense*."

"Shit, you two know how clouded I used to be." Trevor chewed while he spoke. "How... just fucking *out of touch* I was. After that weekend, after we met the doctor..." Again they shared a knowing look. "I see what matters with focal-point clarity. *We* see it. Everything makes sense now." He chuckled, looking at everyone. "It probably sounds crazy to you guys."

"All that matters is that it makes sense to you," Linda said, smiling back at Frank.

He nodded, although he wasn't sure he agreed, for some reason feeling like he was being sold on a time-share. After no contact for several years—neither Trevor nor Dillon had wished Lin as little as a "get well" when she'd been in the hospital—Dillon had emailed out of the blue asking if they'd be interested in a weekend climbing expedition. Frank had agreed reluctantly, as it seemed Linda had wanted to prove herself physically fit again. Linda's active lifestyle had been one of the first things that had attracted him about her. But hearing these two go on about this "method," it sounded like Trevor and Dillon might have gotten themselves into a cult.

"It's not a cult, if that's what you're thinking," Trevor said.

"I wasn't thinking that," Frank lied.

"It's just...it's a very intense experience, isn't it, Dee?"

Baby Clay laughed at her breast. "Clay seems to think so!" she said, and they all laughed with her.

"Is it expensive?" Linda asked.

Gotta be cheaper than a divorce, Frank thought. *And less nasty.*

"Well, it ain't cheap," Trevor answered. "But how can you put a price on love, right?"

Dillon leaned into his shoulder. "Such a big softie."

Trevor kissed the top of her head. "That's not what you said last night, babe." He laughed and everyone joined him, even Frank, who didn't find it particularly funny.

"But seriously, it's the best decision we ever made, right, Dee?"

She smiled up at him from under his chin, and baby Clay gurgled at her breast.

Trevor drew an arm around them, his perfect family.

Frank had never thought he'd see the day, but he had to admit it did seem like their relationship had gone through a massive transformation, cult or not. It had *matured*. Whether that was more down to the arrival of their new family member or a single weekend's getaway at therapy camp, he couldn't say.

But if Linda was willing to try it, he supposed this "method" thing couldn't hurt.

Chapter 3

Authority

S ilence drew out between Frank and Linda as he drove the wide mountain road, looking for the turnoff. Linda wondered if it was as uncomfortable for him as it was for her, but she wasn't about to ask. Instead, she pretended to study directions on her cell phone.

In the week following their climb with Trevor and Dillon, when Frank had blurted out that he wanted to try this "method" and she'd agreed to it, they hadn't argued much. Home life had been civil for the most part. Part of her suspected Frank's reason for suggesting the trip was so he couldn't be seen as the bad guy when their marriage did eventually—inevitably—disintegrate.

He was trying though, and she couldn't fault him for it. If she didn't at least meet him halfway, she'd ultimately be responsible for the death of their marriage, or be burdened by the weight of that guilt, even if she wasn't.

She'd decided not to ruin his gesture by questioning his motives. She let him book the trip, let him put the hefty down payment on their joint credit account and provide Lone Loon Lodge with the make, model and plate number of their hatchback and the names of their next of kin in case of emergency. They'd both undergone physicals and had their physicians fax the results to Lone Loon Lodge, c/o Dr. Kaspar.

The little blue arrow on her GPS blinked for them to take a right at the next turn, and she instructed Frank to do so.

"Thanks." He turned to her briefly. The smile didn't reach his eyes. "How 'bout some music, huh?"

He thumbed on the radio. Fleetwood Mac's "The Chain" came on in the middle of the chorus, *"never break the chain..."*

"Please, God, no," Linda said, rolling her eyes in despair.

"I like that song." He shrugged and changed the station.

A pleasant melody for strings filled the silence. She recognized it but couldn't name either song or composer. She allowed the music to wash over her, soothing her nerves. What was there to be nervous about?

Nine years, that's what, she thought. *This weekend will make us or break us, and honestly, I'm not even sure which I'd prefer.*

If the thought hadn't already spoiled her moment of peace, the police car up ahead with bubble lights flashing did the trick.

Both Frank and Linda glanced at the speedometer.

"What's the speed limit here?" he said.

"Fifty-five, last I saw."

"Me too." He maintained his speed. They passed the cop at two below the limit.

Frank let out a sigh of relief, cut short when the siren blipped behind them. He bristled, frowning at the rearview mirror. "Shit. What does he want?"

"Better pull over."

"What, you think I'm gonna lead him on a high-speed chase?" He flicked on the blinker with a shaky hand and slowed the car.

"Stay calm, okay? It's probably something minor."

Frank gave her a dubious look. "Lin, can you do me a favor?"

"What?" She didn't mean for it to sound aggressive, but it did.

"I've got weed in my pocket."

"Oh, Jesus, Frank! I thought you were gonna take this weekend seriously!"

"I *am* taking it seriously. It's a just in case. Can you just...can you just hide it or get rid of it?"

Linda shook her head in aggravation as Frank began to pull over into the soft shoulder. The hatchback came to a stop, and she gave a faux-casual look out the back window, digging into the front pocket of his jeans.

"That's not it," he teased.

"Do really think now is the time to make jokes like that? Where did you even get this stuff, anyway?"

"Trevor hit me up. He said it's good for pain."

"What pain?"

"My knees were shitty after the climb." He grinned and zipped down the window. "It's a joint for my joints."

"Jesus," she said again, watching the officer leave his patrol car and approach. He was huge in his khaki sheriff's department uniform, even in the side mirror. She slipped the bag of weed out of Frank's pocket and tucked it under the seat, just hoping Frank wouldn't say something stupid and give the cop cause to search the car.

"Morning, Officer." Frank gave the trooper an overly cheery wave. He'd always acted weird with police, more so when he had something to hide. The quirk wouldn't have been so odd if his dad wasn't a retired officer.

"Sir, please keep your hands on the wheel."

The cop leaned down toward the car. Frank jerked his head back at the size of him in the window.

"Is there a problem?" Linda leaned down to get a look at the man. "We were driving the speed limit."

"No problem, ma'am," the cop said. With his mustache and hair slicked to the side, he reminded Linda of Frank's dad. "Unless you're looking for trouble."

"Why would we be looking for trouble, Officer?" Frank asked.

The cop tapped the shield on his lapel. "*Sheriff*, not Officer."

"Sorry..."

"Don't be sorry, just don't do it again."

The sun glimmered off his sunglasses. It troubled her, not being able to see where he was looking. Could he see the weed sticking out from under the seat?

"You passed by my patrol car back there and didn't slow down. Do you realize that's against the law?"

"I..." Frank looked confused. "But you were just parked there."

"When an emergency vehicle is parked with its lights flashing," the sheriff's voice rose in aggravation, "it's the law to slow down. Now since this is only a two-lane highway, I can't expect..."

"Off..." He caught himself. "*Sheriff*, with all due respect, that's a bullshit law."

Linda shot a look at the back of her husband's head. She'd always known about his problems with authority, with *male* authority figures in particular, but she hadn't expected him to be so reckless about it.

"*Frank*," she pleaded.

"Excuse me?" the sheriff said.

Frank turned to her with anger in his eyes, and something else she couldn't quite place. He looked like a little boy who'd been picked on, unable to take any more abuse. "No, Linda, it's a bullshit law. He didn't have anyone pulled over, there was no emergency, as far as I could see..."

Over Frank's shoulder, she saw the sheriff's jaw tighten and his chest expand as his thick fingers gripped the windowsill. He made himself larger, more imposing. He was losing his patience, readying to strike back.

"Sir, step out of the car please."

"Officer, this is..."

"*Sheriff*." The cop rested a hand on the .9mm Glock in his belt holster. "And I am not gonna ask you again."

Frank rolled his eyes at his own reflection in the rearview and opened the door.

The cop stepped aside to give him room, boots clomping. Frank threw a wary glance at Linda as he climbed out. From then on, she could only see their torsos.

"Put your hands on the car, please."

"This is ridiculous," Frank said. His hands thumped down on the roof, and the cop began to pat him down. "I didn't *do* anything. I know my rights. My father's a retired cop."

"Sir, I would advise you to stop talking."

As the sheriff's hands neared Frank's crotch, Frank danced away from him, pressing his groin against the window. "*Ow! What the hell?*"

The cop's hand returned to his sidearm. "*Don't move.*"

Linda willed Frank to listen. To his credit, he immediately put his hands back on the car. "You just jabbed me with something."

"I didn't jab you with anything."

"I *felt* it, man," Frank said. "I'm not making it up."

"Sir, I'm frisking you. It's called frisking. Now don't move again, or I'll be forced to take you into custody."

"All right," Frank said. "Okay."

The sheriff pushed Frank's legs apart with a knee and resumed patting him down. "Sir, what is this?"

"I can't tell what you're touching."

The cop reached into Frank's front pocket, where he'd kept the weed. Linda hoped the baggie hadn't opened and the cop wasn't feeling bits of dried leaf with the tips of his fingers at the bottom of the pocket.

The sheriff removed his hand, holding up Frank's pocketknife.

"What have we got here? A concealed weapon?"

"That doesn't meet the requirements..."

"*Shut up!*"

He pulled out the knife blade with a long thumbnail, its edge glinting in the sun as he examined it. Linda heard him snap it closed. "All right, looks like you're clean." He sounded disappointed. Stepping back, he handed Frank the knife. "You're free to go."

Frank took it and opened the door. He got in with a sulk, slipped the knife into his pocket, and placed his hands on the wheel at ten and two.

The sheriff leaned down with a grim smile. "Next time you see an emergency vehicle with its lights flashing, what are you gonna do?"

"Pull over," Frank said through gritted teeth.

The cop leaned in further, cocking an ear. "What's that? I didn't hear you."

"Pull over, *sir*," Frank spat.

"It's not just the right thing to do, it's also the law." The cop patted the roof, causing Frank to startle. "You have a nice day now."

"You too, sir," Linda called out as the cop rose and stepped back from the car.

Frank said nothing, looking dead ahead as he zipped up the window.

Linda waited for the sheriff to return to his patrol car and whispered, "What the fuck was that, Frank?"

"You know he's just filling a quota..."

"You didn't have to challenge him. You take the ticket and fight it in court."

"You *saw* there was no one there but him." He turned, his lower lip quivering. She could tell he was only gripping the wheel so tightly to keep his hands from shaking. "You know he was waiting for someone like us to drive by just so he could harass us!"

"You don't know that."

"It's what they *do*, Linda. They get off on it."

The cruiser crawled by. The sheriff tapped a finger to his temple and pointed it in their direction.

"Yeah, yeah, fuck you, dude."

"The police aren't your enemy, Frank. It's their job to protect us."

"You would think that. You didn't grow up with a cop for a dad."

"This isn't about your father, Frank. *You* screwed up. You could have gotten us *arrested*. Why can't you admit that?"

Frank sneered. "Maybe I should just turn the car around."

"The down payment is nonrefundable."

"It's a thousand bucks. I'll eat the cost."

"You wanted to do this, Frank. This was your idea."

"Because I thought you wanted it, okay?"

Oh finally, the penny drops, she thought.

"If I'd known how you really feel about me—"

"This weekend isn't about *you*, Frank. It's about us. *Us.* This fucking marriage." She jabbed a finger at her wedding ring.

"You're *making* it about me. Right now. Okay, so maybe I fucked up, but you didn't have to bite my head off. That asshole cop stuck me with something..." He rubbed his hip. "It still hurts. You yelling at me, implying it's all my fault, isn't fucking helping!"

Linda stewed, desperate to defend herself, aware that if she said anymore, it would further cement his opinion. So much for meeting him halfway. It couldn't hurt to placate him, to let go of a little control.

But I'm not fucking apologizing, she thought. *If that's what he expects, he's in for a rude awakening...*

"Forget it," she said. "Let's just...let's just go."

Frank sat a moment, catching his breath. "Forward or back?"

"Forward. To the retreat. We paid for it, we're gonna do it."

Frank put the car into drive and pulled out from the soft shoulder. "Whether it kills us or not," he muttered with a derisive chuckle.

CHAPTER 4
—————

TRUE / FALSE

Frank stepped up to the slab of live edge wood that served as the concierge desk and dinged the service bell. He peered around the large cathedral-ceiling lobby with its second-floor loft, everything glossy wood and clean stone. The lobby smelled like Pine Sol and hot chocolate, reminding him of Christmas at Grandma Moffat's.

"I guess nobody's home." He turned to Linda, who stood in near silhouette against bay windows two stories tall, baggage in both hands.

"Patience is a virtue."

"So is free Wi-Fi." He looked at his cell phone. "I can't even get a tower signal. Why don't you put the bags down?"

"When we get upstairs."

"Well, at least let me carry one."

"I've got them."

Frank sighed and rang the bell again.

"I'll be right there!" a man called from the open doorway beyond the desk.

Frank took a red striped mint from the dish beside the bell, twisted it open, and popped it in his mouth. A moment later, a muscular Asian man emerged from the back in a black t-shirt two sizes too small, showing off the tattoos on his biceps.

"You must be the Moffats." He smiled. "I'm Alex Xiang, the concierge. I'll take you to your rooms."

"Rooms?" Linda asked, emphasizing the plural.

"That's right." Alex stepped around the desk and met them with a bright smile. "Here at Lone Loon Lake, all of our guests have private accommodations."

"It's part of The Method," Frank said. "Right?"

"We just like to make sure our guests are comfortable." The concierge held a hand out to Linda. "May I take your bags?"

She handed the one not containing her toiletries and underwear, Frank noted. Even still, she hadn't hesitated for a moment.

Do you blame her? he thought. *Look at the guy. He looks like the cover of a romance novel. You should just be glad she didn't swoon into his rippling chest muscles.*

Alex lifted her heavy luggage to hip level with a pleasant smile. "Follow me, please."

Right, so my wife can get a good view of your rock-solid buns. Nice try, pal.

Frank picked up his bags and hurried to slip in between them. Linda gave him a quizzical look to which he grinned.

At the stairs, Alex turned back to see that they were following and smiled again. "Dinner is at six. Breakfast from eight to ten. Lunch is served from noon to two. All meals are provided as a part of your treatment package." He began up the stairs. Frank and Linda followed.

Yup. Rock solid.

"You'll find fresh towels in the bathrooms as well as an array of complementary toiletries."

"Ooh," Frank said with a sarcastic edge.

Linda bumped his leg with her remaining suitcase. He turned back with a grin.

"You'll also find a bottle of Dr. Kaspar's homemade wine from his very own vineyard in the south of France. It's a wonderful, fragrant Bordeaux I'm sure you'll both fall in love with."

"That sounds to die for," Linda said.

Frank had never heard Linda utter the phrase "to die for" in his life and bit the inside of his cheek to keep from laughing.

"On your way in, you may have seen the lake." Alex reached the second-floor loft. "The water is...well, it's brisk this time of year, but we do encourage you to take a dip. We also have canoes and kayaks, should you want to take them out. I'd suggest heading out right before dusk. Once the loons start calling and the sun sets over the trees, it really is an experience."

"It sounds lovely," Linda said.

"There's no elevator? No chair lift?" Frank asked.

"Elevator?"

"Frank's an accessibility advisor."

"Oh, that's interesting. The woods aren't exactly the best place for a wheelchair, are they?"

"You make a good point, Alex. In a perfect world, everything would be accessible to everyone. That's how I feel."

"That's a nice sentiment, Mr. Moffat." Alex stopped in front of a door and set Linda's bag down. "Here's your room, Mrs. Moffat." He grabbed the keyring on his belt, selected one, and unlocked the door. He stepped aside with a smile to usher her in.

"Call me Linda, please." Stepping across the threshold, she set down her remaining suitcase and began patting her pockets dramatically. Frank knew this game. She played it just as effectively while passing homeless people in the street. "I don't, uh..."

Alex held up a hand. "Don't trouble yourself, Linda, please. Lone Loon Lodge isn't a conventional hotel. It's a retreat. Any gratuities are included in the initial fee. Even if I was allowed, I wouldn't accept a tip."

"Thank you again," she said.

Frank recognized the smile she gave Alex as her "eager to be left alone" smile.

"You're quite welcome." Before she could close the door,

Alex placed his left red Converse shoe in its path. "One last thing: I'll need to take your cell phone."

"What?" Frank asked.

The concierge gave him an ingratiating smile. "It's our policy. If you read through the contracts we sent you..."

"I don't remember anything about cell phones."

"It's the first article on page six: 'Cell phones are to be relinquished to the Examiners upon arrival.'"

"But why?" Linda asked sullenly, always quick to challenge the rules when they applied to her.

"Cell phones distract us from people. And from ourselves." Alex gave them a sympathetic look. "Trust me, after a few hours here, you'll forget you ever had one."

Frank doubted it. Linda had her phone surgically attached to her hand, constantly checking it for anything work related. She'd only left it behind during their climbing expedition due to Trevor's badgering, and as soon as they'd returned to the car, she'd had to respond to two emails and a phone call.

The entire long weekend without her phone would be absolute torture for her.

Frank, on the other hand, would gladly give up his phone. The only thing he would even consider using it for out here would be for directions, maybe snapping a few photos. Without a tower signal, he didn't expect the GPS would function, and the camera wasn't all that great.

Linda handed over her phone grudgingly. Alex slipped it into the back pocket of his black jeans. Frank gave her a sympathetic shrug she didn't appear to trust.

"Mr. Moffat?" Alex had already moved on. "Come with me, please."

"See you later," Frank said with a small wave.

"Yup."

Alex turned a corner, and Frank followed deeper into the hotel.

"This place is pretty big, huh?"

"You should see Dr. Kaspar's chateau," Alex said. "Sixteen rooms, eight baths... it's hard to believe when his parents fled from Austria they had nothing but the clothes on their backs."

"They were...?"

"Not in the internment camps, no. They left before all that started. His father was a psychoanalyst. Dr. Kaspar said his father saw the change coming like storm clouds descending over the Alps."

"Will we be seeing Dr. Kaspar today?"

"He'll be out of pocket until this evening. He's expected to arrive for dinner though."

"Arrive?"

"Dr. Kaspar's been conducting an experiment at Yale." Alex stopped in front of a door. "And here's your room."

Frank set his bags down as Alex unlocked the door. "That was a big deal for my wife. For Linda. Giving up her phone like that." He reached into his pocket and handed over his own. "I barely use mine."

"Someday these things will do everything but wipe," Alex said. He took the phone and tucked it into the second back pocket.

"Ha. Yeah, probably." Frank picked up his bags and carried them into the room. "So what's the deal with this place? Man to man."

"Man to man?" Alex looked off down the hall as if he were afraid someone might be listening in. "When I first came here, I was on the verge of divorce."

"And now?"

"I'm a widower."

Frank let out a surprised laugh. "Sorry," he said hastily. "I didn't mean..."

"It was a long time ago." Alex put a hand on Frank's shoulder as if he were the bereaved one. "Another life."

"Hmm."

"We think we can only take so much pain." Alex let his hand fall to his side. "That's what we think. But the well always runs deeper."

"That's... that's pretty deep." Frank noticed he'd just repeated Alex's sentiment and chuckled awkwardly.

"Want some free advice, Mr. Moffat? This weekend will make you or break you. Fight for what you love. If it's worth it, you'll know."

ALREADY SLIGHTLY ON edge without her phone, Linda stood looking out the large window at an open field leading into the woods when a knock startled her. She turned to see a sheet of paper slip under her door.

Linda crossed to it, opened the door, and peered out into the hall as a small woman in a white uniform turned into the next corridor. Peering over the landing, she got a decent peek at their host's muscular glutes down in the lobby as he bent to access a lockbox, but she was much more interested in the cell phone he placed inside. He closed it and locked it with a number code.

The big front doors swung open, and a well-dressed couple strode through the front doors.

"We have luggage," the tall, lithe woman with jet-black hair and pale, freckled skin said as she slipped out of her fur coat. The man, equally tall and dark-skinned with a buzz cut, puffed on a cigar.

"I'm sorry, sir, you can't smoke that in here," Alex told him.

The woman looked toward the loft and caught Linda's eye. Both men followed her gaze, and Linda retreated to her room and slammed the door. She fell back against it with her heart racing, as if she'd been caught spying on someone having sex.

Her gaze fell on the slip of paper. It had her name at the top.

"'Individual assessment,'" she read as she picked it up off the floor. "'For evaluation purposes use only. Will not be shared with other participants of Dr. Kaspar's Method.'"

Linda had an affinity for quizzes and questionnaires, and enjoyed speaking about herself and showing off her knowledge. Pride wasn't something to be ashamed of in her family. Frank's false modesty, learned behavior from his father, had begun to grate on her nerves recently.

She smiled to herself and read the first question aloud. "'I often feel anxiety in stressful situations, true or false.' False," she said, and looked around the room.

A queen-size bed with a plain white duvet and large pillows with smooth black cases stood beneath the window. A plush, violet Persian rug with a golden fringe lay under the bed. Beside the en suite was a modern vanity and rectangular mirror, a sharpened pencil and stationary pad laid out on its gleaming surface.

No telephone—this wasn't a conventional hotel, Alex had said. No minibar, which she supposed would at least prevent Frank from getting drunk. No room safe either.

She picked up the pen and stationary stamped with the Lone Loon Lodge name and logo, two loons floating together on cartoon ripples. The mattress felt firm and springy as she sat on its edge to begin her assessment.

"'I feel anxiety in enclosed spaces,'" she read aloud, and checked *False*.

—How often does your partner insult you or talk down to you? *Sometimes.*

—How often does your partner physically harm you? *Never.*

—I have issues with giving up control/letting go. *True.*

—Have you ever been seriously ill/injured? *Yes.*

—I would characterize my relationship with my in-laws as... *Strained.*

—I prefer hands-on solutions to my problems. *True.*

—I love my spouse.

Of course I do, she thought. *I wouldn't be here if I didn't still love him.*

She checked the box marked *True.*

—I have had or thought about having an affair. True/False

She scowled at the question. "That's not fair." Thinking about sleeping with someone and actually doing it were far from comparable, so she couldn't give it an honest answer without implicating herself. Although she supposed the thought of sleeping with someone else once, even more than once, wasn't necessarily the same as actually contemplating an affair.

"No," she said, checking the appropriate box.

The final line was an essay question: "What Brought You Here?"

Linda hesitated, pencil poised over the empty box, still unable to think back to the Year From Hell without choking back tears. Her diagnosis had exploded in their home like a grenade; it had nearly destroyed them, and once they'd finally managed to pick out the shrapnel, all she'd wanted was escape.

She'd thrown herself into work, pushing Frank away every chance she got. He had suffered the sting of her actions and words for months before he'd even begun to fight back, the two of them digging painfully into each other's wounds but careful to shy away from the rot at their core.

She'd survived her yearlong battle with cancer, and now it was their marriage on life support.

Linda swallowed her feelings and began to fill in the box.

***

Frank unpacked tightly folded socks and underwear into drawers, removing his cologne and toiletries and placing them side by side on the dresser in front of the mirror. He sniffed the cologne and each of his armpits before glancing at his reflection in the mirror.

He'd put on a bit of weight since Lin got the all clear from her oncologist. During the Year From Hell, he hadn't been eating much or exercising at all and had lost a fair bit of muscle mass. They used to work out regularly. They'd run marathons and had even attempted an endurance event/obstacle course similar to the Tough Mudder, although the "Electroshock Therapy" obstacle had knocked both of them out of the race short of the end. Last week's climbing trip would have been a walk in the park for them three years ago.

Get out there in the kayak, he thought, squeezing his fleshy arms. *Tread water, do some laps. Maybe get a bit of color.*

A light knock on the door disturbed him as he slipped a clean shirt over his head. He tugged it on, unlocked the door, and peered out.

A small, dark-haired woman stood in the doorway, her olive skin a contrast to the white of her housekeeper's uniform. She smiled deferentially with her gaze on the floor and held a sheet of paper out to him.

"Is this a pop quiz?"

She looked confused. "No English."

Frank took it from her. "*Gracias*," he said, guessing she spoke Spanish, based on her accent.

She smiled again with a small nod, still not meeting his gaze, and walked empty-handed toward the lobby.

Smiling at her bizarre behavior, he brought the assessment to the desk by a window overlooking the sun-dappled lake. He felt a bit unprepared, like those nightmares he still had where someone would hand him a quiz for a class he'd only just joined. It made him slightly queasy.

Linda's probably loving it though, he thought.

In the top drawer, he found a pencil and pad with the retreat's logo, two loons floating side by side. He thought the name and image might have been a metaphor, but it seemed like a misstep.

"'I have an inherent problem with authority figures,'" Frank said, reading the first question aloud. "They must have been reading my mind." He scribbled in the box marked *True*.

—I am prone to jealousy. *False.*

—I sometimes have thoughts that could be considered prejudiced. *False.*

—I have issues with giving up control/letting go. *False.*

—Have you ever been seriously ill/injured? *Yes.*

He'd broken his arm when he was young, falling off the monkey bars on the last day of the third grade, and spent half the summer reading books instead of playing with friends.

—How often does your partner insult you or talk down to you? *Sometimes.*

Especially recently, he thought.

—How often has your partner physically harmed you? *Never.*

—I can admit my mistakes and learn from them. *True.*

He imagined Linda responding to the same statement and wondered if she'd answered *Yes* or lied her ass off.

—If I saw a wounded animal in a trap, I would help it, regardless of my own well-being.

"What is this, a Voight-Kampff test?" He answered *False.*

—I am confident that my spouse has been faithful. True/False

Linda would never have an affair. Frank knew this with absolute certainty. Her mother had cheated on her father and left the two of them behind for another man. Linda still despised the woman for leaving them, and had never forgiven her. She'd even avoided reconnecting when her mother had made an attempt after Lin's diagnosis. Frank couldn't imagine her ever mirroring that behavior.

He filled in *True.*

—I have had or thought about having an affair. True/False

He answered *False* and moved on to the next.

—I prefer hands-on solutions to my problems. *True.*

—I love my spouse. He scribbled in the Yes box and read the final question: What Brought You Here?

Frank scrawled, *I want to reconnect with my wife, why else would I be here?*

He laid the questionnaire down on the desk and looked out the window at the sunny day. A tall woman with long, black hair, dressed in a black, one-piece bikini, strode barefoot to the end of the wooden dock. She bent, giving him a view of the crotch of her bathing suit as she placed something on the dock boards. Without even dipping a toe to check the temperature, she dove off, her ass jostling below the bikini line.

"Well, hello there," he said to himself.

He waited for her to surface, feeling a bit like a creep for watching, but still not turning away. She swam back to the dock and drew herself up onto her elbows, her breasts pressing together over the neckline of her bikini. She lit a cigarette and took a long drag on it, hanging off the end of the dock.

When she looked up, her gaze seemed magnetically drawn to his window.

Frank ducked back out of sight.

Had she seen him? Or had the sun reflected off the glass, obscuring him from view?

Either way, he needed to be more careful. That was someone's wife out there. His own wife was just down the hall.

A knock startled him.

"Mr. Moffat?"

"Frank," he corrected the concierge. "What's up?"

"Have you finished your assessment?"

Frank crossed to the door and unlocked it. Alex stood in the hall with a smile, a sheet of paper in hand.

Linda's assessment.

Alex seemed to note Frank's stolen glance at her assessment. "How do you think you did?"

Frank looked over his paper with a shrug. "You had to take this test with your wife, right?"

"Husband."

"Oh, cool. Linda's best friend is gay."

Alex grinned. "I'll just tuck that little factoid into my back pocket."

"Sorry. That was a weird thing to say, wasn't it?"

"It's okay. And to answer your question, yes, we did take the test. Why do you ask?"

"How did you do on it?"

"Honestly? I lied my ass off." Alex laughed. "I was worried Don would see it."

Frank chuckled, relaxing.

"Trust me, Frank, you've got nothing to worry about. Nobody's looking at these but the doctor himself, and they're really not all that important, just a gauge of your mindset going into your therapy."

Frank handed it to Alex, who placed it with Linda's.

"You guys are gonna make it through this," Alex said. "I can tell."

"You think?"

"Trust me. I've seen hundreds of couples come and go over the years. You get to know the look. You'll survive." He put a strong hand on Frank's shoulder. "And hey, if you don't..." He shrugged. "At least you can say you tried."

Alex turned and headed back down the hall.

As he rounded the corner, one of the assessments fell from his hand and fluttered to the carpet.

"Hey..." Frank began, but stopped himself as the concierge disappeared from sight.

Frank stepped out into the hall, not realizing he was practically tiptoeing until he neared the page. It had landed facedown. He bent to pick it up.

Linda's name was printed in bold at the top.

Don't read it.

He glanced at the first question about enclosed spaces.

"Lying right off the bat," he muttered. "That's an interesting strategy."

He headed for the stairs, meaning to bring it down to Alex. Curiosity got the better of him, and he read the other answers.

Their tests were slightly different, with many of the same questions but in a different order. He wondered if there was a reason for it, but realized these people had known nothing about them prior to checking in, which meant it was likely random.

He scanned the page, looking for the only responses he really cared about. Like his, they were at the bottom.

For "I love my spouse," she'd placed a very Linda-like, neat little checkmark in the box marked *True*.

That was good, at least.

She'd checked *False* for the affair question.

Doubleplusgood, he thought.

In the box marked "What Brought You Here?" Lin had written one sentence much like his own, but with a very different sentiment:

I'm here because Frank needs closure.

He read the words several times, unable to process them, and didn't realize his hand was shaking until the page began to flutter loudly between his fingers and the text became a gray blur.

It fell to the floor, and Frank returned to his room to think about it.

LINDA WAS SCRUBBING makeup off her face in front of the bathroom mirror when the first gunshot went off. She patted herself dry as she stepped out of the en suite, and headed barefoot to the window.

The man she'd seen earlier in the lobby with his runway model–looking wife lowered the rifle and strode through the tall grass toward the woods. Halfway there, he raised it again and fired a seemingly random shot into the air. Linda followed his aim to see a bird fall from the overcast sky in the east.

The man watched its descent and trudged out to where it had landed. He stooped, picked it up by the legs, and returned to the lodge with a proud smile, the dead bird bouncing off his hip.

Beep.

Linda turned back at the sound, but heard only silence. She returned to the bathroom to get her hair ties.

Beep.

The sound came again from the area of her vanity. Without little time to pack, she'd thrown in things she thought she might wear in different weather conditions. She hadn't unpacked yet, which meant a previous guest had probably left something in the drawers.

Linda sat down in front of it and opened the top drawer first, but found it empty. The lower drawers were next, also empty except for a crossword book she found had been mostly filled in when she flipped through it.

Beep.

Not the drawers. The mirror. Right in front of her.

She leaned in closer.

Why would the mirror be beeping?

She tapped the glass. It seemed normal.

Beep.

Definitely the mirror. No doubting it at this distance.

Linda peered around the back of the mirror. If there was anything behind it, it would have had to be behind or even *inside* the wall. Either way, it was too close to see anything but shadow without moving the vanity.

With effort, she pulled one end of the heavy, awkward vanity and then the other, dragging it over the carpet. Once it was far enough out from the wall, she leaned around to peer behind it.

A square hole had been cut into the wall, about six by six inches. At the back of the mirror, a square of the reflective backing about the same size had been removed. She could see right through it.

A small camera was mounted inside the hole, pointed toward the mirror.

Beep. The little red light flashed.

Nervous, Linda hurried to the door and out into the hall. She rounded the corner, stepping over her assessment without even noticing it. There were three doors in this hall, and she didn't know which one was Frank's.

She knocked on the closest one. No reply.

At the second door, Frank called out, "Yeah?"

"*Frank.*"

"Linda? Why are you whispering?"

"Can I come in?"

She heard him sigh heavily. A moment later, he opened the door, looking annoyed. "What? Did the rifle startle you?"

"No. Yes." She shook her head, feeling flustered. "That's not why I came over." Peering over his shoulder, she saw their binoculars on the desk in front of the window. "Are you bird watching?"

"Huh?" Frank followed her gaze. "Oh." He looked like she'd caught him at something. "No, I thought I'd get a look at whoever was shooting, but I didn't see anyone."

"It's the new guests. The husband."

Frank's eyebrows rose. "What the hell's he shooting at?"

"A Canada goose, I think."

"Is that legal here?"

"Maybe. But that's not why I'm here..."

She saw him visibly flinch. "Then why *are* you here, Linda?"

He sounded upset, and she couldn't imagine why, except that she'd interrupted whatever he was doing with the binoculars. "I need to show you something."

She grabbed his hand. He stayed firmly inside his room, arm extended.

"What is it, Linda?"

"Please, you need to come with me."

"All right." He sighed and with a glance behind him, he allowed her to pull him along. "Are you gonna tell me what's the matter?"

"Keep your voice down."

"What's this all about?"

She dragged him into her room and closed the door, locking it.

He looked over her suitcases on the floor spilling clothing. "This place looks like a war zone. What the hell's up with the dresser?"

"I don't know if these things have microphones, but we should probably be careful what we say."

"What *things*, Linda?"

"*This*," she said, pointing at the wall behind the vanity.

Frank approached it, peering around the mirror. "I don't see anything."

"You..." Linda frowned and pushed him out of the way. "It was there, I swear."

"*What* was?"

"A video camera!"

"A video camera?" He looked at her as though she'd gone crazy. "Come on, Lin. You're being paranoid."

"Don't you think I'd know?"

Frank seemed about to retort but closed his mouth and instead looked at the back of the mirror. "Looks like it's part one-way glass." He pointed it out, tracing his finger around the edge.

"That's why I ran and got you."

"How did you notice it? Aren't those things designed to be discreet?"

"It's my *job*," she said, only fudging the truth a little, which Frank seemed to accept at face value. The hole was covered, but the seams in the ugly, patterned wallpaper were still visible. "Look, there was a piece cut out of the wall. You can see the edge."

Frank came over and ran his fingers over the seams. "Weird. You think somebody's trying to gaslight you?"

"I don't know, but I don't like it. I'm going to talk to Alex."

Frank nodded resolutely. "I'm coming with you."

He passed her in the hall. Anger quickening his step, he

bounded down the stairs. She caught up with him at the desk just as he rang the bell.

Alex came out from the back room, where he'd been sitting in front of the office computer. Along the back wall was a row of television monitors, mostly shut off aside from the two that showed the front of the lodge and the lobby.

"Moffats." He smiled briefly. "You look troubled."

"You're damn right we're troubled—" Frank began.

"There's a camera in my room."

Alex looked relieved. "Oh, that! Just act like it isn't there—"

"'Act like'?' You've been spying on my wife!"

Linda patted his hand gripping the edge of the counter. "Hon."

"Don't 'hon' me, Linda. This is unacceptable!"

"It is, but we can handle ourselves with some decorum."

"Fuck *decorum*, Lin. This is about *boundaries*. You can't go around filming people without their knowledge."

Alex dipped behind the desk. Frank leaned over with an angry look. The keypad beeped as the concierge open the safe. He returned with a patient smile and a copy of their contracts.

"Article seven b of the contract you both signed states —" Alex flipped to it and read, "'The Participants agree to be videotaped for the purpose of assessment. This footage shall not be used by the Examiners without expressed written permission.' It's right there in black and white."

"Let me see that." Frank turned the contract around. "Wait a minute." He looked toward the loft with noticeable apprehension. "Are you filming me too?"

"There are cameras in all the bedrooms," Alex said.

"I don't care what we signed, if you're taping me while I'm on the shitter—"

"Bathrooms are designated safe zones," Alex assured him with a patient smile. "Nobody wants to watch you poop, Mr. Moffat."

"Christ, this is *insane*."

"Your payment has already cleared. We can refund your money if you like, but your deposit is nonrefundable as per your contract."

"I don't give a shit about the contract—you can't just film people without their knowledge—"

"Frank, I'm sorry, but if you'd read the contract, it wouldn't be without your knowledge now, would it? You really should read things before signing them."

"He's right, Frank." Linda shrugged. "We screwed up."

Frank's nostrils flared and he sneered. "Fuck," he said finally, letting go of the desk.

"Go cool off in the lake," Alex suggested. "Take out the canoe."

"How do we know there's no cameras out there?"

"I promise you, there are no cameras other than the ones in the lodge."

"What about that maniac? Some guy's out there shooting off a rifle, scaring my wife to death."

"I wasn't scared."

Frank shot her an angry look.

"That 'maniac' shot tomorrow's dinner," Alex said. "A Canada goose, I believe."

"And the gun?" Linda asked.

"Locked up in the office." Alex smiled pacifyingly. "Trust me. You are perfectly safe within these walls."

"How do we know we can trust you?" Frank said, voicing Linda's concern.

"You don't. Just know that when I was in your position, I felt the exact same way you do now." He looked genuinely sympathetic. "That's about all I can offer you."

Frank looked like he was about to start up again before his whole body deflated. He turned from the desk and headed for the stairs.

"I work for a security company," Linda said once Frank was out of earshot. "A very big security company. I know how this stuff works, okay? If you're lying to us, if you're taping us when you're not supposed to be taping us, if you're playing fast and loose with legalities, I will bring a shitstorm down on this place."

"I do not doubt that, ma'am."

"Good." She held his gaze to drive the point home. "I want a copy of that contract."

"I'll bring one right up to you."

"Thank you. And it's still Linda." With that, she walked away.

CHAPTER 5

THE OTHER COUPLE

Frank changed into his swim trunks in the bathroom and headed out into the hall with a towel under his arm and a Ludlum book in hand. As he closed the door, wishing for a lock on the outside, the woman he'd seen—and had considered stroking off to in front of God knew how many cameras—came around the corner, still glistening from the lake, a bright yellow towel wrapped around her hair.

Up close, he could see she was probably in her late thirties or early forties, judging by the crow's feet and the beginnings of laugh lines, but her body was as taut as a twenty-year-old's. He suspected she worked out frequently, and in conjunction with her Egyptian-looking gold and jade necklace, he suspected she was rich enough to put in as many hours at the gym as her husband may have required of her.

A smile crept onto her lips as she saw him. "Well, hello," she said, stopping in front of the door nearest the loft. "I didn't realize we had company this weekend. I was told it was just Neville and I."

"Sorry to disappoint you."

"Oh, I'm not disappointed." She looked him up and down. "It should be fun. Don't you think?"

"Always nice to meet new people."

"Isn't it?" Without turning away, she opened her door.

"Don't catch a chill in the water. It's not quite spa temperature."

"I'm just gonna dip my toes in, thanks. You might want to be careful in here. Apparently there are cameras in all the rooms."

"Are there?" She smirked and raised an eyebrow. "Well... maybe I'll give them a little show."

Frank suffered with the lump in his throat rather than swallow. "Maybe you could do a little salsa dance for them with your Chiquita banana hat."

She reached up and touched the towel before grinning and attempting a quick, dancelike shuffle. "You like?"

"Ha," he said. Of course he liked.

"Well.. . I suppose we'll see each other again at dinner. My husband's shot a goose, the brute."

"Sounds tasty."

"Oh, he's very tasty." She winked. "I presume the goose will be too. Have a nice dip."

"You too. I mean thanks." He twiddled his fingers in a wave, immediately feeling like a dork. "See ya."

"See you at dinner." She grinned as he passed her door.

Frank let out a breath the second he rounded the corner, just as Linda came out in one of her old bikini tops with a towel wrapped around her waist. Her hair was tied in a ponytail, and when she smiled at him, he remembered how good it had once been between them when they'd first started dating, before their respective careers, bills, buying the right furniture, mortgage payments, her cancer, and all of that other joy-sucking stuff had gotten in the way.

He met her at her door. "You look good."

"Thanks." She gave him a tight smile. "I was looking over the contract—"

"Oh?"

"Yeah. So it looks like we've also agreed to something called a 'cleansing.'"

"Like a high colonic?"

"What's that?"

"Colonic irrigation. An enema."

Linda shuddered. "I hope not. I'm thinking it's more likely some kind of hippie dippy thing you won't like, so I just thought I'd warn you."

"I appreciate you thinking of me."

Linda gave him a queer look and headed for the stairs, her sandals clacking on hardwood.

He took up behind her. "I say we just follow the contract to the letter. You know, like work to rule."

"Definitely. I'll look over it tonight."

"I can help."

"It's a one-person job," she said. "You'll just slow me down."

"I read contracts in my job too."

"Not as often as I do."

"What difference does that make?" Frank lowered his voice as Alex stepped out of the back office and took up sentry behind the desk.

"We're just going to take a dip in the lake," Linda said.

The concierge smiled. "Good idea! If you go through this way, you won't have to walk the stone path in your bare feet," he suggested, referring to Frank.

They thanked him and headed through the open French doors to the right of the desk and down the hall. The French doors to the dining room were closed, but Frank and Linda peeked inside as they passed, and he noted a large table and buffet.

They passed the kitchen, where a fat, hairy man sweated in front of a deep, steel pot on the gas range and the small Hispanic woman plucked feathers off the goose, blood spatters on her white uniform.

They passed a closed door labeled MAINTENANCE, and turned toward a sunny hallway. Chairs had been stacked in the far corner. At the opposite end of the corridor, the door had a FIRE EXIT sticker above a reinforced glass panel.

"This door should be closer to the kitchen if it's a fire exit," Frank said. "And I didn't see a single extinguisher."

"*Frank.*"

"Well, it's true..."

He followed her outside. The clouds he'd noticed earlier had disappeared, leaving only pure blue sky. Seagulls glided and dipped high above the lake, which was larger than he'd first thought. Where he'd seen only trees before, he noticed the water curved around a bend between the mainland and a peninsula. This part of the lake was the size of a football field, but it could easily go on for miles beyond the narrow bay. Steel-gray mountains lined the horizon.

Boards creaked as Linda mounted the dock, wobbling underfoot. To the far right were two large wooden racks replete with four kayaks and two canoes, life preservers, paddles, and hanging snorkeling gear. Moored to the dock, a tin fishing boat with an outboard engine drummed against it in a light current.

The dock was still wet where the tall brunette had been stretched out, drying off, her butt print a visible heart shape at Linda's feet. Linda squinted up at the lodge with a hand shielding her eyes from the sun and gave him a shrewd look.

"What?"

"You *were* watching birds. Or *a* bird."

"Don't try to tell me you didn't check out the concierge."

"I generally don't fall all over myself for gay men, Frank."

He scowled. "Is this an inquisition or are you coming for a dip?"

"I need to get warmed up first."

He'd heard those words many times before in a very different context. Linda sat on the dock, avoiding the wet patch —another thing she did under different circumstances—and lay back with her head on her hands.

"That rifle's in the office," she said as he sat down on the edge, dipping his legs into the cool water.

"How did you spot that?"

"It's my job."

It wasn't, not technically, but he let her have it.

"There are two of them locked in a rack. Both have locks on the triggers."

"I'm just gonna tuck that little factoid in my back pocket."

Linda squinted at him.

"What?" he said.

"Don't say that, it's weird. And anyway, those shorts don't have pockets."

"They don't?" He felt his ass and found she was right. She should be, having bought them for him. "You don't think we're in danger, do you?"

"Not from the staff. I don't like that they didn't tell us about the cameras, but it *was* in the contract. Then again, I also don't like guns, especially in the hands of civilians."

"You talk like my dad sometimes," Frank said snidely.

"Well, sometimes your dad talks sense." Her lips protruded in a look of regret. "I'm sorry, Frank."

"Hey, it's okay." He squinted out at the lake. "He was trying to protect me from going through the same thing we went through with Mom. I just... I shouldn't have told you. Not while you were going through..." He hesitated, not wanting to bring up the pain in her past that was still so present between them, no matter how they tried to avoid it. "It was stupid."

He caught the movement out of the corner of his eye, but she retracted her hand as he turned, and she draped her arm over her eyes.

"Sorry," he said. "I know we promised not to bring it up this weekend."

"Don't be sorry. It's silly to think we'll avoid it this weekend. It's a part of us."

He felt tears coming on and hoped getting in the lake would disguise them. "I'm going in."

"Already?" There was disappointment in her tone.

"The water," he explained. He placed his hands on the dock on either side of himself, twisting at the hips to slip backward into the water. "Oh! It's cold!"

The chill spread through his bones, and he front-crawled away from the dock. He spotted a rock in the tea-colored water, and rested the tips of his toes on its slimy surface, using his arms to keep himself afloat.

Linda lay with one leg bent, the toes of the other stretched toward him, an arm draped over her face. He considered attempting to cajole her into sex, but her response to *"What Brought You Here?"* came back and soured the mood.

He swam back to the dock and pulled himself up on his elbows. "Warm enough yet?"

"Getting there." Her voice was muffled under her arm.

Frank watched her a moment, glad to see her looking healthy again. "Let's try to make the best of this weekend, huh?" he said. "It sucks, but we're kind of stuck in it now. No use making it worse by fighting with each other."

Linda raised her arm to squint at him, but said nothing.

"You know the concierge? Alex? He said he came here with his husband. They didn't make it through the treatment."

"I guess it wasn't meant to be."

"I guess not. Anyway, his husband passed, so don't bring it up."

"Recently?"

"No idea."

"So they failed the test, is that how it works?"

"No idea. But he told me he thinks we're gonna make it. Said he knows the look."

"Hmm." She seemed unconvinced. "We should ask him about Trevor."

"I doubt he'd be able to talk about it. Confidentiality and all that."

"True."

"What do you think? I mean about us. Do you see us making it?"

Linda rolled to her side, facing him, and propped up on an elbow. "When we first met, Frank, I could see our entire future plotted out before us."

"And now?"

"You know that expression about not seeing the forest for the trees?"

He nodded, unsure where she was going.

"That's us right now. Only we're chained to trees on opposite ends of the forest." Whatever that meant, she let it hang between them. "This weekend is the clear cut. Total deforestation. And if we're on the trees left standing, maybe we'll be able to see each other clearly again over all those dead stumps."

Frank nodded, pulling himself up onto the dock. "I like that. I mean I thought you were gonna say 'We're the trees,' but I like what you said better."

They smiled at each other as the dock swayed in the light current.

———

FRANK AND LINDA returned to their separate rooms, having agreed to meet in her room after they'd changed out of their wet swimsuits to discuss the contract.

Even in her haste, Linda had thought to bring along the summery dress Frank loved, and she wore it when she opened the door for him. He took a moment to drink her in before stepping inside.

God, she's beautiful.

He felt underdressed in a loose, white linen short-sleeved shirt and khakis.

Linda moved past him and sat on the edge of the bed. Her room was a disaster zone and not just the usual piles of clothes on the floor and beauty products strewn over the vanity. She'd obviously been hunting for cameras and listening devices.

"Find any more?"

She shook her head, seeming oddly disappointed.

Frank closed the door, dragged the vanity chair over, and sat across from her.

"You could've sat with me. We sleep in the same bed at home, it's not like I'm allergic."

"I thought this was a business meeting," he said with a grin.

With a jovial shake of her head, she crossed her shimmering cocoa-buttered legs and licked an index finger to flip through the contract. "The nondisclosure thing is important. We can't divulge anything about The Method or they'll sue our asses off. That's why Trevor and Dillon were so secretive about it, although I'm surprised they mentioned it at all. The language here is water tight."

Frank nodded thoughtfully.

"And here," she said, pointing to a paragraph on the third page. "It says we have to provide a urine sample if asked. I guess they want to make sure we're going into this with a clear head."

"Let me see that." She turned the contract for him to read. "'Participants found to have consumed illegal substances allow the right to search and seizure; should illegal substances be found, the Participant will be ejected from the premises.'"

Frank met Linda's wide eyes. "Have you brushed your teeth yet? My teeth feel fuzzy from lunch."

She caught his slight nod and agreed. "I have to brush mine too."

They both stood as casually as possible and crossed the to the en suite. Linda locked the door behind them and stood very close to him in the cramped room.

"I'd better do something with that weed," Frank whispered. "Doesn't it take a while to get results?"

"Usually twenty-four hours for a negative. If it's positive, they have to do more testing to figure out what drug it is. Either way, best to get rid of it. When did you smoke up last?"

"Couple of weeks ago."

"That's probably fine. Wait...was that at my sister's wedding?"

"Shhh!" Frank said, putting a finger to his lips. "Of course it wasn't."

Even in a whisper, he sounded guilty. She gave him a narrow-eyed gaze.

"Okay fine, I smoked a bit at Laura's wedding. I was stressed. Everyone was asking how you and me were doing. Asking about kids and all that. Danny offered, I said sure. "

"Of course it was fucking Danny."

"He's a wildcard." Frank shrugged. "It's not a big deal, Linda. I'll get rid of it. We'll be—*wait*. Did it say anything about a refund?"

"I thought you wanted to go through with this."

He gave her a mock-offended scowl. "Of course I do, just if they found it already, then we'd get our money back."

"We don't even know if they're going to *do* a drug test. It could be just another head game, like the disappearing camera or those tricky questions on that test."

Frank thought back to the way the test had slipped from Alex's hand and realized there was no way the concierge wouldn't have noticed it fall. Frank had heard it flutter all the way from his room. It made him wonder it Alex had dropped it on purpose for him to find.

To see her answer to that final question.

Closure.

The word made him tense.

"What?" she said.

"Nothing. You're right. We'll have to keep on our toes. Stay one step ahead of the game."

Linda wrinkled her nose. "Okay, you really should brush your teeth. I can taste what you had for lunch."

"Sorry, I had to burp." He picked up his toothbrush from the ceramic holder. "Meet you out there?"

Linda nodded and eagerly stepped out, closing the door behind her.

FRANK SNUCK out the side door to the parking lot and glanced over his shoulder before opening the passenger door of the hatchback and rooting around under the seat. His fingers roamed over crumbs, coins, and small plastic wrappers, until finally settling on the bag of weed Linda had hidden. He palmed it, reached into the glove box, and pulled out the box of Swisher Sweets he'd bought when he quit smoking after Lin's diagnosis. Slipping the baggie into his pocket, he stood with a cigarillo held between his teeth.

As he passed the high-end SUV he supposed must have belonged to the new arrivals, the vehicle's alarm began to blare, and Frank jumped out of the way with a cry of "Fuck!"

The alarm still blaring in his wake, he sauntered down to the dock and lit the smoke with a disposable lighter. Its sweet cherry tobacco smell perked him up. He still missed smoking the real thing, but the Swishers dulled his occasional craving.

When he reached the end of the dock, the alarm stopped with a *blip blip!* He watched the low afternoon sun flicker on the lake, slipped a hand into his pocket, and opened the baggie, ready to dispose of its contents in the water.

"Mind if I join you?"

He jerked his hand free from his pocket. "Be my guest," he said, trying not to sound spooked.

The tall woman wore an ankle-length, jade-green gown, cut low enough in the front that he suspected she'd had to tape her boobs to keep them from spilling out. No bra straps were visible anyway, and from how seamlessly the dress fit her hourglass figure, Frank assumed she wasn't wearing any panties either. Barefoot, she held a pair of heels in her left hand and approached him with a cigarette poised between plump cherry red lips. "Got a light?"

He lit her cigarette, breathing in a citrusy, floral scent that reminded him of the perfume his mother used to wear, Chanel N° 5 maybe. She stepped back, dragging on the smoke as she eyed him with an amused half smile.

"Had to get away from the husband. He's been driving me absolutely bonkers talking about business."

Frank raised his eyebrows noncommittally and puffed on his Swisher.

"He thinks I care about that stuff, but I don't have a mind for boring details. I'm a big picture gal." She gave a wicked look over her shoulder toward the lodge. "Except when he cheated on me, the scoundrel. I wanted to hear every sordid little tidbit about that."

"That right?"

"It is." She squinted at him through a haze of smoke. "So why are you here? You don't look the type to have an affair."

"Ha."

"No offense." She shrugged. "You just strike me as one of the good guys."

He frowned. "I do, do I?"

She nodded slowly, holding his gaze almost sensually.

Frank leaned in conspiratorially. "Well, what would you say if I told you I came out here to get rid of a bag of marijuana?"

She laughed. "Did you? How delicious! But that doesn't make you a bad boy. For all I know, you have glaucoma."

Frank laughed. "All right, so I'm not a bad boy. I was just joking about the weed, anyway."

"No you weren't." She swatted his arm. "I suppose you're not too goody two shoes. I did see you peeping at me from your window up there."

He coughed out a lungful of smoke.

"Don't be embarrassed. I'd have done the same if the positions were reversed."

Frank got a hold of his breathing, swallowing a hard lump of phlegm. "I used to be in better shape."

"The human body is a work of art. We're all painted using different colors and strokes—" Frank noticed an emphasis on the word *strokes*, although he could have just imagined it. "—but there's always something to be admired, even among the grotesque."

"Are you saying I'm grotesque?"

Again she swatted him with a playful grin. "Not *you*.

The chef, for instance. Ugly as sin, but there's a loneliness to those puppy-dog eyes of his that makes me want to snuggle him into my lap and stroke his sweaty, bald head."

"I didn't get that close a look at him," Frank admitted.

"He's a cuddler. Trust me."

Frank laughed again. "You're an interesting woman."

"Oh, I'm a lot less interesting than you might think. I'm just..." She cracked a half-smile. "New," she finished.

Frank wasn't sure how to respond, so he just nodded. "I'm gonna get rid of this weed. Could you make a distraction or something?"

"I could do a little salsa dance for you..."

"Not unless you want me to get in even deeper with the wife."

"Oh no, we wouldn't want that." Her tone said she might find it amusing. "Nobody's watching, Frank. They'd have to have binoculars to see us out here."

Thinking of the binoculars on the desk in his room, he wondered if she'd seen that too. Ignoring the tweak of paranoia, he tugged the baggie out of his pocket and dumped its contents into the lake.

"Oh, look at that." She grinned, watching small fish dart to the surface to nibble on the flakes of weed like fish food. "You've got the little fishies hooked on drugs."

Frank thought about the statement on his assessment, the one about wounded animals, and wondered if it meant something to feel no empathy for the fish gobbling up his drugs.

He pinched out his cigarillo. "I'm heading in."

"See you at dinner." Another half-smile. "Again."

"What's your name?" he asked as he headed up the hill.

"Mrs. Lumley," was all she said.

LINDA PUT the contract away and stepped out into the hall, hoping to ask Alex about the office computer. She'd needed to respond to a vaguely important work email, and it couldn't wait until after the weekend.

Looking up from her thoughts, she almost ran into the Goose Killer. For some reason, it seemed like he'd been waiting near the door for her to step out as his cue to start walking, but she told herself she was being paranoid.

"Oh, excuse me!" He reeled back with a bemused grin, a hand against his heart. "I didn't see you coming out."

"That's okay." She flashed a brief smile. "Cramped hallway."

"Tell me about it, sister." His voice had a deep, familiar rumble to it. His face seemed familiar too, but she couldn't put a finger on where she might have met him. He scratched his temple in curiosity. "Say, did they make you get rid of your phone too? I'm going nutsoid without it."

"Nutsoid, huh? That's a really good way to describe it."

She took a moment to look him over in glances. Square jaw, peppered with half a day's worth of gray and black stubble. He was taller than Frank by a good half a foot, and broader in the chest and shoulders. His shirt and tie coordinated nicely, as if he and his wife might be heading out on the town, without a single rumple in either shirt or pants.

His dazzling green eyes twinkled as he grinned. "I don't know about you, but I can't live without that damn thing."

"Between you and me," she said, catching a whiff of his clean-scented cologne as she leaned into him, "I know where they're keeping them."

"You do, do you?"

"I do."

He pulled back, studying her. "So you're not going to tell me."

Linda laughed. "They're in a safe under the desk. No chance getting in there, but I think I've figured out the first few numbers in the code."

A big smile spread across his face. "You're a bad girl!"

"I was just going downstairs to ask about using the office computer."

"No kidding. I was too!"

"For non-naughty reasons, of course."

He laughed heartily. "Naturally!"

A dress strap slipped off her left shoulder. She let his eyes linger there a moment before putting it back.

"You're stunning." His admission seemed to startle himself. "I'm sorry, that was rude."

"No, it's..." She felt herself blushing. "It's fine. Thank you."

"Shall we walk down together?"

"Sure." She gave him a small smile and stuck out a hand. "I'm Linda."

He shook it. "Neville. Neville Lumley." He grinned as they fell into step side by side on their way to the stairs. "Say, didn't they do a duet together?"

"Who?"

"Aaron Neville and Linda Ronstadt." He sang, "'I don't know much...'"

They sang the rest together and laughed. His falsetto wasn't great, but pleasant enough. They took the stairs.

"I saw your wife. She's gorgeous."

He smiled wistfully. "Lovely to look at."

"How long have you two...?"

"Served?" He chuckled. "Eight years, with time off for good behavior. You?"

"Nine years. Married for three."

Alex wasn't behind the desk when they stepped off the stairs together.

"Looks like we've got the place to ourselves." Neville made a show of peering around. "I'll keep a lookout if you wanna dip around the desk."

She peeked into the office and saw the computer turned on. The sound of utensils clattering and metal clanging from the kitchen wouldn't make it easy to hear anyone coming around the corner, not to mention the two cameras pointed toward the desk from the high corners of the lobby.

"Nah, too risky. Cameras everywhere."

Neville's shoulders sagged. "Yeah, definitely not worth it. Not with what it cost to be here. Friends of ours—Teri's friends, really—took out a second mortgage on their home for a single weekend, but they came back raving about how it saved their marriage, so when Teri suggested it, I thought, *why not?*"

"Wow. Our friends raved about it too. Frank called them recidivists for all the times they've broken up and gotten back together."

"Repeat offenders." Neville grinned. "I like that."

High heels clacked down the hall toward them. Neville stepped back from her and pretended to be admiring the desk, running his hand over the bark. "What is it you call this style? With the bark still on?"

"Live edge." Linda offered his wife a cheerful smile as the woman approached with an obvious twinge of jealousy. She extended a hand. "You must be Teri. Your husband's told me all about you."

"Pleasure." Teri Lumley shook her hand daintily, garishly overdressed in a gown that would have been better at a red carpet gala. "Your husband didn't tell me your name."

Neville caught the jab and gave Linda a brief look of sympathy.

She tried not to grit her teeth as she told the woman.

"Linda. Like the song, right, Neville? 'I don't know much...'" she sang, but no one joined her. She looked them both over and plastered on a smile.

"Well, I'm going to freshen up. Why don't you two..." Teri waved dismissively. "...continue whatever it is you're doing and I'll meet you down here in a mo."

"You do that, sweetheart."

Teri's hips swayed generously as she sashayed toward the stairs like some femme fatale out of an old movie, clearly playing it up.

"Don't worry." He leaned in close once she was out of earshot. "Teri *thrives* on drama."

"I know the type," Linda said, though she didn't feel good about bashing the woman behind her back.

Neville seemed to sense it and touched her arm. "I shouldn't be talking like that about her, I know. It just gets to me, that's all, and I've really got no one else to talk to about it." His hand lingered a moment longer before he returned it to his side.

"I know what you mean."

"Guess that's why we're here, isn't it? We tried marriage counseling. Gestalt. Hypnotism. Nothing worked. Maybe we're just broken."

"You wouldn't be here if you didn't think there was a chance."

"No? Isn't that the definition of insanity? Repeating the same thing over and over again, hoping for different results?"

"If that's insane, the lunatics are running the asylum."

Neville chuckled. "You're an interesting woman."

"I know." She smiled as Frank emerged from the hall, a cloud of cherry tobacco preceding him.

"This must be your fella." Neville stuck out a hand.

Frank's gaze lobbed from Neville to her to Neville again before he put on a friendly smile and stuck out a hand of his own. They shook vigorously, the sort of handshake that seemed more like a pissing contest, neither wanting to be the first to break it.

"Frank Moffat," he said, holding the taller man's gaze.

"Neville Lumley. Pleased to meet you."

"Same." Frank retracted his hand, although it seemed for a moment as if Neville might not release it. "I met your wife..."

"Teri."

"Teri, right. She's nice."

"Don't tell her that, she'll claw your eyes out." Neville laughed uproariously.

"Ha! Good one," Frank said and turned his ingratiating smile toward Linda, who gritted her teeth in annoyance.

CHAPTER 6

POLITE DINNER CONVERSATION

Dinner was served on the hour.

The four of them sat across from each other at the large dining table, all other chairs and place settings removed except for one at the head of the table, where Linda supposed Dr. Kaspar might soon join them. The small Hispanic woman who seemed to perform multiple duties at the lodge circled the table, serving Consommé Olga and a glass of sherry from an ancient sterling silver tray.

Polite dinner conversation followed, interspersed with light slurps. Careers were briefly spoken of, their respective hometowns, and their mutual appreciation of basketball, and although everyone had their own favorite, they all seemed to agree that Frank's Raptors were open to disdain.

The woman cleared their plates and returned with a main course of Chicken Lyonnaise accompanied by a red Bordeaux. Linda sniffed her glass appreciatively, rich cherry and tart lemon.

"Is this Dr. Kaspar's homemade wine?"

The maid gave a bemused shrug. "No English." She continued around the table.

"You know," Teri began, daintily cutting up her chicken, "I think this is the same meal they served on the Titanic."

"Ha!" Frank said with his mouth full. "You think it's a metaphor?"

"Maybe a double entendre," Teri muttered.

Neville greeted this with a smirk. "Well, here's to one or more of us going down tonight." He raised his glass in a toast.

Linda nearly spat out a mouthful of wine laughing.

"What? Nobody?" He lowered the glass with a cheeky grin.

"Hell, I'll drink to that," Frank said.

They clinked glasses. Teri joined their toast. Linda thought, *Fuck it*, although it would take a hell of a lot of wine to put her in *that* mood. She clinked her glass against theirs.

Neville locked eyes with her, a sly grin still on his lips. She felt her cheeks flush.

"I keep getting the feeling we've met before," she said, desperate to change the subject. "Do I know you from somewhere?"

Teri popped her eyes in Neville's direction. He daubed his lips on his napkin and swallowed. "I suppose it's possible. Maybe you've seen me on the news."

"Why were you on the news?"

Teri smiled awkwardly.

"I was accused of insider trading. Totally fabricated, around the time of the financial crisis, the banking scandals, Bernie Madoff. They dropped the charges before it went to trial, but it stuck in the craw of public consciousness. That's likely where you remember me from."

Teri's smile widened as if he'd dodged a conversational bullet. He returned the smile briefly, taking her hand.

"That must be it," Linda said. "I'm sorry to hear it."

"Good thing they acquitted you though," Frank added. "A thing like that gets to trial and it's in the news all the time. I mean, look at Martha Stewart."

"There but for the grace of God." Neville widened his eyes dramatically over a sip of wine.

"How is everything?"

Everyone turned to the doorway to see Alex had stepped in with his characteristic smile.

"Simply to die for," Teri said.

Linda ignored Frank's smirk in her direction. "It's delicious, thank you, Alex."

"Just terrific," Frank said. "Is this Dr. Kaspar's wine?"

"Yes, actually. One of several dozen bottles in the cellar. Isn't it lovely?"

They all agreed it was lovely.

"Will Dr. Kaspar be joining us tonight?" Neville asked, with a glance toward Frank as if he'd wanted to beat him to the punch.

"Oh, no. Unfortunately, he's been called to Switzerland for an emergency."

"What sort of emergency?" Frank asked.

"Some dilettante must have come down with a case of bourgeois malaise," Teri muttered.

"Isn't that why we're here, sweetheart?"

Teri gave her husband a sidelong glance and sipped her wine without comment.

"He should arrive tomorrow afternoon in time for your individual sessions. I am so sorry for your inconvenience."

Those sympathetic smiles of his were starting to grate on Linda. Judging by the looks of mild annoyance from the other dinner guests, she assumed they felt the same.

"I suppose we should be thankful it's a long weekend," Neville said. "Do you people work on Memorial Day?"

"We'll work when Dr. Kaspar needs us to," Alex said, and backed out of the room.

Neville watched the man leave. "That's just great. I could have been at the office today."

"You were there in the morning."

"I can't just skip out on a Friday without sticking my head in the office. I am a VP, sweetheart."

Teri rolled her eyes.

"What about you two? You must be pissed. This is

chump change for me, but a hundred grand means a lot to people like you."

Frank choked on his wine.

"It's definitely not chump change," Linda said, eager to steer the conversation away from the amount of money they'd spent to be here. "Do either of you know anything about Dr. Kaspar?"

The Lumleys shared a look. With raised eyebrows and a wave of her fork, Teri urged her husband to speak.

Neville broke a chunk off the French stick and began to butter it as he spoke. "Well, there's not much known about his early life, aside from emigrating from Vienna a year or so before the Occupation, when Kaspar was three. His father was a colleague of Freud's. His mother was a barmaid. At least that's what I've heard."

He bit off a piece of bread and chewed before continuing.

"In his twenties, Kaspar worked with the CIA. In the '60s, he wrote a few famous diet books, some quit-drinking and self-actualization books, but his most famous was one of those key-to-wealth things, and that book really solidified him in the public consciousness." Neville sopped up some sauce with the bread and took another generous bite. "I like to attribute my first million to my own sweat and blood, but I owe a lot to Kaspar's *Rewire Your Brain for Success*. It really was my bible in the early 2000s. I was pulling in cash money hand over fist, Frank. I'm telling you. And when all the other dotcoms started dropping like flies, I rode that tech bubble like a motherfucking mechanical bull into software development, real estate, finance. You name it."

He finished the last bite and dusted crumbs from his fingers. "Linda, you'd appreciate this. Actually, you should take my card once the weekend's over. I might have some business for you."

Teri rolled her eyes. "I'm *sure* you do."

"Thank you, that's kind," Linda said, ignoring the woman.

"Long story short, Kaspar pulled a Chappelle and went into hiding at his family castle in France. He only recently came back into the public eye with The Method, though it's so exclusive even celebrities haven't heard of it yet. I doubt it's the sort of thing that would make a *New York Times* best-seller if he ever did write it all down. Not exactly a ten-step program, from what I hear."

"What have you heard?" Frank asked.

"Not much. But my lawyer said the nondisclosure agreements have their own nondisclosure agreements." He grinned. "It's like *Fight Club*. You do not—"

The men finished the quote in unison, grinning amiably.

Teri rolled her eyes again.

"We saw that," Linda said. "Our friends were pretty secretive about it too."

"Exactly. We thought Teri's friends might have joined a cult at first."

Teri chuckled along with him.

"So did we," Frank said.

"The funny thing was," Teri added, "I'd just seen Celia for coffee and she was fine, but when we met the week following their Method weekend, they were all banged up and bruised. Rick said they'd been in a car accident."

Neville nodded. "That was a bit odd. Their car looked fine. A shitbox, but fine."

"Maybe it was their other car?" Frank said.

Teri shook her head. "They only have the one."

"That's weird." Linda turned to Frank. "Because our friends were all banged up when we saw them too. They said they'd gotten in a motorcycle accident."

"That is odd," Neville said, wiping his hands on his napkin.

Frank sipped his wine, seemingly in deep thought. "What are the chances of that?" he asked. "Two couples in separate accidents right after they've been here for the weekend?"

A silence fell over the table, not even an audible clink of cutlery.

"It would be *even more odd* if it was the same accident. Wouldn't it?"

"*Neville*," Teri said. "What happened to polite dinner conversation?"

"I'm just saying. Hey, we're all in this to win this, right?" He picked up his knife, red with caramelized onion and wine sauce, and studied it.

"Our friends were here three weekends ago," Linda said. "When were yours?"

The Lumleys gave each other a look. "Same," they said in unison.

"Are any of you getting the idea they're gonna pit us against each other in some kind of battle royale situation?" Frank half joked, raising his glass to look at the claret liquid.

Teri popped her heavily mascaraed eyes at him.

Neville laid his knife down on the plate. "Beats me. But if there *is* something nefarious going down here, I think it would be wise to know about it ahead of time."

"Agreed." Frank downed the glass in one gulp.

CHAPTER 7

MIXED SIGNALS

Frank sat on the edge of his bed, pondering the conversation at dinner.

Trevor had called it "unconventional therapy," but the scenarios running through his mind couldn't be considered therapeutic by any stretch of the imagination.

They were violent. They were vicious.

Deciding he was being paranoid, he flicked on the television to take his mind off it. The news didn't lessen his anxiety, and when a knock came at his door, he jumped, spilling his pop on the bedspread.

"Coming!" he said, using his damp towel to mop up the spill.

Frank opened the door without looking through the peephole first, expecting Linda. Instead, Teri stood in the doorway in a silky nightgown, her face scrubbed of makeup and somehow more beautiful as she shot paranoid glances down the hall. "Can I come in?"

"I don't think that's—"

She slipped past him before he could finish and sat down hurriedly on the bed. Her eyebrows knotted and she shifted positions, touching the spill she'd sat on. "When you said you were coming, I didn't think you'd meant that way."

"Ha! Spilled some pop." He left the door open, not

wanting to give the impression he had anything to hide should Linda or Neville come knocking.

"Pop?" She sounded distraught. Confused.

"Soda," he explained. He'd lived in the United States almost fifteen years and still hadn't gotten used to calling it *soda*, since most people he'd met in Seattle had called it *pop* just like he did. "What's this about?"

"It's Neville." She smoothed the hem of her nightgown on her thigh. "He thinks you two, you and your wife. Linda. He thinks the two of you are plotting to kill us in our sleep." She looked up at him then, her blue eyes wide. "You aren't, are you?"

He approached the bed, stopping short of sitting down beside her. "Teri... why would we do that? We're here for *therapy*. We just had a nice meal. These people—Alex, that strange little Hispanic lady—they are nice hospitable people. There's absolutely no reason to be paranoid."

If only I believed it myself, he thought.

"I know." She nodded, holding his gaze. "But he's convinced himself—"

"He's wrong, okay? Nobody is going to *kill* anybody."

He realized how stupid his paranoia had been as he spoke the words. No one would be hurt this weekend, aside from a potential broken heart or two. The idea that Kaspar's method involved pitting two couples against each other in a fight to the death was so laughable he did so aloud.

Teri looked up at him, her gaze darting back and forth between his eyes like an actor in a love scene. His pants felt suddenly constricting.

"I think there's something wrong with him. With Neville. He's always had a paranoid streak, but tonight...I don't know if I can trust him anymore. I certainly won't be able to sleep..."

Frank sat down opposite the wet spot, closer to the pillows. "Teri, everything's going to be okay. He's just stressed, that's all. I mean it's been a pretty strange day in a strange place. Tomorrow will be easier. Go back to bed. Get some sleep. Okay? Lock your door if you're worried—"

She reached out and snatched his hands, drawing them into her lap. "Will you walk me to my door?"

Frank tore them from her grip and shot a glance toward the camera he'd found after dinner. "Teri." He tried on a smile. "You'll be fine. It's literally right across the hall."

"Then watch me." Her eyes were full of desperate fear. "From your door. *Please?*"

He shrugged, not seeing the harm in it. "Okay." He stood and waited for her to follow.

She tugged down the hem of her nightgown, and when she finally stood, she was bare inches from him, heat radiating off her body as if she'd just been in a sauna. Her head lowered, her eyes downcast, moist lower lip pooched outward.

He thought again about closure, all the hurt welling up inside, and when she raised her head, their lips met as if they'd been drawn together. He didn't know whether she'd started it or he had. All he knew for certain was that it was wrong, but it felt so goddamn good to touch someone again, to feel human contact.

She grasped the back of his head and he pulled away sharply, thinking there might still be a chance to save his marriage, but not if he continued kissing a stranger, no matter how badly he wanted her in that moment, no matter what offences he felt Lin had committed.

Backing into the nightstand, he knocked over the glass and spilled the rest of its contents on the rug. "You need to go."

"I'm sorry." Her eyes downcast again, that pouty lower lip. He felt a sudden strong urge to slap her, as if she were the only one at fault.

"It's okay, just go. Please."

She apologized again and left the room, leaving the door open behind her.

Frank let out a deep breath and looked at the camera. He

shook his head and threw up his hands, hoping if anyone was watching, they would understand he was as mystified as they were by what had just happened, with both of their spouses just a few doors down the hall.

Adjusting his pants, he flopped down on the bed, sitting right in the wet spot. He stood abruptly and headed for the bathroom where he washed his lips, tasting soap, and brushed his teeth.

He stepped out into the hall to find Linda, creeping past Teri's room so as not to alert her of his presence outside her door. She'd probably spend a few restless hours shifting uncomfortably in bed, but sleep would eventually come. After what just happened, he doubted if he'd get any sleep himself.

THE TV in Linda's room came on suddenly as if someone had switched it on from outside the room or it had been on a sleep timer.

Startled, she rose on her hands and checked the blanket, thinking she must have sat on the remote. She spotted it on the table beside the TV, and she crossed the room to turn it off, but she had to stop to gawk at the screen.

It was the camera feed from Frank's bedroom.

Frank was seated on his bed beside the Lumley woman. They were talking, but Linda couldn't hear what they were saying. She felt the sides for volume buttons and cranked it up as far as it could go, but still couldn't hear them. No audio. It might have come as a relief when she'd first discovered the cameras. It only fueled her anger now.

What the fuck is she doing in there? Why did he let her in?

Teri Lumley grabbed Frank's hands and put them in her lap. Linda balled her own hands into fists.

I'll kill her.

Frank looked directly at the camera, directly at *Linda*, and pulled his hands away.

Good boy. Now go to bed, bitch.

He faked a smile and said something, giving her reply a cautious nod.

Frank stood first. Teri Lumley followed him a moment later and stopped much too close to him.

The kiss happened so fast Linda couldn't tell who'd started it, and it wasn't as if she could rewind the tape and see an instant replay. One moment they were standing in front of each other, and the next, they were kissing.

Her heartbeat quickened, dumping poison into her veins. "Son of a bitch." She slapped at the screen as if doing so would make it stop. *"Son of a bitch!"*

Over the past year, she'd hardened her heart toward Frank and wasn't prepared for how much seeing him with someone else would hurt. As she headed toward the door to confront him, she marveled at just how far she'd come from the sibling-like love she thought she'd felt for him only moments before to the murderous rage this one brief infidelity had caused.

When she turned back to the screen, Frank had already pulled away from the Lumley woman and was pointing at the door. It didn't negate the fact that he'd kissed her, but at least he'd stopped himself before it could go any further.

Linda relished Teri Lumley's look of disgrace as the woman left Frank's room.

Less than a minute later, Frank was knocking on her door.

"Go away," she snapped.

"Hon, it's me."

"I said go away!"

Her voice broke. She hadn't even realized she'd been crying. Her gaze fell to the handle as he jiggled it. Worrying she'd left it unlocked and he'd see her standing there crying, she pressed her palms flat against the door.

"Linda, what's wrong?"

If she hadn't wanted to hide the evidence of the pain his

betrayal had caused, she might have opened the door just to slap him in the face.

"I don't want to talk to you. Just leave me alone!"

She stood watching the empty room on the TV screen for Frank to return until she grew annoyed and turned it off. In the blank screen, she caught a glimpse of her harrowed reflection.

First thing in the morning, she was leaving whether Frank came with her or not. Refund or no refund.

Nothing was worth so much pain.

As she decided this, the shouting began in the room next door.

FRANK HAD no idea what had gotten into Linda, but he wasn't about to stand outside her door all night waiting for her to come around. He lingered a moment longer before moving next door and knocking.

"That you, Ter?" The voice behind the door sounded groggy.

"It's Frank."

"Frank?" Glass clinked inside. "Hang on a second, buddy."

Time drew out long enough for Frank to regret his decision to speak to Neville, but before he could excuse himself, Neville opened the door a crack.

"Hey, Frank!" He seemed overly chummy, his eyes slightly bleary. "What's up?"

"Can we talk?"

"Sure." Neville opened the door to a room in complete disarray. Frank smelled the wine on the man's breath as he stepped in. "To what do I owe the pleasure?"

"Doing some redecorating?" Frank crossed a pile of clothing and open suitcases to the desk Neville had pulled away from the wall. He sat in the chair.

"You know they put cameras in our rooms?"

"I saw that."

Neville nodded and poured himself another glass of wine.

"Where'd you get that bottle?"

"Snuck down to the cellar." He winked. Indicating the second glass, he said, "Care to join?"

"I'm good, thanks."

He winked again, as if he was in on the joke. "Got to keep the mind sharp, hey?"

Frank ignored the insinuation. "Your wife visited me just now."

"She did, did she?" Neville turned away with a dismissive shrug. "I *thought* she might have had her eye on you..."

"It wasn't like that," Frank said hastily. "She said that you've been talking about me and Linda."

Neville flopped back against the piled pillows with an exasperated sigh, somehow managing not to spill his wine.

"Well, have you?"

"I may have said a few things..."

Frank's pulse quickened. "Like?"

Neville sharpened his gaze. "Like if this is gonna be a battle of wills, you and your pretty little lady love are gonna come up short."

"Look, man, I don't know what you think is going on here—"

"Don't *bullshit* me, Moffat." Neville rose angrily from the pillows, fell back against the headboard and struck his head. He shook it clear. "You want to win this as much as I do."

"There's nothing to win! Jesus, man!"

"You said it yourself, Frank. A *Battle Royale*. That's what you said, isn't it?"

"I was being sarcastic."

"Oh, were you? Because you looked dead serious to me." Neville showed his teeth in a grin, stained red from the wine. "Now get the fuck out of my room." He picked up the remote and flicked on the television.

He blinked at it blearily. Frank followed his gaze to the screen, where Neville's wife lay sprawled on her covers, eyes closed, stroking herself through the silk of her nightgown.

The two men turned to each other for a long, tense moment.

"Turn it off," Frank said.

Neville tried. "The remote won't work." He turned a thunderous glare back to Frank. "Don't *look*, goddammit!"

Frank pulled his attention away from the screen.

"What is she *doing*?" Neville said. "I told her there's a camera..."

"Did you turn this on before? Were you watching her room?"

Neville scowled at the implication. "What the hell business is that of yours?"

"Were you, or not?" Frank asked, more irritably than he'd meant to.

"Are you implying I've been spying on my own *wife*?" He got up wearily.

"Where are you going?"

"I'm going to tell her to fucking stop."

Frank grabbed the man's arm as he passed, but Neville tore it free and punched him in the jaw. Stars flooded Frank's vision, and he fell against the TV stand. The television tipped back against the wall, and Frank's cheek pressed against the image of Teri Lumley masturbating.

"Stop looking at her!"

Neville launched himself at him. Frank slipped out of the way a moment before the fist connected with the television and the screen split and went blank.

He saw Neville stagger back to swing again in the blank screen, and he kicked out at the man's feet. Neville tripped and sprawled drunkenly over the bed. He lay there panting for a long moment.

"Are you okay?"

"Fuck you." Neville rolled over onto his back and looked up at Frank with surprisingly clear eyes. "You want

to fuck my wife? Be my guest. This isn't even *about* that anymore."

"Goddammit Neville, nothing *happened* between us!"

Neville rolled over and squeezed his eyes shut with a growl. "I am so fucking done with this shit, man. Just let me sleep."

"Neville—"

"*Let me sleep!*"

The words rang in Frank's ears. Holding his sore jaw, he turned and left the room. He looked out over the railing at the empty lobby below before knocking again on Linda's door.

"Linda? I know you can hear me. I just want you to know I'm going home first thing in the morning. You don't have to come with me. I'll take a cab if I have to, but I can't stay here anymore. I know I pushed you into this. I know you don't really want to be here. You can stop pretending for me now, okay?"

He leaned his forehead against the door, breathing deeply out his nose, waiting for her to say something. *Anything.*

But she remained silent.

"That's all I wanted to say." He pushed away from her door. "Except that I hope you'll come with me, okay? Goodnight."

LINDA STOOD by the door until Frank disappeared out of sight from the peephole. She changed into a long t-shirt and slipped under the sheet, the blanket pushed to the foot of her bed, the room too warm. She tossed and turned for a long time, unable to sleep.

Somehow Frank had known she'd only come here to placate him. Somehow he'd been able to see right through her facade, while his own motivations remained a complete mystery to her.

It's over, she thought. *I shouldn't care that he kissed an-other woman.*

She rolled over and stared up at the moonlit ceiling.

I shouldn't care. But I do.

Her head swam in the darkness. She'd overindulged with the wine and aperitif, and drunken overthinking never led to productive solutions. Fed up, she flicked on the light. The room stopped spinning.

Linda couldn't remember being this drunk since the last time she and Frank had gone on vacation together, shortly before her diagnosis.

It had been a honeymoon destination, several months after the wedding. Palm trees, beaches, and late nights spent drinking and dancing. Frank only danced when she got him drunk enough, and that night, both of them had consumed just enough tequila to lose their inhibitions. When they'd returned to their room sometime after three in the morning, they'd already half undressed.

The hotel room had overlooked the ocean. They'd opened the shutters wide, and she'd sat on a wooden storage chest in front of the window. Frank had slipped off her panties while she'd stroked him hard and pulled him inside of her, and the two of them had fucked right by the open window until they came together.

No sleep for me tonight, she thought, feeling the familiar throb between her legs. *Not now.*

She crept to the door and opened it quietly, fearful of waking the others.

Frogs chirped and moonlight cascaded through the front windows, giving the lodge an eerie, bone-white glow when she stepped out into the hall. Though the night was still warm, she shivered when a loon called out over the lake.

She went to the bathroom first. Her bladder never quite felt completely emptied since her surgery, even though it had been a kidney they'd removed. She'd have to pee again first thing in the morning or maybe again in the night. It was an annoying side effect—something she'd gotten used to, but it still caused frustration. But it was better than the cancer.

I'd rather pee in a bag the rest of my life than go through another year like that, she thought as the toilet gurgled.

Linda stood in front of the sink and rinsed between her legs. The cold water against her skin didn't dull the urge to fuck, but somehow made it stronger. She wanted nothing more than to jump someone's bones. Anyone would do and as soon as possible. Quickly, she washed her hands and patted herself dry with a hand towel, which she tossed in the hamper.

She pictured Neville's muscular body as he slept naked under the sheet, and she fought the urge to knock on his door. Even if she could have brought herself to cheat on Frank, if she'd still been angry about the kiss, it was highly possible Neville would reject her. Attempting it wasn't worth risking the hit to her ego at such a fragile moment.

She found Frank's door unlocked as though he might be expecting company. The brunette bitch across the hall, maybe.

No. He's not a door locker. How many times have I walked in on him while he's on the toilet? Too many to count.

She peered up and down the hall and slipped into his room.

An angular slat of moonlight illuminated his bed. He lay on his back under the white sheet, sleeping like a vampire, like the dead. She crept to the bed and lowered herself onto the mattress. His breathing remained even, in and out through his nose the way it always did when he slept.

Under the covers, she slid her hand over the light hairs on his thigh until she found his cock, already semi-hard. He must have been having good dreams. She stroked him a few times, but his breathing never increased.

Still asleep, she thought. *Good. He won't question it. Won't ruin it with talking.*

Raising the sheet, she straddled him. The flood of relief

as she felt his hardness inside her lasted until Frank opened his eyes.

"Linda?" He blinked, looking confused and hopeful.

Guilt threatened to derail her desire, and she placed a finger on his lips, rising on her knees until he was about to slip out of her. "Shhh." She lowered herself, twisting her hips. She rose slowly and descended, twisting until she grinded against his thighs.

Confusion forgotten or simply set aside, Frank grasped her hips.

She rode him harder, allowing herself small moans of pleasure, still very aware of the cameras. The thought that someone might be spying on them—Alex maybe, even Teri—increased her enjoyment until her whole body shuddered in orgasm, squeezing him to his own climax.

She collapsed on top of him with her head against his on the pillow, facing away, feeling his chest rise and fall, his wild heart beating out of sync to hers.

Her eyes felt heavy. It would be too easy to fall asleep here and fall back into the pattern.

Would it hurt so much?

She forced her eyes open.

Not me, maybe, she thought. *But him. Best to tear the bandage off quickly.*

"I should go," she said, rising from the bed.

"Linda, what—?"

"We'll talk in the morning." She pulled down her long t-shirt and stepped out into the hall, closing the door behind her without looking back.

She heard hushed voices in the main hall and paused before turning the corner.

"—you just know Harriet's gonna want a little extra something on her check for pulling that stunt in her room," Neville hissed.

"If she wants to renegotiate her contract next time, that's up to—"

Alex hushed. The silence drew out.

Certain she'd been caught, Linda turned the corner.

The men stood Neville's doorway. They saw her and stepped into his room without acknowledging her, closing the door behind them.

Linda returned to her room, wondering what the hell that was about.

She didn't waste much time thinking about it, having already decided to leave with Frank in the morning. Maybe they could separate amicably. Maybe it would be a difficult break. That look of hope in his eyes told her it would likely be the latter.

But they would do it themselves. This place had only confused their predicament.

She flicked off the light, exhausted and mostly satisfied. When she laid her head against the pillow, she immediately fell into a deep and restful sleep.

CHAPTER 8

DOGS

W hen Frank stepped into the dining room the next morning, Linda was already eating scrambled eggs and toast. He'd had trouble sleeping after Linda left, uncertain what had caused her 180 from being pissed off at him to jumping his bones within the span of an hour.

"Someone's got an appetite," he said with a playful smirk.

Linda looked up at him, scooped another forkful of bright yellow egg into her mouth, and chewed.

"Oh, okay, we're not talking now? Because it seemed like you were real interested in me last night."

She sipped her coffee. "I wasn't the only one interested in you last night."

"Oh, so that's what this is about. You saw what happened with Teri Lumley. I told her not to come in, Linda."

She didn't look up from her plate. "You didn't kick her out."

"I knew it. I knew you saw. That's why you came into my room last night, isn't it? You got jealous so you had to prove you still own my dick, right?" He realized how self-satisfied he must sound and changed tack. "I mean, what was I gonna do, physically push her out the door?"

Linda shrugged.

"She came to me because she was concerned about her husband, okay? I didn't *want* that to happen."

"Yes you did, Frank. You just didn't want an audience."

"Fine, okay, *part of me* wanted her. I mean, obviously, or it wouldn't have happened." He pulled out the chair across from her and sat. The steaming cup of coffee between them smelled strong and black.

Like Neville, he thought.

"Like you've never had thoughts about other men."

Don't give her any ideas, Frank.

"I wouldn't act on them," she said.

"And I didn't! I stopped it, or did you not see that?"

"It was hard to tell with all the groping."

Frank shook his head. "You've gotta be crazy."

Linda shrugged, not looking up from her food. "I get it, Frank. She's an attractive woman. We hadn't been intimate in a long time. Shit happens."

"You say that, but I don't think you mean it."

Her eyes met his, clear and unwavering. Thinking back to what she'd written on her assessment steeled her resolve. Those words unchangeable, graven on paper.

"Forget it. If the tables were turned, I might have done the same."

"You—" He chose to ignore it. "Those two. I don't even know if they really are who they say they are. They could be —I don't know. I mean, for all we know, they're in on this, right?"

"It doesn't matter. We're leaving, aren't we? That's what you decided?"

"We're leaving," he agreed. "But I don't want to leave if we're going back to separate beds. Separate lives. I'll stay here as long as it takes. I just want us to be good again. Like we used to be."

Linda blew on her coffee. "Honestly, Frank, I don't think that's ever going to happen."

She took a casual sip from the mug emblazoned with the Lone Loon Lodge logo, and Frank held her gaze. When he realized she wasn't backing down, he pushed up from the table, scooped himself some eggs, plated bacon, toast, some jam packets, and a carton of milk and returned to his seat.

"You sure got a funny way of cutting ties, slipping into my room in the middle of the night. Once more for old times, eh?"

"It was a mistake, Frank. I'm sorry, but that's all it was."

Frank bit his lip and nodded. He had no appetite, but he ate anyway, supposing he'd need sustenance for the long drive ahead of them.

Linda waved her fork in the direction of his face. "He hit you?"

"Yeah he did. Sucker punch." Frank touched the large purple bruise on his jaw. "Will you do me one favor before we go?"

Linda finished chewing. "Depends."

"Come for a walk with me."

"That's it?"

He saw her words on the page between them as if they'd been written on her face: *I'm here because Frank needs closure.*

"That's all," he said. "You don't have to forgive me. We don't even have to talk about it if you don't want. Just take a walk with me in the woods. It's a nice day. The sun's shining. Who knows when we'll ever get to do that again?"

Linda chewed thoughtfully before shrugging. "I can't see any harm in that."

"Great." Frank smiled and began to eat. "This bacon's to die for," he said, but the reference failed to return a smile.

THE LUMLEYS never made it to breakfast, and Alex was nowhere in sight when Frank and Linda rang the bell in the lobby. She knocked on the office door and jiggled the handle but found it locked, so they headed out into the woods to the east of the lodge, circling the lake, which grew much wider the farther they got from the other buildings.

They'd been walking maybe twenty minutes through the dense forest, sweating under the hot morning sun, when they first came upon the tree with initials engraved in its bark: **HK + JD**.

The letters had mostly grown over, and sap had oozed from a long, vertical gash above them into the woody notches. Frank ran his fingers through the grooves of the K as they passed.

"Wonder if these two are still together," he said.

A few paces ahead, Linda glanced back. "That's got to be at least twenty years old. If those two are still alive, they probably don't even remember each other."

Frank rolled his eyes.

They trudged onward, over a washout caused by a nearby beaver dam and up a hill to where the widely spaced giant redwoods creaked and groaned, their gently swaying canopy high above, turning day to dusk.

"Sounds like a haunted house out here," Frank said.

Linda peered over her shoulder with a quizzical look.

"All that creaking," he explained. "When's the last time you heard a bird?"

She stopped a moment with an ear cocked, and Frank caught up to her. "There's one."

Frank listened. After a few seconds, he heard a single bird calling from a good distance away. "Kinda sounds like a monkey."

"I'm pretty sure they don't have monkeys in Montana."

"I didn't say it *was* a monkey. It does sound like it though, doesn't it?"

"Kind of, I guess." She shrugged. "Whatever it is it sounds like, it's laughing."

"You think it's laughing at us?"

Linda gave him a look of annoyance and continued ahead.

"Are we gonna talk about this, Lin?" he called after her.

She didn't slow her pace. "Haven't we done enough talking? All we do is talk talk talk, blah blah blah blah blah. It's worse than C-SPAN."

"So you're done, are you? Just because of a kiss?"

She rounded on him. "I don't give a shit about the kiss, Frank! It's a symptom of the larger issue. We're incompatible."

"We used to be compatible."

"We *used to be* in our twenties. We used to run marathons and screw in strange places. We *used* to make time for each other."

"Don't lay that shit on me—"

"I'm not *laying* anything on you, Frank. I'm guilty of it too. And that's my whole point."

Frank shrugged. "We gave up a long weekend to save our marriage. I could be relaxing. You could be getting work done. But we came here."

"And we couldn't even make it through the night."

"Those two crazy people—"

"It's not *just them*, Frank! It's *us*. Nine years ago we would have never let something like that come between us. Because we *cared enough* to fight for us. Because there was something to fight *for*. Now all we do is fight each other."

"We still want the same things."

"Do we? When's the last time we talked about the future? When's the last time we planned anything together?"

Frank thought to mention this weekend again, but decided against it. "We planned a climbing trip with Trevor and Dillon."

"You don't even like them."

"But I went. I went for you."

"I don't *want* you to have to do things because *I* want them, Frank."

"Well, we can't always want the same things. I mean, isn't that what a marriage is? A series of compromises?"

"If that's what you think marriage is supposed to be—"

"Not just for me," he said exasperatedly. "For you too."

"Oh, well thank you for including me."

"Jesus Fucking Christ, Linda! Remember last year when I wanted to do that locked room mystery thing, but you thought it was corny? And I mentioned it a couple of times, so you backed down and we went and you ended up having a good time?"

"It was tolerable."

"That's compromise."

She rolled her eyes.

"Well, isn't it?"

"I thought you wouldn't stop talking about it if I didn't go."

"Regardless, you could have ignored me. You could have told me to shut up about it. But you went with me and you had a tolerable time."

She said nothing, only trudged onward into thick green underbrush. "Ow!" She stopped walking and raised a bare leg to look at her calf. "Don't walk in this. It's prickly."

"That's juniper," Frank told her. "It's what they make gin from."

"Thanks for letting me know."

"I didn't see it until you were in it."

Linda stepped out of the bush and walked around its outer edge where the juniper grew taller and thicker, the branches like dry, twisted vines.

"Lin, I know I messed up last night. If I could take it back, I would—"

"I feel like we're going around in circles," she muttered.

"Maybe we are. But just tell me you don't love me and I'll—"

"*No*, Frank. We're just going around in circles! There it is again!"

"There *what* is?"

She pointed to it.

The tree with initials carved in its bark.

"*One...*"

The agony as the trap snapped closed on Frank's leg, crippling him.

"*Two...*"

The revelation of the chain, linking the trap to the tree with a declaration of love carved under its oozing gash.

"*Three!*"

Linda pried open the metal jaws, tearing her fingernails to the quick, and before she could even get it wide enough for Frank to pull out his foot, it clamped down harder, opening the wound further and bringing fresh blood.

The barks of dogs somewhere in the woods met Frank's agonized howl, and the barks grew nearer.

Frank and Linda's eyes met in shared fear.

"Probably just hunters," she assured him.

The barking grew vicious, as though the dogs had found their quarry and had begun salivating to tear it to shreds.

The first appeared over the hill, where the tops of the ancient redwoods swayed and groaned in the hot summer breeze. Even from a distance, it looked big and mean and nothing like a hunting dog, fangs visible as it bolted down toward the valley where the two of them sat, completely exposed.

"Go," Frank said.

"I'm not leaving without you."

"Fine. We'll do it together."

Linda nodded, and the two of them pulled the jaws apart. On the verge of passing out, Frank added very little strength, but with both working together, the bloodied metal teeth snapped open just as the dog hit the leafy valley floor and set its sights on them.

Linda grabbed Frank's hand and pulled him to his feet.

The Rottweiler charged forward, kicking through underbrush and dry branches without taking its beady, brown eyes off them. It was so close now they could hear its panting and the trundling of its paws on hard-packed earth.

Frank tripped on a loose stone, and his leg gave out. He

fell back on his ass, bringing Linda down to her knees beside him.

She closed her fingers on his and they pushed to their feet, but the dog had closed the distance, its snout wrinkled in a snarl, strings of saliva dripping from its yellowed fangs.

Linda shouted, "*The trap!*"

The dog was less than ten feet from tearing the two of them to shreds. They wouldn't make it far before they'd have to fight or die.

Nearest to the chain, Frank tore his hand from hers and jerked the trap closer. The jaws snapped down so hard on the dog's front leg that Frank heard the bone crack as he and Linda skittered out of its way.

The chain pulled taut, and the dog's forward momentum whipped it around in a tight half circle. It slammed down into the dirt, its muscular body scattering leaves, and yelped as it licked its injured leg.

Frank paid it only a moment's attention. Two more Rottweilers had appeared over the ridge and barreled down toward the valley floor.

"Come on!" Linda cried.

She rushed toward the patch of junipers and plunged in, gritting her teeth against the prickles. Frank hesitated only a moment before following, knowing it would be more painful for him without a shoe and with the fresh wound exposed on his ankle but aware they were short of options. With no second trap to ensnare one more dog, let alone the two of them, he hoped the juniper would deter the dogs long enough that they would give up the chase and go home.

A high, single-note whistle stopped the charging dogs in their tracks. They panted halfway up the hill, torn between hunger and loyalty. Another whistle made them dart around and tear back up the hill.

The dog in the trap lay on its side and howled.

"This way," Linda said, stepping out of the brush.

Frank hobbled along behind her. They were lost, but she often managed to find her way as long as the sun was visible.

With any luck, they would get back to the lodge or at least as far as the lake before the dogs found them again, or their master saw what they'd done to the first dog.

Frank's leg hurt like hell. Dried leaves stuck to tacky blood on his sock and ankle, and every time he put a little bit of weight on his leg, he felt like he might black out from the pain.

But they were alive and they were together.

That had to count for something.

Chapter 9

Refuge

On the verge of passing out several times, suffering under the midafternoon sun, Frank stumbled along behind Linda on his injured leg. After walking for what seemed like hours, they finally came to a clearing with a small body of brown water, little more than a pond.

Frank dropped to his knees on the pine-carpeted shore and splashed his hands in the water. He doused his hair, neck, and armpits with the gritty water. Despite being on the verge of dehydration, he didn't dare drink any. He'd seen enough survival reality shows to know it was a surefire way to get sick.

When he looked up from the water, he saw the cabin.

The way the sunlight flickered off the old graying wood and sloped roof, he wasn't sure if it was real or a mirage until Linda confirmed it.

She favored him with a sympathetic look. "Think you can make it?"

"We've come this far."

Linda helped him to his feet, and they followed along the edge of the pond, pushing aside low branches and sidestepping marshy areas.

Nearing where the woods had been cleared to build the cabin and had since grown over, Linda stopped. "What if this is where the dogs came from?"

"I need water," Frank said. "A phone. If that place has either, I don't care if they're breeding those motherfuckers."

She nodded and continued. At the edge of the trees, she surveyed the area. Beyond a patch of dead leaves surrounding the cabin was an open field of scrub grass and stones. A two-rut road led from there into dense woods.

No vehicles in sight. Better yet, no sign of any dogs.

"Okay." She drew his arm over her shoulder. "Let's go."

They walked side by side to the back porch, Linda carrying much of Frank's weight as he hobbled along beside her. Crickets chirped somewhere in the bone-dry field. Brittle grass swished at their feet.

On the porch, they navigated broken boards and loose nails to reach the door. Frank leaned against the splintered railing, taking the weight off his bad leg while Linda peered in through a window coated with grime, soot, dust, or a combination of all three. Flies buzzed inside so loudly Frank thought there must be hundreds of them.

"Well?"

"Well, I don't think anyone's been in here in decades," she said. "There's a phone, but I doubt it works. I didn't see any cables, did you?"

Frank shook his head.

"There's a sewing machine. Maybe there's some thread we can use to sew you up."

"Small miracles," he said despondently.

Linda tried the handle, and the door creaked open on a gasp of dust that swirled in the sunlight. Frank thought of the cigarillos he'd left in his room. He would have killed for one of them right now.

"Check for traps," he said.

Linda spooked, withdrawing her foot. She looked back with a scowl.

"Trip wires. Stuff like that. I mean, you can never be too cautious."

Linda shook her head and stepped in quickly to spite him. She turned and threw her hands out. "No traps. See?"

Frank lingered a moment, still nervous.

She pouted. "You want help?"

Linda felt bad teasing him when he'd done such an admirable job following her without much complaining on their way here. But she'd found in her time living with Frank that he tended to work better with a little push.

"I can do it," he said, grunting as he pushed off from the railing. The board split under his weight, and he stumbled forward, pain shooting up his leg as he lurched through the doorway to where Linda caught him, his head nestled against her breasts.

She patted him on the back. Frank couldn't tell if she was genuinely sympathetic or patronizing him, but it felt nice. "It really does hurt, you know."

"It *looks* like it hurts. We'll get you fixed up." She gave him a brisk stroke between his shoulders. "Come on. Sit down over here."

She helped him to a metal-frame desk chair, its blood red vinyl cushion burst open like a zit, dirty, yellow foam scattered around it on dusty, plastic tiles. She swatted dust and buzzing flies from the seat and eased him onto it.

He sighed, glad to finally be able to rest both legs.

The whole place smelled like stale beer, mustiness, and copper. Maybe fifteen feet at its widest, the floor of the small hunting cabin was littered with newsprint, pine needles, and crushed beer cans, flies darting in and out of their open tabs. Cupboards lined the wall to his immediate left, with a few dusty food tins and boxes visible on doorless shelves. Below the cupboards was a counter lined with old newspapers and a sink with a hand pump.

Chains hung from the ceiling at the center of the room with fat hooks fastened at the ends. Frank guessed they must be for stringing up deer and gutting them. More flies alighted on the old bloodstains below.

Against the opposite wall stood an old push-pedal sewing machine. Beside it was a black iron stove with a white enamel oven door, the stovepipe broken and bent a foot below the roof. Water dripped from the remaining pipe segment left in the ceiling, clanging on the copper kettle that was perched on the stovetop.

Linda didn't like the look of those hooks hung from the ceiling and gave them a wide berth on her way to the sewing machine in search of needle and thread. The drawers reeked of animal urine, their bottoms littered with turds. She found a scattering of various needles and a few spools of thread in various colors in the last drawer and brought them back to Frank.

He'd been staring vacantly at the single painting beside the stove, a plain-looking watercolor of a pot of flowers that didn't seem to belong in a place like this.

"Here we go." Linda knelt down in front of him. "I'm gonna have to take off your sock."

Frank nodded and looked away, as if not seeing it might lessen the pain. Linda gingerly peeled the blood-encrusted sock away from his flesh, rolled it off his foot, and tossed it aside. Inspecting the wound, she saw it was actually two separate gashes, one deeper and wider than the other. Fortunately, the two hadn't connected at the front or the back of his leg.

"Do you have your lighter?"

"I think so..."

Frank dug into a pocket and handed it to her. Linda struck the wheel multiple times before it caught, and she held one of the thicker needles she'd found over the flickering yellow flame until it glowed red, scorching her fingers. She winced and blew on the needle to cool it, then looped a strand of forest-green thread through the eye. Once she'd doubled it, she fixed Frank with a sympathetic look.

"I'm not gonna lie and say this won't sting."

Frank nodded, already steeling himself against the pain. "Are you sure we should do this? I mean, it could be infected. That trap was pretty rusty."

"It's still bleeding though. If I don't sew it up and we

don't get you to a hospital soon, you'll lose too much blood. Pass out. I don't think it hit your femoral artery—"

"I'm guessing that would be bad."

"That would be extremely bad. But it has torn the muscle." Linda tried to look at the wound with clinical detachment, but it nearly made her vomit when she saw how the skin and muscle had peeled back to reveal naked bone. She swallowed hard. "Nothing looks broken, thank God. Can you rotate it?"

Frank tried. The enormity of the pain caused stars to flash in front of his eyes, and he couldn't tell if it actually worked until Linda said, "Good. Tendons are fine. If only we had some rubbing alcohol or something to clean the wound."

"I've got my flask." He groaned against a wave of pain. "Left cargo pocket."

"Never in my life have I been gladder for your addictive personality." Linda grinned as she reached into his pocket.

"That's not it," he said.

She raised an eyebrow. "You're gonna try that one again, are you?"

"Hey. Laughter's all I got."

She gave him a wry look and removed the flask, unscrewed the top, and sniffed it. "You don't drink vodka."

"Less of a smell," he explained.

"We all have our priorities, I guess." She raised his foot and held the flask over the wound. "Ready?"

"As I'll ever be."

She squeezed her eyes shut and tipped the flask.

Vodka splashed over Frank's calf, the wound burning so badly he expected to see the flesh bubble. The searing liquid and blood dripped pink on the grayed tiles. Gritting his teeth and balling his hands into fists, he still nearly blacked out.

"You alive?"

"For now," he grunted.

"Okay." She let out a tortured breath through her nose. "Now the real fun starts."

Linda rested his foot on her thigh and hesitated with the needle poised over the raw flesh surrounding his wound.

"I can do it if it's too much for you," he said.

Linda swallowed hard. "I'll be fine."

"Sure you will." He pasted a smile on his sickly, pale face. "There's got to be at least a part of you that's wanted to torture me for a good while now. You've got this."

Linda smiled back, thankful for the levity and the vote of confidence. She poked the needle into him, surprised at how much the flesh stretched before it finally tore through. To his credit, Frank merely grunted, squeezing high on the thigh of his uninjured leg as if to balance out the pain.

The second jab went smoother, since Linda knew how much pressure was required, and she drew the thread all the way through to the knot she'd tied at the end, pulling the wound shut.

"You have really hairy legs," she said, jabbing the needle in and pulling it out the other side.

"I know. It's what kept me from my dream of swimming in the Olympics."

"You could've just used Nair." She pulled the flesh together.

"You know, I never thought of that. I guess it's too late for that now." He watched her face as she worked. "What about you? How does someone grow up on the ocean and never learn to swim?"

"I can swim."

Frank grinned. "Yeah? What would you call that stroke you do? The 'eggbeater'?"

"It's a dog paddle."

"A three-legged dog," he said.

Linda remembered the injured dog whimpering in the trap, and instead of sympathy, she felt cold fear. Frank tried to cover the gaffe with a weak chuckle.

Fingers quivering, she dug the needle in and pulled it through, closing it in a crooked, puckered smile. She bit the end of the thread, tasting Frank's coppery, salty blood, and tied it taut.

"One down, one to go," she said, attempting a brave tone.

"I think I'm gonna need some of that vodka."

She passed him the flask and he swigged. "Want some?"

"I'm good," she said, threading the needle.

He downed the rest and screwed on the cap. "Okay. Let's do this."

Linda rotated his leg and poked the needle through, careful not to puncture the exposed tendon. She pulled it through the other side, drawing the skin together.

"*MOFFATS!*"

The voice startled her, and her next stitch split his skin open to the wound.

"*Ah!*"

"*Sorry.*"

"It's okay. Was that Neville?"

"I think so."

"*Frank! Linda!*" Teri called, singsong. "*Where are you two?*"

"We're in here!" Linda shouted. She turned to Frank. "You okay for a second?"

"Yeah, of course."

"Hold this." She handed him the needle and set his foot down gently before crossing the cabin to the front windows.

"*LiinnnnDA!*"

She saw the couple crossing the open field, hand in hand. Neville wore ankle-length slacks and an open-collared, short-sleeved shirt that rustled in the same breeze fluttering the hem of Teri's short sundress. Neville had to keep a hand on his fedora to stop it from flying off his head. Both of them wore overly large sunglasses. Together, they looked like a fashion ad.

"In here!" Linda called out again.

The Lumleys turned quizzical looks on each other as if they might have only heard her faintly.

Linda rubbed dirt off one of the panes with her sleeve and waved at them, but she realized the sun would be in their eyes, so she yelled out, "*We're in here!*"

A gunshot drowned out her cry.

She saw the bullet explode out of Neville's chest a moment later, and he dropped to his knees with a stunned expression, pulling Teri down with him until she tore her hand free of his grasp.

Linda dropped down below the window, heart racing.

"Was that Neville?" he asked, thinking the crazy son of a bitch had brought along the rifle Linda had seen him with the other day.

"*They shot him.*" Linda said, barely able to believe what she'd just seen with her own eyes, despite the image of it sun-blasted onto her retinas.

"*Shot him?* Who? Jesus, is he...?"

She nodded.

"Jesus Christ."

Out in the field, Teri screamed.

Frank began to push himself up from the chair.

"*Stay down.* If they see you..."

"What's going on out there? What the fuck is *happening?*"

"I don't know."

He limped over, hunched down so he wouldn't be seen through the window.

If she hadn't just been dealing with Frank's injury, Linda thought she might have lost her mind with fear in that moment. "They shot him in the chest. It just *fucking exploded.* But Teri...she's still out there."

"Fuck..." He shook his head. "We've gotta help her."

"*How?* We'd be fish in a barrel."

"*Well, we can't just let them kill her too.*" He scrutinized her. "We have to do *something.*"

Linda shook her head. When she closed her eyes, she saw Neville drop to his knees again and again like an instant replay, so she forced herself to look Frank in the eye. "I don't know what to do. I don't know."

A high, single-note whistle pierced the sudden silence.

Teri's terrified whimpers stopped abruptly.

Linda and Frank peered over the windowsill and out through the dingy glass.

Neville lay where he'd fallen, face down in the grass about twenty feet from the cabin. His hat had caught in the wind and rolled toward the house. Teri sat on her Ugg boots beside him, the hem of her dress riding high on her thighs, her whole body quivering as she wept.

A man emerged from the trees, then another, both dressed in bulky camo and both carrying rifles.

"What the living fuck?" Frank muttered.

The men took their time crossing the field as if they couldn't care less whether or not someone happened to see what they'd done. Teri staggered to her feet, raising her hands to protect herself as the men drew nearer.

"We ain't gonna hurt you, pretty lady," the heavyset man to her left said, just barely audible from the cabin. His face was all beard aside from his nose and small forehead, between which the same rainbow-tinted sunglasses Trevor had worn reflected a glint of sunlight in Frank and Linda's eyes. "What in Jesus's holy name you two doin' out here dressed like that?" He sounded exasperated, as if shooting Neville had spoiled an otherwise good day. "Holy hell, lady, don't ya'll know it's huntin' season? Ya'll should be wearin' one of them orange vests or some shit, that's why your man got shot right there."

"Don't cuss, Jackson." The second guy wore camo face paint on his face and walked favoring his left side, loping like a man with an old injury. He held the stock of his rifle in his last remaining arm. "There now, angel, he's still breathin'." His voice was soft and soothing. "He ain't dead."

Teri said something, but neither Linda nor Frank could hear it through the window.

"It was an accident, princess. You got us all wrong. It's

like what Jackson said, if you'd-a been wearing vests like you s'posed to, your man wouldn't-a gotten himself shot now, would he?"

"He's lying," Frank said.

Linda agreed with a solemn nod. If they'd been in the middle of the woods, it might have been accidental. But Neville and Teri had been out in middle of a wide-open field. No hunter who'd spent that much money on camo and weaponry would have ever mistaken them for deer.

They'd been *aiming* for him.

"Go on back and get Keith and the four-wheelers," the one-armed man said to the guy with the beard.

"Nuh-uh, how come I gotta get him?"

"'Cause I said, that's why. You wanna carry this fella on your back be my guest, but I ain't takin' turns."

The bearded guy turned in a huff. The one-armed man watched him lumber off toward the woods a moment before approaching Teri. She raised her hands, begging him to spare her in a voice too quiet for Frank or Linda to hear.

"He's gonna kill her," Frank said.

"If she's lucky."

His eyes widened at the implication.

"It's like my friend said, princess, we ain't gonna hurt you." The man flashed a dark grin. "What kind of hosts would we be if we done that?"

An engine fired up in the woods. The one-armed hunter cocked his ear toward the sound, smiling wide.

Teri threw herself over Neville's body to protect him from further harm.

"He's *dead*, princess."

She shook her head, throwing weak punches at the man's leg. The hunter stepped back from her fists with a toothy grin.

"Well, I don't s'pose there's much point puttin' up the pretense if you ain't gonna play along!"

He faked a lunge and Teri scrambled backward.

"Please, please just let me go, I didn't see anything, I swear!"

The man grabbed her by the hair, his rifle swinging on its shoulder strap. She screamed and pulled away, but he dragged her forward.

"What are we gonna do?" Frank asked.

"I don't know," Linda said, although she realized he was probably talking to himself.

The ATV roared out of the trees then, the guy the one-armed man had called Jackson standing on the pedals. He revved the machine, tearing up dirt and grass on his way to the murder scene.

"We have to do *something*."

"They've got *rifles*, Frank. We do anything, they'll kill us too."

Frank sank against the wall. "I can't sit here and watch it. They're gonna *kill* her."

He was right. But Linda couldn't take her eyes off them. Someone had to bear witness, despite the horror of it.

The one-armed man pulled a knife from his belt. Behind him, Jackson stopped the ATV and jumped off.

"Where the heck is Keith?"

"He's back there with the dogs. They been actin' real cagey since what you done to Biscuit."

"Puttin' Biscuit down was a kindness. She wuddn't no good to nobody with her leg all jacked up like that."

Jackson shrugged. "Still. Pro'ly figure if you'd-a done that to their momma, you'd do it to them too."

"Good. Let the little mutt's know their place. Now what are we gon' do with *this* li'l doggy?" The one-armed man still had Teri held by the hair. She hung from his clenched fingers, docile, arms limp.

"Shit, Colby, I bet I can think of a few ideas."

"Watch the cussin'. Go on an get him on the back there, I gotta get L'il Miss Priss to the prom, don't I, princess?"

The man made her nod her head. Jackson uttered a high giggle.

Frank had been staring at the out-of-place painting, focusing all of his fear and anger toward it when it suddenly fell from the wall and landed on its front, shattering the glass.

Linda gave him a furious look as if he'd knocked it over via telepathy. He shrugged innocently, shaking his head.

"What the heck was that?" Jackson said.

The one-armed man, Colby, let go of Teri's hair, and she slumped over her husband's lifeless body as the two men raised their weapons.

"Somebody in the cabin?"

"I look like a redneck magician to you?" Colby asked. "Hustle your fat butt over there an' go check."

Jackson kicked a patch of dirt and grass into the air in a huff and began trudging toward the cabin.

"How the fuck did that fall?" Frank whispered.

"We have to hide. Block the door. *Something*." Linda scrambled to the other side of the cabin. "Get behind the stove."

"I can help."

"There's no time. *Just do it*."

Begrudgingly, Frank dragged himself under the window and crawled between the stove and the wall.

"I can still see your foot."

He drew his injured leg painfully close and felt a sharp pain in his ass. The needle still hung from the thread looped through his wound. He snapped it off and tossed it aside.

Linda scrambled to find something heavy to put in front of the door. Pulling down one of the shelves or dragging the sewing machine over would be too noisy. She settled on the chair, brought it to the door, and wedged it under the handle.

Jackson's boots clomped on the creaky, busted porch. He moved past the window, no more than a dark blur through dirty glass.

She pressed herself against the wall on the far side of the door.

The handle rattled. A panel split as the big man threw his weight against the door, but the chair held firm.

"What's the holdup?" Colby shouted.

"Door's stuck!"

"Well, push it, ya dang pansy!"

"I *am* pushing it!"

The porch groaned as he moved to the window and peered inside, tenting his fat fingers over his eyes. His shadow drew long over the dirty tiles.

Linda held her breath.

"Pitcher fell!" he shouted.

"How come it fell?"

"I look like a redneck magician?"

"You look like a fat idiot, which is what you are."

Jackson muttered, "*Fuck* you" under his breath as his shadow and footfalls retreated from the window.

Frank peered out from behind the stove. He saw Linda holding still against the wall, clearly not daring to move until she knew they were gone, and he shuffled as quietly as possible to the window to look out.

The man called Jackson had stopped in the window directly above Frank, and he squinted up at something. "The shit is this? Aw hell, they got cameras!"

He thrust the butt of his weapon upward. Plastic and glass crunched, and the hunter sidestepped as electronic parts rained down.

"What are we gonna do, Colby?"

"Hang on a dang second, I'm thinkin'. An' watch the cussin'."

Frank couldn't see Teri with the bearded guy taking up much of the window, but he heard her whimper.

"*Shut it!*" Colby snapped.

The sharp slap that followed silenced her.

Linda scuttled over to the window beside Frank, risking a peek over the sill. She watched Jackson tromp away from the cabin toward his friend.

"All right, only one thing we can do far as I can see,"

Colby said. "Gotta recon that fancypants resort on the way back to camp. Make sure nobody seen what they got on that tape."

"What if they already seen it, Colby? What if they done called the cops?"

"Would you calm the heck down? I'll handle Gus, all right? Most important thing right now is we got to erase that video before some idjit puts it up on the innernet. All you gotta worry bout is gettin' him on back-a the quad—"

"—an get him back to camp. I'll figger out the rest."

"Sarge gon' be pissed, ain't he?"

"You just worry bout gettin' this critter back to camp. Let me handle Sarge."

"All right then." Jackson scooped up Neville's limp corpse and hauled him up over his shoulder.

Teri lunged at them on her knees, crying out, and sprawled prostrate in the grass.

Colby sidestepped her fall and turned the movement into a little jig, wearing a gleeful grin. "Aw, beautiful, I'd love to, but you know my dance card's all full!"

Jackson lowered Neville's body onto the back rack. Neville's limbs hung limply over the sides. The big man let them hang and mounted the seat.

"Bungee cord him or he gon' fall off," Colby instructed.

Jackson climbed off in a huff and strapped Neville to the back with the bungee cables already hanging from the bars. "Anything else, your highness?"

"Yeah, why don't you go on and kiss my butt for me real quick?"

Jackson flipped him off and jumped back on the quad. He revved the engine, tore up clumps of dark earth, and roared off toward the trees.

Colby slapped dirt from his cargo pants. "I apologize for my associate's language. He hasn't been housetrained."

"*Fuck you!*" Teri screamed.

"Now what kind of way is that for a lady to talk?" The man tutted and grabbed her around the waist, scooping her up under his arm. He carried her kicking and screaming toward the woods.

Frank slammed a fist against the floor. "Fuck! *Fuck fuck fuck!*" He shouted until his hand bled, and he drew it to his chest with a wince.

"There was nothing we could do, Frank."

"Who the fuck *were* those maniacs?"

Linda shrugged, a steady unpleasant throb in her temples. "Hunters. Some sort of backwoods militia group maybe. Whoever they are, they're too dangerous and too well armed for us to deal with."

He was looking at the floor where his fists had unsettled years of dust.

"Frank. *Frank.*"

He looked up at her.

"We can get help. We just need to get to a phone."

Frank looked far less convinced than she felt, but he nodded, and Linda thought that was something she could build on.

"This fucking painting," he said suddenly, and scuttled across the cabin to the broken frame. "What's this?" He flicked aside shards of glass.

"What?"

"It's a notebook." He showed it to her, a small pad with a worn green cover. "You need to see this."

She came to his side and saw what someone had written neatly in ink on the cover:

$$HK + JD = PAIN$$

"Same thing we saw on the tree," she said.

"Except they solved the equation. What does it mean, you think?"

Linda frowned, thinking. "What's Dr. Kaspar's first name? Do you remember?"

"I don't think anybody told us. I mean, if they did, I don't remember."

"H.K.," she said. "H. Kaspar. Herbert, Hans, Heinrich..."

"Why was it hidden behind the painting? And then it just falls off the wall on its own?" He thumbed through the pages, every bit of space filled with small, neatly penciled letters, but he could only understand the first two words underlined at the top of the first page: *DIE METHODE.* "What language is this?"

Linda snatched it from him. "I recognize some of these words. *Das, die, ein.* Didn't Kaspar's family come from Austria before the war? They speak German there."

"Is 'die' the same in German as it is in English?"

"It means 'the,'" she told him.

Frank considered it. "All right, but that doesn't help us, does it? We still need to get back to the lodge and get the police involved."

"But it *does* help. The trap, the initials, the chain..." She shook the notebook excitedly. "*H.K. plus J.D. equals pain.*"

"Fuck," Frank said as it dawned on him.

"This whole thing is a trap. That's why Trevor and Dillon and the Lumleys' friends were all banged up and bruised like they said. They didn't get in an accident, Frank. They were *fighting for their lives.*"

"We can't trust anybody here. Can we?"

"Just the two of us," she said.

Chapter 10

Fubar

F rank tapped his fingers impatiently while Linda sewed up the second wound, so keyed up thinking about everything that the pain barely registered.

"I don't think the painting fell by accident," he said as she closed the wound.

"You think...what?" she said, the needle clenched between her teeth.

"A trick hanger, maybe. Like in those poltergeist prank videos."

"They would've had to know exactly what was going on at that exact moment."

"There was a camera outside. We never checked in here. This place could be wired just like the lodge."

"You're right." She frowned. "But if they're in on it, then maybe..."

"What?"

"I don't know, but it doesn't *feel right*. You know?"

He nodded. None of it felt right. Not since what had happened last night with the TVs in their bedrooms. If the whole thing had been part of The Method...how could they be sure what just happened with Neville hadn't somehow been faked?

Yeah, like the moon landings, he thought derisively, gritting his teeth against the pain as Linda pulled his flesh together. *The 9/11 conspiracies. Roswell. It's all a great big social experiment by some clandestine government agency.*

He let out a guttural chuckle, and Linda looked at him queerly.

She bit the thread and tied it off. Looking over her handiwork, she felt satisfied with it, hoping it would hold up to the trek ahead. "Let's get out of here."

She helped him out of the chair, and he tested his leg. The stitches creaked, but the wounds remained closed. They walked to the door with his arm over her shoulders.

"Wait here," she said once they reached the porch.

Avoiding the broken railing beam, Frank leaned his weight against a post while Linda went around the front to check the area. She found Neville's fedora in the grass. Blood had spattered its cream fabric.

Nearby, a wallet lay open in a bare patch of grass. She bent to examine it.

The driver's license belonged to a man named Jamal Reed. The man had Neville's charming smile, the same dazzling green eyes, and the rest of his very familiar face.

Curious, she flipped through the rest of its contents.

Sixteen dollars in the billfold. A US visa issued to a Jamal Reed from Canada tucked in behind the cash.

In the wallet slots, she found more proof of fraud or deception. What she didn't find was any evidence that Neville Lumley or Jamal Reed or whoever the hell he really was also happened to be a millionaire businessman.

"You all right?" Frank called from the cabin.

She said she was fine, though she felt woozy, honestly, and returned to the porch with the wallet.

"Whatcha got there?"

"Turns out Neville wasn't really Neville."

Frank gave her a confused look. She showed him the driver's license in its clear plastic slot. "Jamal Reed?" He shrugged. "Maybe he changed his name."

"Look at the rest."

He flicked to the back. "Not a lot of cash for a supposed millionaire."

"No. And no platinum credit card either. Looks at the rest."

Frank pulled out a $10 Starbuck's gift card with the PIN reveal scratched, a Cineplex points card, a debit visa, an organ donor card, and a card for his low-tier healthcare plan.

Lastly he found Jamal's Screen Actor's Guild card. "He's an actor."

Linda nodded. "That's why I recognized him. I must have seen him in something and just assumed we'd met before."

"But you saw him get shot."

"Maybe...I don't know. But maybe it was like those things they use in the movies."

"A squib? You think so?"

"I don't know. I don't know what to think anymore." She leaned against the window and shut her eyes against the sun. "Could this...this whole thing, could it be part of The Method?"

"A trick, you mean?" Frank jumped at it, eager to have his theory confirmed, despite what it might mean. "Like what happened with the cameras in our rooms?"

"It just seems like everything is linked. The trap was real, and the dogs... but was Neville or Jamal...? We never *saw* them shoot those rifles, Frank."

Frank closed the wallet and tucked it into his cargo pocket alongside Kaspar's notebook. "That way of thinking could get us killed if you're wrong," he said. "This isn't a game, Linda. Not until somebody says 'olly olly in come free.' If we don't treat it like a real threat, we could die in this fucking place."

The desperation in her eyes as she nodded showed him the sentiment had sunk in.

"We've got to get to the road, but that means we'll probably have to go to the lodge. We've to be careful about this.

Jungle warfare, Lin. Stealth and vigilance. You hear anything, you give me a signal."

He took her hand and squeezed it. She looked at him. He stood in silhouette, but her vision adjusted to the light, and the fire in his eyes reminded her of how he'd looked as they'd planned their run through the endurance event they'd participated in years ago.

"We've got this," he said, just like he'd said then.

Only this isn't a game, she thought. *This is real. Lives are at stake.*

"We can make it, Lin. I know we can."

And we never beat the endurance event. We crapped out at the electroshock.

Linda managed a weak nod, if only to bolster his courage.

IT TOOK over an hour to find Lone Loon Lake through the bush, and they'd had to backtrack another twenty minutes once they'd reached the main bay and realized they had been following the shore in the wrong direction.

Frank had dunked his head in the water and rinsed fresh and crusted blood from his leg. Linda had squatted for a pee in the bush before splashing her armpits and the back of her neck under her hairline to cool off. By the time they reached the lodge, it was well past noon. She had peed twice, and Frank had sweated through his shirt and the crotch of his shorts, his leg throbbing and itching like crazy.

They stood hunched in the woods and surveyed the area. The dock swayed lazily on a light current. Their hatchback and the Lumleys' shiny SUV remained in the lot. Three four-wheelers stood near the side door.

The grounds themselves appeared deserted. No movement inside or out.

"Where is everyone?" Frank said.

As if on cue, the side door swung open. Frank dropped

behind a felled tree, pulling Linda down with him. Its bushy branches provided adequate cover, but they could still see through the needles in some spots, well enough to watch the new guy who'd emerged from inside.

The man leaned against one of the vehicles to light a smoke, dressed in a cowboy hat and a long brown duster which, combined with a goatee, reminded Frank of *Walker, Texas Ranger,* although Frank suspected Chuck Norris didn't smoke. The man had no visible weapon, but if he was with the men they'd seen at the cabin, he was likely to have at least a single handgun holstered under the jacket.

"We've gotta lure him away from the door," Linda whispered. "We need to get to that phone."

"The SUV's got an alarm." Frank nodded toward it. "It went off when I was getting rid of the weed. Could we throw something at it? Would that set it off?"

Linda shook her head. "It'd have to be something big. It sounds like it might be a proximity alarm, but it probably also has motion sensors. A piece of gravel or something small like that won't do it."

Frank hummed, deep in thought.

"What about..." She paused to weigh the options. "What if I ran over there, set off the alarm, and ran down to the dock to hide?"

"I can't let you do that."

"Well, you can't do it, not with your leg. I'd at least have a chance. Then you could hobble over to the door while they're looking for me."

"And leave you trapped outside? No way."

"It's the only chance we've got. You get to the phone, lock yourself in the office, and call the cops."

"No." He watched Walker take another drag on his cigarette. "It's too dangerous. Let's just follow the road. Go find help. Maybe that cop's still out there in the speed trap—"

"They could all be *dead* by then. What if those guys have men out on the road waiting on the police? I love you,

Frank, but you're louder than a moose limping around on that leg of yours. There's no way we could outrun them."

"We're gonna go in there up against three heavily armed dudes, maybe more? You said it yourself. We don't stand a chance."

"Neither do Alex and Teri. Or the other people here. These guys aren't heavily armed, Frank. The fat guy has a single-shot rifle. The other guy's is bolt action, but he's only got one arm to shoot, cock, and reload. We don't even know if the guy in the long coat is armed or not." She was determined now. Fear and excitement pumped her limbs full of adrenaline, perking up her senses. "I've already seen a man die today. I'm not gonna hide in the bushes while those motherfuckers slaughter everyone else. At least we'd have the element of surprise."

Frank studied her face. She had a wild look in her eyes, like in those first few years of their relationship when they'd sneaked off to screw in various public places just barely hidden from sight.

"I'm not asking your permission, Frank. I'm telling you to be ready to run. Hobble. Whatever. I'm asking you to be strong for me."

Frank knew she was right, but fear held him in place. "This is crazy, Linda," he breathed in one last attempt to change her mind, to stop her from what would surely be committing suicide.

"The whole world is crazy," she said. "The lunatics are running the asylum now. The only way to stay on top is to out-crazy them." She gave him a fierce look, gripping his shoulder. "We can do this, Frank. You said it yourself."

He nodded, holding her gaze. "Okay. Okay, but you be careful. I want you coming home in one piece."

Linda leaned in and kissed him on the forehead. He smiled, fighting back tears.

"The second he's out of range," she told him, "you make a run for that door. Use the kitchen phone, get a knife, and wait for me there."

He nodded, his eyes welling up, about to spill over.

Linda took a deep breath and exhaled it shakily.

Then she darted across the lot in a crouch.

Frank blinked away tears and watched Walker. The man smoked leisurely, looking off toward the road. Linda dropped down behind their car. The man didn't appear to see her.

On her haunches against the trunk of the hatchback, she briefly considered getting in and driving over to the edge of the lot to pick up Frank. Even if she could have somehow managed it without alerting the guy in the long coat, both vehicles sat on slashed tires. They wouldn't make it far driving on bare rims on a gravel road.

This was the only way.

She peered around the rear bumper and saw the man in the duster crush his cigarette under a cowboy boot. As he turned his back, she dashed around to the SUV.

The alarm began to bleat before she had a chance to touch the side panels. Panicking, she bolted for the dock and crawled out of sight, hoping the man in the long coat hadn't seen her.

Frank watched Linda disappear down the embankment as Walker rose from his lean against the four-wheeler and strode toward the noisy SUV.

"Wait for it..." Frank told himself.

Halfway across the lot, the man reached into one of the deep pockets of his duster, brought out something small and black, and aimed it at the vehicle.

The key beeped. The SUV alarm blipped twice and turned off.

"*Shit.*"

In the silence, the man in the duster put two fingers to his lips and whistled a single high note.

"Shit, not the dogs, not the *dogs*..."

Frank braced himself, listening for the barks. If the dogs came now, he knew they would sniff him out. They'd have gotten his scent from the bear trap, the same trap that had caught their mother. They would want his blood.

Walker returned to the ATVs as Colby came around the corner, rifle at the ready.

"That them?"

"Can't be sure." Walker spoke with a Southern drawl, a slow cadence the others lacked. He whipped open his duster and drew a chrome, long-barreled revolver from its holster. "Could just as easily have been a squirrel. Best check the perimeter anyway. They're the only ones left who saw what you did, and we need them alive."

"Copy that."

While Colby headed toward the SUV, Walker hung by the door, peering out into the woods. He holstered the pistol and lit another smoke.

Left with no other option, Frank retreated further into the trees. Once he'd gotten enough cover, he limped down toward the lake.

Through the trees, he saw Colby try the hatchback doors. The one-armed man approached the SUV and tried to get a look into the tinted windows. He tried the doors and found them locked.

Colby turned in Frank's direction. Frank's limbs seized in fear. Slowly, he flattened himself against the earth as the man's boots crunched gravel toward him. Terror magnified every sound. The blood in his ears was thunderous, the rustle of leaves like a hurricane.

The one-armed man stopped at the edge of the woods and shaded his eyes with his hand, maybe fifteen feet from where Frank lay.

Frank held his breath. If Colby caught him now, he just hoped Linda would remain safely hidden. She could still help the others. She could still make it out of this alive.

Frank's elbow exploded with red-hot fire, and he withdrew it from the dirt, rolling onto his side. Little red ants scurried away from the collapsed dirt mound he'd been leaning on. Several had stung him in self-defense. He plucked a flailing insect off his skin and flung it away, the skin around the sting already turning an angry red.

Down at the dock, an engine sputtered and started.

Colby turned toward the lake and raised his weapon as he headed down the slope. Frank saw Walker toss his cigarette and follow suit, leaving the vicinity of the door.

A moment later, the tin boat zipped away from the dock. Frank couldn't see the driver, but he had to assume it was Linda.

The men rushed down to the shore, leaving the side door unguarded.

Now or never, Frank.

Frank hobbled out of the woods and across the lot and ducked down as far as he could manage while limping on his bad leg. The whole foot had long since numbed from the pain of his injuries, and he barely felt the jagged gravel as he made his way to the car on one bare foot.

"Shit," he breathed. The hunters had slashed all four tires.

He hurried to the door and gripped the handle when a burst of rifle fire tore through the sunny silence. The sound rocked him. Heart stuttering, he chanced a look out at the lake, where the boat continued toward the far shore, unimpeded.

All he could do now was hope like hell the shots had missed her and use the chance she'd provided him to get help.

Frank jerked the handle. The door swung open on an empty hallway. The air conditioning chilled the sweat down his back as he scurried toward the next corridor. He found the maintenance door still locked, and he hobbled past, pressing himself against the wall to peer into the kitchen.

The room smelled of bacon grease, French fries, and industrial cleaning fluid. A pot bubbled on the stove. The mop and bucket stood in the middle of the room beside the rolling steel counter, the dirty mop head dripping on the floor. The heavy door to the walk-in fridge lay open.

The wall phone had no dial tone, so he limped over to a set of sharp knives hung from a magnetic strip on the wall beside the grill. He pulled a cleaver off the strip and hefted its weight.

"Bad *ass*," he muttered, and shuffled over to the walk-in.

The cooling unit rattled and hummed at the back of the fridge. There was plenty of room to hide, and it wasn't quite cold enough to make a prolonged stay painful if necessary. The door locked from the inside, as well as out, with a metal pin hung from twine. The shelves were lined with enough food for days: large plastic condiment tubs, chopped veggies and leftovers under cellophane, wax-coated boxes of vegetables and fruits, and a box of fish on ice, heads and scales intact. The Canada goose hung from a hook near the back, its feathers plucked and washed clean of blood.

Frank had always hated the birds. They were vicious and shit everywhere. But he felt a sort of strange kinship with it, and not because it was named after his homeland. He sympathized with its current predicament. He felt strung up himself, stripped and at the mercy of cruel hunters.

He grabbed a hunk of sharp cheese and a handful of cookies and ate them greedily, not feeling very hungry, only knowing he'd need his strength if he wanted to survive.

Knife at the ready, he checked the hall and stepped out. The maid had cleaned after breakfast. The dining room was empty. He continued to the open French doors to the lobby.

Cleaver held above his head, he staggered in.

The lobby stood in disarray, chairs overturned, the front doors flung wide, items strewn on the floor. He staggered over and peered behind the desk.

No one was there.

Eyes on the loft, he crossed to the front doors and bolted them, although he supposed the entire wall being glass made the action pointless. He returned to the desk and picked up the telephone receiver.

"Must have cut the lines," he muttered.

What about the cell phones? Are they in the office?

He scuttled around the desk and tried the door. "*Yes!*" Opening it all the way, he saw the computer screen on and the monitor wall flickering.

Internet?

He hurried in and locked the door behind him. No movement in any of the rooms on the monitors. The desk drawer held scattered office supplies and candy wrappers tied in bows, but no keys for the rifle rack or the rifles themselves.

He scanned the narrow room. Files littered a second desk and the top of a filing cabinet. An old TV sat on a rolling cart, like the kind they used to use for presentations in school before the advent of digital. A first-aid kit hung on the wall nearby. He opened the kit, sprayed Bactine on his wounds, covered them with a layer of cotton batting, and wrapped them in gauze.

While he fastened the bandage, he looked up at the framed photo beside the hooks where the kit had been. A bearded man in a brown suit stood with his arm around the shoulders of a clean-cut blond man in a lab coat, the two of them out front of an old building. The handwritten caption below read *Dr. Kaspar with Stanley Milgram at Yale, 1963.*

The name of Kaspar's companion held no meaning to him, so he returned his attention to the computer. The soul-crushing alert had appeared: *There is no Internet connection.*

Without access to the Internet or a telephone, their entire plan was shot.

Shot, he thought, cold terror gripping his innards as he worried he'd never see Linda again.

In a sudden fury, Frank picked up the keyboard and smashed it against the desk. Several keys snapped off and clattered on the floor. He let the keyboard fall at his feet and leaned back, stretching out his limbs, looking up at the monitors to see if he could spot those murderous fucks outside. The grounds appeared to be as deserted as inside.

He scanned the other monitors, looking for signs of life. In what looked like his room—the Ludlum book and empty glass still stood on the nightstand, the suitcase spread out on the bed the way he'd left it—the maid lay sprawled on his bed, a red stain blossomed on her white uniform.

He watched her for several seconds. She didn't move.

"Jesus," he muttered.

As he eased out of the chair, his gaze fell on the monitor showing the first-floor hall. In the same instant, Jackson emerged from the maintenance door and locked it with a key. He shook his head in aggravation as he made his way down the hall toward the lobby.

Frank tensed. The bearded man's image grew as he approached the camera, rifle held in both hands.

"What's he doing?"

Jackson turned at the kitchen. Frank followed him to the next monitor, watching as the man headed toward the walk-in fridge, stooped at the door, and laid his rifle against the wall.

Now's your chance, Frank.

Jackson stepped inside the fridge.

For Linda.

Frank pushed himself up. He spotted the thick yellow cable leading to the monitors and tore it from the wall with a buzz of electricity, leaving all the monitors with blue screens and "NO SIGNAL" alerts.

Satisfied they wouldn't be able to see his comings and goings throughout the lodge, Frank opened the door and staggered out into the lobby. Clouds had covered the sky in a dull gunmetal gray. No one stood out front.

He limped to the French doors, peered down the hall, and pushed himself onward, hoping Jackson was still inside the walk-in.

Heart in his stomach, he stood against the doorjamb and leaned in, half expecting the man to blast a hole in his head right there.

The rifle remained against the wall, its owner still in the fridge.

Frank scurried to the steel counter and ducked. The pot hissed on the stove, steam rising. He scuttled around and crouch-limped toward the fridge and the gun, thankful for the rattling hum of the refrigeration unit, aware of how loud his shoe sounded as it slapped against the tiles.

In the doorway, he saw Jackson loading up a plastic bag with food from the shelves. Frank stepped out of sight behind the door and reached for the gun.

The door swung open and struck his funny bone. His arm numbed, and he dropped the cleaver. It hit the tile and skittered out of reach.

Jackson spat out a hunk of cheese and threw the bag of food at Frank.

Deflecting a rain of cookies, rolled lunchmeats, and chunks of stinky cheese, Frank spotted Jackson reaching for the rifle, and he swung the heavy fridge door at the man. It slammed against Jackson's shoulder, and he stumbled away, sprawling over a counter. Eggs spilled from their packaging, rolled off the counter, and cracked on the floor.

Crouching painfully on his bad leg, Frank grabbed the cleaver. He rose just as Jackson went for the rifle again. The big man slipped in the yolky mess, missed the gun, and lurched toward Frank with his arms pinwheeling.

His full weight struck Frank dead center, and Frank toppled backward. He hit the floor hard, breath exploding out of him as the big man landed on his chest, crushing his ribs, his lungs burning.

Any remaining doubt these men posed a legitimate threat evaporated.

This was no game.

Unable to breathe, Frank struggled under the larger man's girth, grunting, the hand holding the cleaver pinned. Jackson rose on his belly, allowing Frank a single breath. Cheap aftershave and cheese breath filled Frank's nostrils, and the man grabbed Frank's wrist and bashed his hand against the floor, trying to make him drop the knife.

Despite the pain, Frank held firm until his fingers went completely numb and released the cleaver of their own accord.

The big man grabbed it, eyes wild, and raised it over his head with an animal roar.

LINDA HESITATED FOR ONLY A MOMENT.

With the one-armed man just feet from discovering Frank in the woods, she rolled out from under the canoe where she'd hidden and scurried down to the dock in a crouch. Throwing a glance over her shoulder, she couldn't see the one-armed man beyond the small hill leading to the lake, and she hoped he couldn't see her.

She crept toward the fishing boat, willing the keys to be in the ignition, hoping the sound of the engine would draw the men away from Frank and the side door so he could get inside.

One last chance.

Linda crouched, unlatched the boat, and stepped one foot onto the driver's seat. The steering wheel was stiff and wouldn't budge without serious effort. Perfect. An orange floatable foam key fob hung from the ignition. Unable to believe her luck, she turned the key, praying it would start on the first try.

The engine roared to life. She thrust the lever forward, and as the boat tore away from the dock, she slipped feet first into the water, plugging her nose and squeezing her eyes shut.

She knew the dock was raised on floats, but the motor had churned up sediment in the tea-colored water, making it difficult to tell where anything was down there.

Peering around anxiously, as terrified of being underwater for the first time since a childhood friend had pushed her under as she was by the fact that the one-armed man was surely running down to find the source of the noise, she managed to find the underside of the dock and struggled to reach the surface.

She rose from the water and sucked in a sharp breath.

Boots clomped on the boards overhead. The man stopped directly above her, blotting out the sun. Linda blinked, wanting desperately to clear the water from her nostrils, but not daring.

The man gripped the rifle.

The burst of fire magnified to deafening proportions in the cramped space under the dock, and for one terrifying moment, she thought he'd shot down at her. But she was still breathing. She was still wet and uncomfortable. Still terrified.

He'd fired at the boat still retreating across the lake. With any luck, he would assume she'd ducked from the shot, and the two men would head out on their ATVs to hunt her down.

A second pair of boots rocked the dock, making the hinges squeak. "You let them get away," he said. She recognized the voice. The man in the long coat.

"That boat was 'bout halfway across the dang lake when I got down here," Colby said. "Maybe it wasn't them."

"Take the quad and recon the other side of the lake. After you just put the fear of the founding fathers in them, they're bound to be sloppy. They'll leave a trail. But *don't* kill them. We need them alive." He laid a hand on the other man's shoulder. "I'll cast an eye on how Jackson's faring with the ones in the cellar before I radio back to camp for more artillery. We do not want this getting away from us anymore than it already has."

"Are we FUBAR, Sarge?"

"You'd better hope not, fella." She saw the man in the duster poke the other man in the chest. "Or the next bullet's got your name on it."

Sarge walked away, leaving the one-armed man with something to chew on.

THE CLEAVER BLADE suspended above his head in Jackson's meaty fist, Frank drove his knee upward into the man's groin.

Jackson groaned and rolled off him. Frank twisted out of the way, and the blade clacked against the tile close to his head, skittering away.

Jackson lay on his back, groaning and gripping his testicles.

Now or never.

Frank crawled for the gun. His hands slipped in the sticky egg slop, and he almost fell face first, but righted himself at the last second. His fingers slick with egg, he gripped the rifle and drew it under his arm, falling back against the wall.

"*Fuck*," the large man groaned.

With a primal scream, Frank squeezed the trigger, preparing for the recoil.

Nothing.

Jackson began to giggle. "You asshole. You forgot to take the dang safety off."

Frank twisted the weapon and flicked the toggle. "Thanks."

The big man's eyes widened in realization of his error, and Frank pulled the trigger.

White-hot fire exploded from the muzzle. The bullet tore a bloody hole in the large man's chest. The man's whole body seemed to deflate as he expelled one final breath and was still.

The rifle barrel smoldered. Arms still reverberating from the recoil, Frank cast the weapon aside in disgust.

No choice, he told himself. He would have been killed himself if he hadn't shot the man, but it didn't make him feel any better about it. He felt no pleasure and only little relief.

As he looked down at the dead man, a familiar voice called his name.

AFTER SHE HEARD the ATV rev up and head away from the lodge, Linda pulled herself onto the dock and lay there a moment, catching her breath.

Then she was up and on her feet, dashing up the ramp onto land and running in a crouch up the hill, where she paused on the ridge to survey the area.

She watched the man in the duster enter the side door, and she hurried across the parking lot herself. At the door she paused, considering her next move, thinking he might have seen her approach and was lying in wait for her to step in. She wasn't sure he had a weapon, but there was no reason to believe he didn't.

One thought got her moving: *Frank.*

He was inside. He might be dead already if the man with the beard had found him. If he hadn't, if Frank *was* still alive, he'd have even less of a chance of survival against two men with guns than just one.

She opened the door.

The hallway was clear.

Linda stepped in, crept down the hall, and chanced a look around the corner just as the door marked MAINTE-NANCE swung shut.

Her gaze fell on the stacked chairs.

It worked before, she thought.

She raised a heavy chair off the top of the stack and brought it to the maintenance closet. Wedging it under the door handle, something metallic clattered down the hall, catching her attention.

She headed for the kitchen. From the doorway, she saw the large man's camouflaged legs stuck out from behind the steel counter. In the next moment, a rifle opened fire and the man's legs kicked, his boots squeaking against the tile.

She drew back against the wall, heart hammering, not knowing what to do next.

The weapon clattered on the floor on the other side of the counter.

"Frank?" she ventured, raising her voice over the rattling fridge unit.

"Lin?"

"Are you shot?"

"I'm okay!"

"Is he dead?"

A pause. "If he's not, he's a pretty good actor."

Pounding down the hall made her jump.

"Ma'am?" The man in the duster's voice came from behind the door. The door rattled, shaking the chair.

"We've got a gun!" she shouted at him. "Your friend's dead!"

"Who is it, Lin?"

Linda ignored Frank, her eyes on the door, watching for movement.

"If you mean Clara's boy, he wasn't my friend," the man said patiently. "I didn't even particularly like him. Open the door and let's talk. I like to look a man in the eye when I speak with him. Or *her*, as the case may be."

"You stay away from us!"

She saw Frank hobble over without the gun, and she jabbed a finger at it repeatedly until he looked down and reluctantly picked it up. He limped over to her side and gripped the doorjamb to hold himself upright.

"Ma'am, if you don't open this door for me, I'm gonna have to blow a hole in it, how about that?"

"You shoot through that door and you're next!"

The man said nothing.

Linda gestured impatiently for the rifle. Frank handed it to her. She hadn't fired a weapon since the last time her father had taken her to a gun range before she'd met Frank, but there wasn't much to it beyond point and shoot.

She aimed it at the door.

"Linda—may I call you Linda?"

Frank gave her a look of concern. She supposed they could have gotten their names from Alex or the logbook, but it made no difference. When she didn't reply, the man continued.

"Linda, my name is Gary Hill. My friends call me Sarge. Most of my enemies do as well, I suppose." He chuckled softly. "Now Linda, I know you're frightened. I know what you saw out there by the cabin. It was a terrible mistake, and it shames me to no end to admit that it happened on my watch. See, he'd meant that bullet for someone else. Someone who'd been fixing to steal something near and dear away from me."

Like that makes a difference, she thought, but said nothing.

"Now I know what you're thinking. Murder is murder. Well, what one of you has clearly just done to my subordinate proves that's just not true. There's murder and there's protecting what's yours by rights. Whether it be your life or your livelihood...or land your kin have lived on since the Hellgate Treaty of 1859."

She turned to Frank. He shook his head in confusion.

"But this...*unfortunate incident*, let's say...has put me in a bit of a pickle. See, I want to set these fine folks down here free. I *want* to let you leave here in peace, despite what you just did to Clara's boy." He paused. "Trouble is, if I do, you'll go straight to the police, and my men and I will spend at least a few years in the prison industrial complex, and while we're indisposed, cowards operating under the employ of the Divided States of America, whose authority I *do not* recognize, will strip my family of our lawfully owned land."

She heard him take a deep breath in and out through his nostrils.

"I cannot let that happen, Linda. I *will* not. Hence the dilemma we find ourselves in at the moment. Holding guns on each other through a door."

"What do you want?" she asked.

He let the question sit a moment. "I want your word. That's all. Your word that when my people walk away from this, you'll take it no further. What happens here stays here, as the saying goes."

Frank nodded eagerly. Linda considered it for only a moment.

"How are we supposed to trust you? Your one-armed pal just shot a boat he thought I was in. Damage control doesn't leave room for witnesses, does it?"

"Ma'am. Take a moment to consider what I could have done while you've stood there pointing Jackson's peashooter at a door. I *could* have walked calmly downstairs and put a hole the Chinaman's head and the cook's. But I did not. That's not to say I *won't*."

Frank grabbed for the rifle. Linda jerked it out of his reach.

"Open the door, Linda," the man called Sarge said. "Let's handle this like civilized people. Don't make me kill these innocent men."

With no other choice, she reached for the door handle.

"Linda, no," Frank said.

"What choice have we got, Frank?"

With no idea how many rounds were left in the clip and how much ammunition this "Sarge" carried, with more ammunition and more men on the way, cutting a deal was the only chance any of them had of getting out of this alive.

"Do you honestly think they're going to *let us go*?"

She didn't. But she couldn't stand by while the man on the other side of the door executed Alex and the cook. She wouldn't be able to live with herself.

"What was the name of that treaty you mentioned, Mr. Hill? Hell something?"

"Hellgate," Sarge said.

Frank could practically hear the smile in his tone.

"We're going to draw up a treaty," Linda said. "Both parties sign. Then we go our separate ways." She let him consider it. "Agreed?"

"That sounds more than fair."

"I'm opening the door." Linda reached for the chair. "If you shoot, I shoot."

"Understood."

Linda grasped the chair, aiming the rifle with her right hand. She knew the shot would go wild if he forced her to fire on him, but she hoped it would at least strike enough fear in him that he'd stagger a few steps down the stairs, maybe even fall if she was lucky.

She slid the chair out from under the handle.

The door tore open before she could react. It struck the rifle and sent the thing flying out of her hand. Sarge kept on charging, slamming into her and driving her to the floor.

She saw Frank lurch toward the rifle in the split second before Sarge drove the butt of his revolver into her forehead.

Frank saw Linda's eyes flutter shut as she lost consciousness. Crying out in anger, he reached for the rifle.

Sarge spun the barrel toward Linda's forehead, chrome gleaming under the hallway lights.

Frank froze, his whole body trembling with fear and adrenaline.

"I wouldn't do that if I were you." Sarge rose from his knees, keeping the revolver leveled at Linda.

"You made a fucking deal," Frank said.

The man in the duster sneered. "Tell it to your Congressman."

Chapter 11

Right Place, Wrong Time

Frank hobbled down the stairs at gunpoint, holding the handrail to steady himself.

"It truly shames me I was forced to strike your wife," the man in the duster said at his back. "Especially as there are few things I find sexier than a lady with a gun."

Frank gritted his teeth and continued down the steps. One of his stitches had popped, and he was babying his leg, walking on the ball of his foot, hoping the other stitches would hold. The stone floor felt cool as he limped to the end of a short hall lined with wood wine racks stained red. He eyed bottles of various shapes and colors in individual cubbyholes. He considered using them as weapons, but Sarge prodded him with the gun barrel, urging him forward.

In the main cellar, several corked wooden barrels stood alongside more wine racks, every bottle gleaming in the yellow glow of several wall sconces, not a speck of dust on anything. No sign of Alex or the cook either.

A heavy wooden door with a round window at head height stood at the far end of the room. Sarge slipped past and opened it, revealing a sauna carved jaggedly out of the bedrock and a wood-paneled heater stacked with black rocks at the center of the room.

Alex and the cook sat slumped against the wood benches, beaten to the point of unconsciousness. Sarge and his thugs had left them gagged and tied at the wrists and ankles.

Frank shook his head. "You guys really fucked up, didn't you? I mean, you shit the bed."

Sarge pushed the muzzle into the meat between Frank's shoulder blades. "Was it Lincoln who said a man shouldn't crack wise with a gun at his back?"

"Sounds more like Yosemite Sam."

The man in the duster chuckled. "Have a seat beside the Chinaman."

"His name is Alex."

"*Sit.*"

Frank gripped the wall and eased down onto the stone floor. Sarge reached into one of the large pockets and threw a pair of handcuffs in Frank's lap.

Frank picked them up and dangled them in front of his eyes. "You know I heard you militia guys had a thing for dildos, but I didn't know you were this kinky."

"*Put them on,*" Sarge grunted.

Frank snapped the cuffs onto each of his wrists. "You know what I don't understand? Why don't you just kill us all now and get it over with? I mean that's how this ends, isn't it? There's no way Linda and me are gonna walk out of here. Why beat around the bush?"

Sarge got down on his haunches and fixed him with his blue eyes, his freckled cheeks and nose riddled with pockmarks. As he came closer, Frank noticed the kerchief tied around his neck like an ascot, only slightly redder than his goatee.

"Much as you might think my men and I are cold-blooded murderers, Frank, killing a man is always a last resort." His eyes narrowed. "We're not bad men. Colby, Clara's boy, and I, we're freedom fighters."

"So is it ironic that you're keeping people hostage, or are you just plain fucking stupid?"

Sarge smiled bitterly. "What's that Dr. John song? 'Right Place, Wrong Time'?' Any other weekend, you and your wife would have had yourself a relaxing time in the beautiful wilds of northwest Montana. The fishing out at the old place is a real treat. I once caught a brookie the size of my—"

Eyes twinkling, he paused and looked over the two badly beaten men. "I'm being disrespectful. Now is not the time for fishing stories. Mr. Moffat, what you and your lovely wife have found yourself caught up in is a decades'-old battle between a group of sovereign citizens and a violent, oppressive regime."

"Lucky us."

The man began to tie Frank's ankles. "That's a nasty wound you've got there. I noticed it before, but it looks much more serious up close. I don't approve of forced vaccinations, but I sincerely hope you've had your tetanus shot."

Frank didn't reply.

Sarge tied the final knot so tight it cut off circulation, then stood. "Now should I carry your wife down, or would the two of you prefer separate accommodations?"

"If you hurt her again, I swear to God—"

"Are you a God-fearing man, Moffat? Seems to me you liberal types are all atheists these days." Sarge awaited Frank's reply. Receiving none, he nodded and headed for the door. "I'll get your wife."

"What did you do with Teri Lumley?"

Sarge stopped in the doorway. "The brunette with the model good looks? She's at the homestead. My wife and sons are taking good care of her. Don't you worry."

His spurs jingled as he ambled around the corner and up the stairs.

Frank began to work at the knot around his ankles.

"*Are you crazy?*"

Alex's face was so battered he could barely open his eyes. "They'll kill you if you run, Frank. Just like they did to Maria Luisa."

Frank gave up on the knot, tied too tight, and started trying to pull his hands free of the cuffs. "Who are these people?"

"The Hill family owns most of the land surrounding the lodge," Alex said. His busted nose whistled as he exhaled. "The guy with the hat, Gary Hill, he's been trying to scare us off for years. Says our 'people' have a bogus claim on this property, that his grandfather's crooked lawyer sold it to Dr. Kaspar illegally. I don't know about that, but I've seen the deed, and it has Heinrich's name on it."

"They killed Neville over a land dispute?"

Alex shrugged up his shoulders and winced from the pain. "I guess so. I didn't even see what happened until they made me delete the videos. They saw you and Linda were in Dr. Kaspar's old cabin, and that's when the one with the beard hit me with his gun. When I woke up, I was tied up down here with Mathias."

The cook, Mathias, breathed deeply, either unconscious or sleeping.

"The guy with the beard—he's dead."

Alex's eyebrows rose. Blood from a wound on his forehead trickled down his cheek. "After what he did to Maria Luisa, I can't say I'm upset. Did you—?"

Frank nodded solemnly.

"Good. If I had the chance, I might have killed him myself."

Sarge's spurs jingled as he clomped down the stairs. Frank stopped working on the handcuffs and assumed a relaxed position. Alex eased himself back against the wine rack with a slight grimace and shut his eyes, faking unconsciousness.

Boot falls on the stone floor echoed in the outer room. When Sarge appeared around the corner, he had Linda slung over his shoulder in a fireman's carry. He stepped into the sauna, lowered her gently onto a bench, and rolled her onto her side.

"You made quite a mess of Clara's boy." Sarge stood back and gave Frank a look of admiration. "Color me impressed. He'd always been a bit of a dullard, truth be told. Lazy too. I suppose I'd always assumed someone would get the upper hand on him someday. Just not today." He uttered a bitter chuckle. "That's about as good a eulogy as the boy earned."

He began to draw a length of yellow rope from the duster's deep pocket, like a magician's trick, until its frayed end dangled. "I suppose you've heard the expression 'quick draw,' and I've no need to impress upon you the fact that if you mess with me while I tie up your wife, the two of you will be dead before I even break a sweat."

Frank nodded.

"Good." The man knelt and bound Linda's legs like a rodeo calf roper, the nylon making *zip zip zip* noises as he looped and tied. With the same rope, he tied her hands taut behind her back and positioned her so she faced Frank.

Linda's hair hung in her face, but Frank could see the large welt already forming on her forehead and a slash along her left eyebrow trickling blood down her cheek.

She seemed to be breathing fine. He was glad for that at least.

Sarge hunkered down in front of him and held out the handcuff key. "I want those cuffs put round behind you."

Frank raised his hands.

Sarge unlocked the right cuff. "Round the back."

Frank did as he was told.

"Scooch over. Now you kick me while I'm down here and I'll empty this cylinder on the rest of these folks and save the last dance for you."

The man eyed him until he seemed certain Frank would comply, and he reached behind him to cuff his other hand. When he'd finished, he stood and looked down with a self-satisfied half smile crooking his goatee.

"Are you aware how many civil liberties you've signed away to these people?" Sarge rummaged in a pocket and drew out several folded sheets of paper. "'The Participants release the Examiners from all liability and waive the right to sue in the case of injury, loss of personal property, or accidental death.'" He looked up from the contract with an expression of incredulity. "How desperate were you to sign this? Did you even read it?"

Alex's nose whistled in the silence.

Sarge glanced at the concierge before raising an eyebrow at Frank. "This place is some kind of marriage counseling retreat, is that right?"

Frank nodded.

"So you paid these people an ungodly sum just to have your head shrunk for a weekend? Have yourself a pedicure?" He gestured toward the surrounding stone walls. "Maybe take a steam? Let me guess: this was the wife's idea, wasn't it?"

"I don't have to talk to you."

The man smirked. "You know this place used to be a government facility? Or did they neglect to mention that? Got rid of everything but the cameras, from the look. The lodge wasn't always here either. When I was a boy, there used to be a big, gray windowless building stood right here. You know." He winked, grinning. "The kind of place with something to hide."

"Are you trying to scare me?"

"What I'm trying to do is impress upon you that things aren't always what they seem. This...*place*...this land...it's never been peaceful. When my kin bought it around the time of the Hellgate Treaty, the Blackfoot had just massacred a whole family of Flathead Indians and tossed their corpses into the Loon. That's the kind of place you paid to stay. Now my family has protected this land for four generations until my granddaddy caught diphtheria after the war against the Krauts, and his shyster lawyer sold it part and parcel to a Mr. Roscoe Hillenkoetter of the Central Intelligence Agency."

More conspiracies, Frank thought. *This place just keeps getting crazier.*

"My daddy told me," the man went on, "that they did all kinds of experiments here. Men in black suits and men in white coats. Paid people a few bucks to participate in studies, so he said, and then dosed them up with LSD and messed with their heads in all kinds of fucked up ways. People died."

He fumbled in a pocket and brought out a pack of cigarettes. He shook one free. As he lit it, he said, "We'd see smoke coming up the chimney at night, and my daddy would say, 'Nother one's gone to the incinerator. May the good Lord bless him and keep him.'"

He blew out a lungful of smoke, his blue eyes focused on the wall behind Frank. His mind was elsewhere, in the past.

"But it wasn't always men they tested on, Moffat. There were women too. We saw the men in black suits driving folks to that windowless building in their sleek black cars." The cigarette crackled as he dragged on it, the cherry glowing like taillights. "Not everyone drove back out. My daddy said he saw a man in a hospital gown run off into the woods one night when he was fishing. A man in a white coat come out behind him just as calm as you please and shot the other man in the back of the head."

Frank shook his head, not sure if he could believe a word the man said, but unable to keep from listening.

"You scoff at men like me and my fellow patriots, Moffat. But it's only because you're afraid to face the truth. In your heart you know it's true. Your government has been lying to you since you were old enough to listen."

He looked down at Frank, the twinkle returned to his cold blue eyes.

"They have enslaved us and put us to death to fuel their prison–industrial complex. They have sent God-fearing men and women to die in unjust wars to protect a corrupt system. They have *cheated us* and *stolen from us* and *trampled us* underfoot!"

Cheeks flushed, his words rang in the enclosed space. He dropped the cigarette as Frank's feet and crushed it under a boot heel. "And now is the time to stand and say *no more*. This here." Sarge pointed at the crushed cigarette, catching his breath. "It's been a long time coming. Right place, wrong time, Moffat. Right place, wrong time."

Frank studied him in the silence than followed. "Just so we're clear, you're gonna die here to take back a couple of acres of scrub brush some relative you never knew stole from the natives a hundred and fifty years ago."

The man regarded him with narrowed eyes. "I love this land, Moffat. She's beautiful and dangerous and *alive*, and I love every inch of her just as if I'd created her myself."

His gaze fell on Linda, lying unconscious and prone on the bench, before returning to Frank. "She may not be perfect. She's got her share of secrets. Some of them dark, quite dark. But I will fight to the death to get her back, you understand? And mister, if you don't have something in your life worth fighting for..." He shook his head in disdain. "Well then, I pity you."

FRANK WAITED several minutes after Sarge closed the sauna door before trying to rouse Linda. She moaned, her brow furrowing. Her eyes didn't open.

"Linda, wake up."

"Be careful," Alex said.

Frank looked over his shoulder and caught him opening the less puffy of his eyes.

"If she's got a concussion, you shouldn't move her head."

"Thanks."

"I told you that guy was crazy, didn't I?"

"What he said about this place being a government building," Frank said, working on the cuffs behind his back. "Is that true?"

"I don't know, man. A friend of ours turned us on to this place a little over ten years ago. It was already Loon Lake Lodge. That's the first I'd heard of it."

"Why did you stay?"

Alex rolled his head in Frank's direction. "This was the last vacation Don and I had together before he got sick."

Frank paused a moment. "I'm sorry to hear that."

The concierge's broken lips upturned in a smile. "It's okay. It was a long illness. ALS. After he passed, I just felt so aimless, you know? Drifting through life. I sold everything we owned and drove out here. I just wanted to be someplace he'd *really lived*. We argued a lot the weekend we came here, but it was the last time I remembered the two of us ever being happy together. I held on to him so long...all the pain he went through...trapped inside himself. If I could do all it over, I'd load him up on painkillers and let him drift away."

"I definitely understand that impulse. I lost my mom to colon cancer when I was young. I still can't go home without seeing her dying in that bed in the spare room all over again. Then when Linda was diagnosed a couple of years back, I was sure I couldn't go through it again."

He licked his lips, wishing they'd been tied up closer to the wine instead of in this cramped little room filled with the smoke of Sarge's cigarette. He was thirsty, but mostly he wanted to get drunk.

"Near the end with my mom, my dad said it's crueler to keep fighting. He said, 'What we're doing to your mother is one of the most selfish things a man can do. We're keeping her alive for ourselves, not for her. To hold on to the memory of her just a little while longer, to—to spare ourselves the guilt of *letting go*. Who are we to decide whether she wants to go on living or not?'" Frank shook his head, feeling the pain the old man's words dredged up. "'What gives us the right?'"

He turned to Linda. "I think about that when I look at her now. If we hadn't kept on fighting, if we'd just given in, let the cancer take her kidney and waste the rest of her away...I don't think I could have lived with myself."

Linda began to stir.

"I think she's waking up," he said.

Her eyes fluttered open. "What...?" She tried to move her arms, and when she couldn't, she grew anxious, tugging on them. Her head hurt badly, and her left eye wouldn't open all the way.

"Relax, Lin. You'll hurt yourself."

She calmed at the sound of Frank's voice, her eyes coming into focus. "I thought we were back in the hospital for some reason. Isn't that weird?"

"No, honey. The man in the duster hit you on the head and took us down here. Alex and the cook—"

"Mathias," Alex groaned.

"They were here already."

Linda struggled to get upright but only managed to roll enough on her shoulder to see the closed sauna door. "Did anyone try the door?"

"It's locked from the outside," Alex said.

She squinted at Frank. "Did you ask him about Jamal?"

"I was just about to when you woke up."

"Who's Jamal?"

Linda rolled onto her hands, wincing at the pain of the movement, and pushed herself to a sitting position. "We found his wallet. We know he's an actor. Everything that happened last night with the cameras in the rooms, Teri Lumley coming on to Frank. If that is her real name. We know you people set this all up to fuck with our heads."

She blinked at the too-bright overhead light, her own head throbbing.

"Okay." Alex's nose whistled as he exhaled. "It's true. Jamal and Harriet are actors. We hire them to play the Other Couple. It's an important part of the process."

"And the militiamen?"

Alex blinked. "Are you kidding me right now? You think those freaks are with *us*?"

"Honestly, Alex, I don't know what to believe anymore. Why do you people have cameras set up all over the woods? Why are there *bear traps* chained to trees?"

"Mrs. Moffat, you have to trust me. I would never go along with something I knew would put your lives in danger. Look at my face! I look like plastic surgery gone wrong!"

"Lin. *Linda*." Frank waited for her to look at him. "I killed a man up there, Lin. We killed a *dog*. If this was a game, they'd have pulled the plug the second I stepped on that trap."

Her head hurt far too much to think too deeply on the subject. She could only take his words at face value. If he'd killed a man and all of this really was a game, they would have had to stop, legally, if not out of moral obligation.

Boots sounded on the stone floor outside the room, drawing her attention to the door. As they neared, she made out two distinct sets, one heavier footed, the other dragging his heels.

A moment later, an indistinct face loomed beyond the window, hot breath fogging the glass. The man behind the door rubbed away the condensation with his forearm and peered inside. His eyes flashed with malevolence when he saw Frank.

The knob turned and the door tore open.

Colby swaggered in with a wide step, a grin spread all the way across the camo paint on his face.

Another man shuffled in behind him, shoulders hunched and dragging his feet. His almost nonexistent forehead and the eyebrows drawn together gave him a wolflike appearance, despite the too-light scruff on his cheeks and upper lip. This wolf-boy held a screwdriver loosely at his side.

"Well *well*," Colby said as he stomped up to the heater full of rocks. "The gang's all here."

Nobody said anything. No one dared.

"Sarge tells me you were the one kilt my battle buddy and *maimed my dog*." He jabbed a dirty finger at Frank. "But that couldn't be right. You don't look like you could kill a deerfly."

In one swift movement, he bent to snatch a rock from the heater and threw it.

Frank ducked, the rock exploding against the wall. A hail of fragments struck the back of his head, reminding him of the rock Dillon had kicked loose during their climbing trip. The fear he'd experienced hanging from the edge of that cliff was nothing compared to this. At least then he'd had a rope to save him.

Or to hang himself with.

Colby jabbed a finger toward him, nostrils flared. "That's the last time I miss, I promise you that. When Rebel an' me get through with you and your wife, you're gonna wish Jackson kilt you." He turned on his heels and grabbed the kid. "*C'mon.*"

The wolf-boy's gaze lingered on Linda a moment longer before he followed, dragging his feet along behind his master.

"Close the door, you idiot."

The wolf-boy slammed it and eyeballed them through the window as he jammed the screwdriver between the door and the frame.

"We're screwed," Alex said.

Frank chuckled at the unintended pun. "There's still a chance. That door isn't locked. It's just wedged shut. If the three of us push on it together—"

"*We can get out of here,*" Linda said, hope returning to her bloodshot eyes.

"Then what?" Alex said. "We can't leave Mathias here. And how are we going to get up the stairs with our feet tied?"

"I've got a lighter." Frank pushed himself up onto the bench beside Linda. "The cellar is full of alcohol—"

"Wine isn't flammable," Linda said.

Alex shifted, nostrils whistling as he raised himself up on his ass. "No, but scotch is. Dr. Kaspar has barrels of it out there."

"What then?"

"We start a fire," Frank said. "Sarge's smoke got me thinking. If we get a fire smoldering out there, they'll have to come down and check on us. But they won't be able to see through the smoke. Then we hit them with everything we've got."

Linda followed his gaze toward the heating rocks. "Rocks against guns, Frank? They'll kill us."

"By the time they realize it's a trap, we'll be on the floor. They'll be aiming high. You said all he's got is a bolt-action rifle. Sarge has got a handgun, that's it. That's what? Seven bullets max?"

Linda considered it. "That's a lot to risk on a long shot, Frank. What if the smoke doesn't get thick enough? What if it does, and they leave us down here to choke to death?"

Alex agreed with a fearful nod.

"Lin. Of all people, you know it's better to fight back with everything you've got than to just give up and die. You too, Alex. These people are *terrorists*. They'll kill us the second they realize we're useless to them, when the police or the FBI or whoever storms this fucking place."

"He's right," Alex said. "That fat dude laughed when he shot Maria Luisa. Men like that have no concept of honor."

"That's how these things end, Lin. You *know* that. This is our only chance."

She saw the sincerity in her husband's eyes. He'd looked at her the same way sitting by her bedside while she'd recovered from surgery and during every chemo session. He'd held her hand for as long as she'd let him, and despite the awful way his mother had died, he had remained strong and by her side, to give her hope.

He needed her to be strong now.

"Okay," she said, rising up on the bench. "But we'll need to burn more than wood if we want to make a lot of smoke."

CHAPTER 12

FIRE IN THE HOLE

Frank's lighter melted through the nylon ropes easily, dripping black gobs onto the benches and stone floor. While Linda made her way around the room freeing the others, Frank worked on getting his hands out from behind his back. His injured leg made the task unbearable. He worried about popping more stitches. And every time he pulled the leg close enough to his body to slip the cuffs out from under his foot, his leg began to jitter, and the pain nearly caused him to black out.

With a gasp, he stretched both legs, giving up on getting out of the cuffs for the moment. He'd need professional medical assistance soon, or pain wouldn't be the only thing he'd have to worry about.

Mathias had regained consciousness while Linda freed him. A tall, beefy man, hairy and ogrelike, his sloped forehead gave him a permanent glower, and he spoke very little as Linda outlined the plan, communicating mostly in grunts and nods.

He stood beside Frank and Alex by the door. Each of them rested their shoulders against it and rammed the door on Linda's count of three. The door ripped free of the frame with a splinter of wood and slammed against the wall.

Alex bent to pick up the screwdriver, brandishing it like

a weapon. Mathias hoisted the rock basket off the heater and carried it into the main part of the cellar. Linda helped Frank stagger out behind them, his hands still useless behind his back.

"Ready?" Frank looked over their battered faces and saw a glimmer of hope as all three nodded. "Okay. Let's do this."

While Frank stood by the corner watching the stairs, Alex, Linda, and Mathias began to undress. Stripped down to a pair of purple briefs, Alex's tattooed torso glistened with a sheen of sweat. Bruises spotted Mathias's hairy belly and chest under the bloodstained cook's shirt. He dropped his loose mushroom-print pants, revealing a ratty pair of tighty whities and graying tube socks.

They all put their shoes back on, so they'd be ready to run when the time came.

Linda pushed aside the feeling of self-consciousness standing among a bunch of strange men in her one-size-too-big bra and granny panties with the ugly scar from her surgery clearly visible. Instead, she focused on business, bringing her t-shirt to the closest barrel, wiggling out the cork, and dipping the shirt into the golden fluid that gurgled out. Then she threw it into the pile of clothing in the middle of the room and bent to light the fire.

The lighter wheel spun and sparked, spun and sparked. Sparked. Sparked.

She almost threw it across the room in a fit of rage.

Frank looked back over his shoulder. "What's going on?"

"The lighter's dead."

"You gotta be kidding me." He glanced up at the stairs, willing Colby and the wolf-boy to keep doing whatever it was they were doing for just a few more minutes. "Did you shake it?"

"What's *shaking it* going to do?" Linda hissed.

"You can find out if there's any fluid left."

She shook the lighter close to her ear. Fluid sloshed inside. "There's some left."

"It's too draughty down here." He came over. "Try again and I'll shield the wind."

He sat down beside her and cupped his hands around the lighter. Linda flicked it. A weak flame rose from the spark.

"Yes!" she cried, lowering the flickering flame to her t-shirt. Blue fire engulfed it immediately.

"Teamwork," Frank said.

Linda grinned and helped him to his feet while the rest of the pile caught fire and a foul-smelling smoke began to rise. Mathias and Alex snapped strips of wood from the rock basket and added them to the blaze.

"All right, everybody grab some rocks and take positions," she said.

Frank returned to his post at the entrance to the corridor while the others scooped up rocks from the basket and fell back against the corners of the room, with the entrance within sight.

The smoke thickened, the odor less foul now, more woody, and almost pleasant. After about a minute, Linda could barely see Alex a few feet to her side, let alone Frank, who had all but disappeared.

"Help!" Frank shouted, watching the smoke roll through the hallway and drift lazily up the stairs. "Fire!"

Linda dropped low where the smoke was less dense, where the men would be less likely to shoot if they came down prepared for a fight. She saw Alex and Mathias had done the same, according to plan, rocks at the ready.

Frank coughed. "*Helllllpp!*"

His voice broke, tearing his throat. Soon the smoke would consume all the air in the wine cellar, and he'd have no breath left to shout.

The wine would put out the fire if it spread to the shelves, but it would be cold comfort if Sarge hadn't maintained orders to keep everyone alive and Colby and the wolf-boy let the four of them choke to death down here.

"FIRE!"

He broke into a coughing fit and eased down to the floor, eyes burning. The fire continued to rage at the center of the room. The stairway door disappeared behind a gray haze.

Linda coughed behind him. Then Alex or Mathias, he couldn't tell which. The room erupted with a symphony of coughs, like a contagion.

The stairway suddenly brightened. Smoke rolled out around a man standing in silhouette in the open doorway above.

Frank crawled back on his butt until his back struck bottles. He lay down flat against cool stone, waiting.

Boots trundled down the steps.

"Jesus H. Fucksticks!" the kid said, and coughed.

"Cover your mouth," Colby said. "And watch the cussin'!"

Shadows swirled in the smoke at the end of the hall. The orange flames illuminated their shapes, but the smoke kept them in a haze. One was tall, the other short and hunched.

"*Now!*" Frank yelled with his last breath.

Rocks clacked against the shelves, smashed bottles, and made fleshy thuds.

Colby and the wolf-boy cried out at the unexpected assault. Frank saw them shielding themselves with their arms —*arm* in Colby's case—as they retreated into the hall.

"*Hold!*" Frank said.

The others stopped throwing their rocks. Already the fire was dying, the smoke beginning to clear.

The kid had left the door open upstairs.

"How they get untied?" the kid asked.

"Doesn't matter," Colby said. "They'll run out of rocks soon. You know that, right?" He was addressing them, glee audible in his tone. "What did you expect was gon' happen? Knock us out with a handful of sauna rocks and run off hand in hand into the sunset?"

"Fuck you, you inbred prick!" Linda screamed. Frank

could see her now through the thinning smoke, lying on her side with a rock poised.

"I done told you about the cussin', lady—"

Linda threw the rock. A bottle near the entrance to the hall shattered and Colby shielded himself, ducking out of the way of the glass.

"One more rock and I'm gon' send the boy upstairs to get Petunia. You don't want to meet Petunia. I guarantee you that. She got a hair trigger and a loud mouth, an' she just loves to get the last word."

An animal roar exploded from the corner of the room. Mathias had gotten to his feet and charged, kicking through the fire toward the men in the hall.

"Fall back!" Colby ordered. "Get the guns!"

The big man collided with Colby, smashing him against the shelf. Bottles shattered and fell around them as the wolf-boy disappeared into the retreating smoke and bolted up the stairs.

Colby grabbed a fistful of the cook's chest hair. The big man growled and smashed his massive forehead into Colby's nose.

Linda winced, hearing the cartilage crunch from where she lay by the sauna door.

The cook grabbed Colby's throat in his meaty fist. From where Frank sat, he could see Colby's eyes bulge and his face turn purple, veins standing out in his temples.

Frank got to his feet, ready to run.

Colby reached back blindly for a bottle.

"Look out!" Frank cried, but he was too late.

Colby tore the bottle free and smashed it over Mathias's head. The big man stumbled back, blinking rapidly, a hand clapped against his forehead. Blood poured down his face, and he staggered back into the shelf behind him. Bottles rained from their cubbies and smashed at his feet.

Without a second's hesitation, Colby grabbed the knife sheathed at his hip and stabbed Mathias several times in the gut. The wounds oozed gouts of dark red down the cook's hairy stomach and onto his graying underpants. His eyes fluttered, and he slid down the wall.

Colby turned his gleaming eyes toward them. He breathed heavily through his nostrils like a wild animal, blood streaming from them. The knife dripped gore, its haft connected to the sheath by some kind of cord or cable. "Anyone else wanna dance?"

The smoke had cleared, leaving the living prisoners exposed. No one dared say a word.

"Aw, all these critters are in their skivvies 'cept you and me," the man said to Frank. "How come we didn't get no invite to the slumber party?"

"You're a sadistic fuck, you know that?"

Colby's smirk vanished. He pointed the dripping knife at Frank. "You watch the cussin' now, fella."

"You're in it for the pain, aren't you?" Frank continued, undeterred. "That's why assholes like you join militias. You probably don't even give a shit about Sarge's politics or his family's land."

Snarling, the man sheathed the still-dripping knife and began his approach.

"Maybe you got bullied in school and you want to take out your rage on innocent people, trample women and children under your jackboots."

The man stopped in front of him, looking down with a sneer. "You best shut your mouth."

"Or what? You're gonna hurt me? Big deal. You think I haven't been hurt before?"

Colby's left eye twitched. "Not like this you ain't."

"Then do it. Show me pain." The man didn't move. "Show me pain, you fucking coward!"

The arm snatched out and grabbed Frank by the jaw, squeezing his face in a vice grip. "*Shut. Your mouth,*" he growled, his head trembling with rage.

Linda rose to her feet. "Let him go!"

"You one-armed fuck." Frank spoke with a lisp with his

lips mashed together. "You can't even hold me and hit me at the same time."

"*Watch the cussin'.*"

Colby let him go and backhanded him across the jaw with the practiced expertise of a pro wrestler. Frank fell on his hands, tasting blood. He spat on the floor at the man's feet.

"You call that pain? My dad hit me harder than that when I was six."

Colby's knuckles cracked as he clenched the hand into a fist.

"*Frank, don't,*" Linda pleaded.

"You don't have to feel guilty anymore, Lin." He turned to see tears in her eyes. "Before he's done with me, you walk away, okay?"

She let the tears fall. "I won't leave you."

"You stand up and walk out of here and don't look back, Lin."

Colby flashed a look in her direction. "She ain't goin' nowhere!"

"Three of us and one of you," Frank said. "How are you gonna catch us with one arm?"

The fist darted out, mashing Frank's ear into his skull. Stars flooded his vision.

"*Frank!*"

As his vision cleared, he saw blood dripping from the man's sheath almost as if the knife itself was bleeding. With his brain rattled, he couldn't quite comprehend what he was seeing. He only knew it was wrong somehow.

"Go, Linda!"

The fist struck him again, and this time when the stars came, his vision didn't immediately return. Something inside his head had broken. One or two more punches and he'd no longer be useful to anyone, except as a punching bag.

Alex stood alongside Linda.

"Rebel!" Colby called over his shoulder, his eyes darting between the prisoners in something approaching fear.

Frank fought through the pain to push himself up as the world came into focus around him. When Colby turned back, Frank charged him with a shoulder.

Caught unaware, the man's eyes bulged and he toppled backward.

Linda rushed him and kicked him in the chest and stomach. It felt like his torso was padded, but she kept kicking, only wanting to hurt the man as he curled himself into a ball.

"If I'd known you were having a campfire, I'd've brought marshmellers."

She got in one last good kick and turned to see Sarge standing over Mathias's dead body, wafting away smoke with one hand, his pistol in the other. Two large men with balaclavas pulled down over their faces stood behind him at either shoulder, both men armed.

"What in the hot hell happened down here, Colby?"

Colby rolled onto his back. "Sorry, Sarge. They surprised us."

"You're on KP duty for a week, how's that for sorry?" Sarge looked around. "Seems like you all just about got the upper hand on us again, Moffats. Right place, wrong time." He chuckled. "Langford, get the Chinaman. Gitmo, you and I'll rustle up the Moffats. *Colby*," he barked.

The man looked up, shamefaced, from where he sat holding his gut.

"You get to carry this fat dead bastard up the stairs."

The man in the maroon balaclava grabbed Alex by the shoulders. The concierge didn't even put up a struggle, just hung his head and went along with his captor. Sarge and the man in the green balaclava—the taller man he'd called Gitmo—approached Frank and Linda.

Sarge sneered as he passed Colby. "Get your sorry ass up off the floor."

Gitmo grabbed Frank by the shoulder and squeezed his thumb into the divot above his clavicle. Sarge stood in front of Linda and looked her up and down.

"Say, where'd you get that scar?"

"None of your fucking business."

He nodded as if she'd made some philosophical statement and he was taking it under consideration. "Well, we'll swing you by your room for some fresh clothes before we move on to the Old Place," he said finally. "These men are animals, Linda. Believe you me: you give them an inch of skin, they'll want to take it all."

CHAPTER 13
———————

THE OLD PLACE

The truck rolled over uneven terrain, engine growling. With a black bag over his face, Frank had no idea where they were being taken. All he knew for sure was that the heavy chains linking the cuffs on their hands and ankles wouldn't be as easy to escape as the ropes had been, even if Sarge hadn't confiscated his lighter.

Escape would take a miracle, and Frank didn't believe in those.

Colby drove the pickup angrily. An old-time country singer's "lonesome cattle call" blasted from the speakers loudly enough to scare off all the wildlife.

Gary "Sarge" Hill and the man he'd called Langford had stayed behind to take care of Alex and give the Mathias and Maria Luisa a "proper Christian burial," according to Sarge. As they'd left, he had instructed Colby to take Frank and Linda to the Old Place, which Frank had taken to believe must be Sarge's old family home.

The hood kept touching his lips and leaving a salty taste. The fabric smelled like sweat and blood, neither of which belonged to him. He was hungry. He was hurt. And he needed to piss something awful.

"I have to pee," Linda said, mirroring his thoughts.

"Hold it," Gitmo shouted over the music, his voice baritone.

145

Linda bit her lip and drew her legs to her chest. Gitmo had leered at her then, and the additional clothing Sarge had allowed her to put on hadn't curtailed his ogling. She could feel his eyes on her now.

"Why do they call you Gitmo?" Frank asked, tasting the salty hood. "Were you stationed there?"

Gitmo didn't answer, and Linda was glad for it. She didn't care whether he'd been the architect of the torture that had gone on at Guantanamo or had suffered through it. She already dreaded what might happen once he got them alone at this "Old Place" Sarge mentioned. Knowing the place of anger her impending abuse came from would be worse.

"Duck," Gitmo said.

Branches slapped against the roof of the truck. She ducked as bristly needles brushed the top of her hood.

Frank caught a branch in the face an inch or so above where Colby had punched him in the ear. He felt it well up immediately, blood trickling a prickly trail down his stubbled cheek. He tried to press the wound against his shoulder, but the injury struck the fat length of chain. "*Motherfu—*"

Gitmo prodded him with a thick finger.

"Better not curse. Colby don't like it when you curse."

"Fuck Colby," Frank said. "Who names their kid after a cheese anyway?"

Gitmo chuckled. "Heh heh heh."

The howling cowboy gave way to the DJ: "*That was Slim Whitman going way back to 1954 with the old cowboy classic, 'The Cattle Call.' Next up, we've got Tammy Wynette, who's got a word for all you fillies out there in radioland. 'Stand By Your Man,' darlin'. On Montana's Classic Country, 98.5.*"

Guitars twanged and Tammy Wynette began to croon. The truck went over a big bump, and Linda fell against Frank, their chains clanking together.

"You okay?"

His words prickled her neck through the fabric.

"I'll be fine."

She felt like she could lie against him forever, feeling his warmth, breathing in the familiar smell of his sweat and a lingering hint of cologne, but Gitmo roughly pulled them apart.

"*No talking.*"

She felt their separation like a wound. She hadn't felt so close to Frank since the Year From Hell, nor had she needed him so much. With the hood covering her face, she didn't bother to hold back the tears, letting them soak into the dark fabric.

Whatever this "Old Place" was, Linda knew it was the last place they would ever see.

The truck tore up dirt as it came to a jerky stop. Colby shut off the engine, and the music died with it. She heard the driver door open. The truck rocked as Colby stepped out and slammed the door.

"Rock and roll, Gitmo! Let's get these critters in the house."

Slap slap. He pounded the truck by Linda's head, making her jump. The chassis rocked again as Gitmo climbed out and his boots thudded on soft earth.

"Where are we?" Frank asked.

"That's for us to know and you to find out," Colby said. "Jeez, that Tammy Wynette always puts me in a hurtin' mood!" The tailgate creaked as it was lowered. "Up and out, Moffats! Up and out, you critters!"

Frank struggled to get up, but fell to his knees on the corrugated truck bed. With his hands cuffed in the front, it was easier to move around, but the heavy chains weighed him down. He was pushing himself up again when something zapped his spine, and he sprawled face first on hard plastic.

As she patted a hand along the side of the truck to find her way to the edge, Linda cringed at the crackling sound. Frank thudded heavily near her feet with a groan.

"New rule," Colby said. "Don't follow my orders fast enough you get zapped."

The zapper, whatever it was, struck her left buttock, a low-watt sting like the bite of a large bug. It was nothing like the ten thousand watts she'd experienced during the endurance event three years back, but still startling. She gripped the side of the truck to keep herself from falling.

"You also get the other one zapped, so think on that. The key here's to *always follow orders.*"

Linda steadied herself and stepped off the truck, judging the height by memory. The ground she landed on was flat. Leaves crunched underfoot.

The Old Place, she thought.

One of the men hauled Frank up by the chains criss-crossing his back and dragged him along the corrugated floor. Suspended in midair for a panicky moment, Frank was sure they'd dropped him. But they were lifting him by the chains. They let him go and he slumped to the ground, not far, but enough to lose his breath. When he tried to stand, someone kicked him back down into the crackling leaves. He pushed up on his hands and knees, sick of being beaten down, but helpless to do anything about it with the chains and the bag covering his face.

If he couldn't see, he couldn't fight back.

He no longer contained the strength to fight back with words. All he felt capable of was crying out and moaning in the hope these men would show him mercy. But neither of their captors seemed aware of the concept.

Another zap to his spine. He clenched his jaw against the sudden jolt of pain.

They struck Linda next. He heard the crackle and her grunt from where she stood above him.

For no reason.

"These men are animals," Sarge had said. He'd set the animals loose on them.

At least they didn't bring the dogs, Frank thought, and immediately worried he'd jinxed them.

"That was just 'cause we can," Colby said.

Gitmo uttered his deep *heh heh heh* in reply.

They hauled Frank to his feet.

"Frank?"

She was close to him, not touching, but close. Her voice was muffled behind her hood and further muffled by Frank's own hood over his ears. They were close, and yet, he'd never felt so far away from her, each in a separate dark ocean of pain and fear.

"I'm here."

Another zap. He fell forward into something. He could tell it was Linda when their chains clinked together.

"Don't give up." Her shaky voice was so close to his ear he could feel her hot breath through the fabric.

The men pulled them apart.

"No talking," Gitmo said.

Someone turned him around. "Get movin'," Colby said from behind him.

Frank did as he was told, wary of the zapper at his back. It was likely a cattle prod and not a Taser, or the two of them would be in far greater pain. He staggered forward, doing his best to walk with the chains at his ankles and his injured leg throbbing like an infected molar. He feared it wasn't fast enough for their captors and hoped he wouldn't make them zap him again and zap Linda for his mistake.

Linda's tears dampened the hood as she stumbled forward. They'd treated her roughly, but Frank had gotten the brunt of it. He was strong. If he hadn't already shown it at her bedside during the Year From Hell, he'd proven it and more today. But she feared that soon he would crack.

Hell, she was close to cracking herself.

Her left foot struck wood, and she stopped just short of tripping.

"On your knees," Gitmo said.

She hesitated. Frank's chains rattled like Marley's ghost beside her as he sank to the ground obediently.

Gitmo jabbed a finger into her old scar, of all places he

could have hit. The scar tissue itself was numb, but it still hurt with enough pressure to the area. She dropped to her knees with a cry of pain.

"Move forward, critters. Hands and knees."

Frank crawled, certain they had a good, painful reason for making them go on their knees. He felt splintered wood under his palms and briefly considered skirting the obstacle. The thought of the cattle prod kept him moving forward, despite the splinters and the uneven boards pressing through to the bone and tearing at his injuries.

He moved forward for Lin. If there was ever a time and place to stay strong, it was right here and right now.

But where is here exactly?

The Old Place, Sarge had called it. There'd been something almost reverential in the way he'd spoken of it, his ice blue eyes twinkling as if this place, wherever they were, held sentimental, if not mystical value.

A church in the woods maybe? Is that why they've got us on our knees?

Crawling forward, Linda put her hand down on a bent nail, and it tore through the side of her palm. She winced.

"Suck it up, princess. Keep movin' till I say stop."

She reached out gingerly, crawling on the tips of her fingers instead of her palms.

"Stop," Gitmo said.

Linda stopped immediately. The cattle prod jammed into her side, and she twisted away from it in shock.

"I said 'until *I* say stop,' not Gitmo. Even a dang dog knows how to follow orders."

They zapped Frank. He barely felt it, just kept moving.

"Stop," Colby said finally.

Frank heard boots fall on the uneven boards near him and heard the door creak.

"All right, get up."

He stood cautiously.

"Walk forward."

Frank began to walk, but someone grabbed him by the chain and held him back.

"Ladies first," Colby said. "Where'd you learn your manners?"

Linda felt Gitmo's large, gloved hands take her by the shoulders and dance her sideways. He let her go like a toy he'd wound up. She moved forward, feeling the threshold with her foot and stepping inside.

Even through the hood, she could smell the beer, dust, and old blood of the cabin.

The Old Place, she thought. *Wasn't this Kaspar's cabin?*

The way Sarge talked about it, she'd expected it might have been his old family home.

She heard Frank hobble in behind her, recognizing the *thud-slap! thud-slap!* of his shoe and bare foot.

Gitmo—she assumed it was still Gitmo—stomped along behind her, prodding her forward until something heavy struck her forehead with a metallic rattle, and she remembered the hooks and the bloodstains below them.

Her whole body began to shiver uncontrollably.

"Raise your hands," Gitmo said.

Again, her hesitation got her jolted, this time on her scar. Another zap followed, but Frank only grunted.

Linda raised her hands. Gitmo grabbed them and fastened her cuffs on the hook. She let her tired arms hang in front of her, glad they would protect her face from further abuse. The bruise on her forehead felt bigger than a softball and throbbed dully. She would have killed for an aspirin.

"Keep movin'."

Colby. Talking to Frank.

There was nowhere left for her to move.

The two- or three-foot radius the chain would allow her to move was where she would die, strung up like an animal on a hook.

Frank limped ahead. He'd heard Gitmo's command followed by their mutual zaps and the rattle of Linda's chains.

He knew the tall man had secured her to one of the hooks at the center of the room, the ones he'd naïvely assumed were for cutting up venison. And he knew his chains would be next.

If he remembered their height correctly, they were too low for hanging, unless Gitmo and Colby were able to raise the hooks.

Not so long ago, Frank had had a romantic notion they would die side by side of old age in a matching set of recliners. Linda's battle with cancer had changed his vision of their future as she'd wasted away before his eyes the way his mother had. But she'd fought through it. She'd persevered. She'd come out stronger, and their marriage had suffered. He hadn't been so naïve not to see her growing apart from him, the two of them unable or unwilling to stop themselves from pushing each other away.

He'd imagined separate futures, living new lives apart from each other with new lovers, maybe children, although neither had craved them before, at least not openly. They wouldn't mourn each other's passing. Others would mourn in their place.

Now, here they were together in the place where today's horrors had begun, likely to die side by side again, but nothing like how he'd imagined it.

"Raise your hands."

Frank raised them. Colby grabbed his wrists and attached him to the hook. He let the hook take his weight, glad at least to able to rest his leg.

"Linda," he said.

"No talking."

"I love you."

Frank tensed against the expected zap. Instead, they shocked Linda.

She startled, more from the unexpectedness of Frank's words than any pain. "I love you too," she said.

"*Shut up,*" Gitmo said, thrusting her forward.

Her feet left the ground, and she swung, suspended by the chain. She found her footing again and staggered back to center, sensing Frank's presence beside her, calming her.

"You wife's a sturdy woman, Moffat," Colby said at his ear. "She gon' wish she'd never heard your name when me an' Gitmo's done with the two a you."

Frank held his tongue, knowing anything he'd say from now on would only cause Lin more suffering.

"We gon' finish what I started back there at the lodge. What was that you was sayin' about me holdin' you and hittin' you at the same time?"

Frank felt the punch in his side like a cannonball. He staggered back to the length of the chain and fell forward, suspended, until he was able to right himself. He stood up as tall as he could manage on one good leg with a stitch in his side.

"I gotta hand it to ya, Moffat, you can take a wallop. Jackson, he was handy with a firearm, but hand to hand, he wuddn't much more dangerous than a teddy bear. Still, we seen combat together. He was like a brother to me."

Frank heard the man breathe in deeply through his nose, preparing for something.

"This one's for him," Colby said.

Frank's ear split against the man's knuckles. He saw stars and nearly blacked out, the only thing keeping him conscious the thought of what they'd do to Linda while he was out cold, not that he could prevent them from harming her anyway.

"Stop!" Linda cried. "*Why are you doing this?*"

"Why?" Colby clomped over to her. "*Why?*" She felt his breath on her neck, his face an indistinct, black shape through the mask. "Might as well ask the snake why he bites."

"Heh heh heh."

"You might as well ask the dog why he gotta *piss* all over his yard. We're *animals*, princess, or did you not hear what the Sarge said? This is *our* territory, sugar, an' roun' here you gon' follow *our* rules!"

"You're a maniac!"

She saw him pull back from her and turn away.

He let out a short, sharp laugh. "Missy, you ain't got no idea. But you're bout to find out, I guarandamntee it."

Chapter 14

Love Is Pain

Linda knew pain.

She knew fear. Shame. Humiliation.

Most people thought they knew these things, but Linda knew them acutely. They'd been intimate. Spend nearly a year pissing yourself, shitting yourself, puking and pissing blood, losing your hair, losing your mind, terrified of falling asleep because you could die during the night, wasting away to less than nothing...those agonies had stuck in her mind. The memory of physical pain had long since dissipated, but the sheer torture of those individual moments had added up and conditioned her brain to expect nothing from the world but further abuse.

Linda knew fear...,but not like this.

The first thing they did was take off her hood so she could see.

Light flooded her vision, so bright she had to close her eyes until the pain dulled and the world around her filled with muted colors.

Then they took off Frank's hood. He turned to her, the whole side of his face a mass of bruises. Sweat had matted down his hair. Blood dripped from his ear onto his shoulder and chest.

The men cast the hoods aside and got to work.

Linda knew pain, but now she'd been given front row

standing admission to the Torture of Frank Moffat. While one man worked him over, the other held her head steady so she couldn't look away.

Set out on the counter lined with newspaper was a toolbox. Gitmo opened it and spread out an array of torture implements almost lovingly. He unzipped a small carrying bag the size of a lunchbox and took out a video camera, which he set beside the tools aimed at Frank and Linda.

The camera beeped when he pressed record. The red light winked on.

Gitmo selected a shiny chrome wrench and approached Frank. His dark-brown eyes gleamed from the holes in his green balaclava.

"Subject: white male, approximately thirty years old." His words were constricted by the tight mouth hole of his ski mask, but they were clearly audible. He cocked his head, looking Frank over. "Five nine. Maybe one hundred and seventy pounds."

"I woulda said a buck sixty," Colby said close to Linda's ear, gripping her neck with his rough thumb pressed under the base of her skull, making her watch.

"Subject has received multiple injuries to the face and torso, as well as what appear to be insect bites on the left forearm, possibly ants. Two wounds on his left calf appear to have been inflicted by an animal trap and crudely sewn together using cotton thread. Discoloration surrounding the wound indicates it may be infected."

"Why are you filming this?" Linda said.

"Shut her up."

Colby grabbed a fistful of Linda's sweat-dampened hair and yanked her head back. She cried out as much from the hairs he'd pulled out by the roots as the unexpected strain to her neck muscles.

"Okay! Okay!"

He let her go, leaving her a moment's respite before he gripped her neck again.

Gitmo raised the wrench above his shoulder for the benefit of the camera. "First implement is an open-end wrench, which I will use to strike the humerus."

Frank danced away, wild eyed, fairly certain he didn't know which bone was the humerus and wouldn't have been able to defend himself even if he did, Linda shut her eyes.

She heard the wrench ping against bone. Frank screamed.

"If she won't open her eyes, punch her in the kidneys," Gitmo said.

Linda forced herself to keep her eyes open. She saw Frank swing from the chains with his legs drawn up, weeping audibly. A pink runner of drool spilled from his lips and pattered on the stained floorboards. The fresh wound on his right forearm already matched the angry red of the bug bites on the left.

"Please," she said. "Please don't hurt him anymore."

Colby let go of her neck, and she tensed her muscles against the impending blow. His fist struck her just under the lowest rib, barely an inch from the tingling numbness of her scar. He snatched out for her neck again without giving her a second to absorb the pain.

Breathing in deeply through her nose and out through her mouth, she let the pain settle, let it dissipate the way they had taught her after surgery.

Her own pain she could abide. Frank's pain, she couldn't absorb so easily.

Somehow these men understood this and were using it to their advantage.

Gitmo returned the open-end wrench to the counter and plucked up another tool. He held it in front of the camera, and the lens twisted to focus.

It was a box cutter.

"Second implement is a utility knife." He raised the knife and studied it as he approached Frank. "Pick the spot, Moffat."

Frank shook his head, lips tight.

"Pick the spot or I'll cut your goddamn throat—"

"*Watch the cussin'.*"

Gitmo turned his fury on Colby. Linda felt the man shrink back, his grip on her neck loosening slightly.

The torturer returned his attention to Frank and the blade. "Pick. The spot."

Frank raised his injured leg from the floor. "My leg! My leg!"

"Good choice."

Gitmo bent and slashed Frank's uninjured leg on the upper thigh. Frank screamed through his teeth as his shorts ripped open and the exposed flesh became red.

"Too bad. I know it's already numb. Be specific next time, Moffat."

Blood soaked through Frank's shorts. His eyes looked heavy.

"Now..." Gitmo turned to Linda, the bloodied blade held before him. "Pick the spot I cut her or the same rules apply."

Linda shied away. Colby's rough hand held her steady.

"Pick the spot, Moffat."

"Cut my arm!"

Gitmo shook his head. "You don't get to choose." He showed gleaming white teeth. "You'll get your chance to play."

He was less than a foot from her now.

"Cut her arm!" Frank sputtered. "Upper left arm!"

"There you go..." Gitmo's eyes flashed and he struck out.

Linda felt the skin tear open and bit her tongue to stifle a cry. She couldn't let Frank believe he'd hurt her. She wouldn't let them win.

"*Very good*, Mrs. Moffat. You've got a fine woman here, Moffat. She won't break easily, I'll tell you that."

"She's stronger than all of us," Frank grunted, and he meant it.

Gitmo turned on him. "Nobody said you could talk." He returned to the counter, set the box cutter down, and selected another tool. Considering the lack of deliberation, Linda thought he must have been following a plan.

"Third implement: a barbecue lighter."

He turned with the object held out. He depressed the trigger, producing a small yellow flame. Linda heard it hiss.

"Since you two like fire so much," Colby said at her ear.

"Heh heh heh." Gitmo stopped in front of Frank. "Who gets burned, Moffat? You or her?"

"M-me," Frank stuttered.

"I knew he was going to say that."

"So'd I," Colby said.

Gitmo approached Linda. "Pick a spot, Moffat."

"No."

"Pick a spot or I'll burn her hair off."

"*Okay*," Frank cried, eyes bugging out.

Linda knew what he was thinking in that moment and promised herself that if it came down to it, she would die for him. Though she knew he worried about the pain it would cause her, that wasn't what terrified him.

It was losing her hair. He'd seen it happen to his mother and then to his wife. For one it had meant death. For the other, rebirth.

Linda had already fought death once and survived.

Frank had fought death twice and seen his mother perish. He'd fought just as fiercely to hold on to a wife who'd rejected him almost as soon as she'd recovered.

He'd fought for them, and in her fear, she'd pushed him away.

All this time, she'd lived with the guilt of her decision weighing her down, unable to tell him the real reason she could no longer be with him, knowing he would never understand.

Would he understand now? she wondered. *Is it too late to ask?*

"Burn my heart," she said.

"You don't get to choose."

"No, Linda."

"Let me take it. Frank, I've been horrible to you."

"It's not just you—"

"You've just been retaliating," she said. "Like an injured animal."

The hand on her neck squeezed so tight her vision grayed. "*Shut it, princess.*"

Gitmo cocked his head to the side, curious. "Let her talk."

"Frank," she gasped as the pain on her neck dissipated, "the reason I've been fighting you, it's because of what your dad said. I thought a lot about it, that it's unfair for you to have to keep fighting, and I thought he was right." Bitter tears stung her cheeks. "I thought about what would happen if the cancer came back, if you had to go through it again, if you lost me this time like you did your mom." She tried to shake her head, but Colby's fingers tightened. "I couldn't live with that. I couldn't put you through that pain again."

"Linda—"

"But he was wrong. I know, Frank. I know that now. *Love is pain.* Love is scary and—" She swallowed. "And messy, and it doesn't always turn out the way you planned it. It's tears and blood and swearing at each other until three in the morning when you have to get up to go to work in the morning. It's sickness." Her chest hitched as she sobbed. "And eventually it's *death*. We say that in our vows. But I think we forget that part. Frank, I love you." She smiled through her tears. "And if this really is the end, I'm glad we'll die together."

Frank smiled back, teeth stained pink with blood.

"So burn my heart," she told the torturer. "Because it's been cold for so long, and it needs to burn again."

"*Phew!*" Colby chuckled. "That's drama, folks! I'd clap if I had two hands."

"Hold her steady," Gitmo said, seemingly unmoved.

The hand tightened as Gitmo pulled down her shirt collar low enough to reveal the tops of her breasts and sternum. He depressed the trigger, letting the flame dance in front of her eyes for several seconds, heating the metal.

He seemed almost apologetic when he said, "This is gonna hurt."

Then he pressed the tip of the lighter into the soft flesh above her left breast.

Red-hot metal seared through layers of flesh. He held it there as the skin around it bubbled and oozed.

Linda steadied herself, breathing into the pain, and locked eyes with Frank. He didn't look away, feeding her his strength.

I am steel, she thought, the way the pain management consultant had taught her at the hospital. *I am steel and you can't hurt me.*

But steel didn't melt so easily, and it *did* hurt her, the foul stink of charred flesh stinging her nostrils until the metal had cooled, and when Gitmo pulled the smoldering thing from her chest, her flesh pulled like taffy, and blood oozed from the hole.

She felt her bladder loosen with no chance to stop it. Hot, prickly wetness saturated her underwear and trickled down the inside of her thighs.

"Oh my dear," Gitmo chuckled as he stepped away, looking down at her crotch. Her shirt fell back into place, the collar stretched loose where it rubbed against the open wound.

Colby danced back from her, grip loosening. "Jesus Christ, did she *piss* herself?"

"It's okay, Lin," Frank said.

Humiliation pushed her over the edge and she wept.

"She told you she had to go. If you'd just let her."

"She'll survive." Gitmo sneered at the burned chunk of flesh on the end of the lighter and returned it to the counter. He picked up the video camera and returned to where Frank and Linda hung with it held in a gloved hand.

Colby's rough hand released her neck.

"Are you ready to talk to the camera?"

Linda wasn't sure she'd heard him correctly. "W-what?"

Gitmo reached into the pocket of his coat and pulled out a folded, crumpled sheet of paper. "Sarge wants you to read this."

Linda wouldn't allow herself to feel relief until they unlocked the chains. Her damp thighs and the burn above her breast itched like crazy, blood already seeping through her shirt. "That's it? It's over?"

Gitmo thrust the paper toward her. "If you do good."

"What is that?" Frank squinted, trying to get a look at what was written on the page.

"Sarge wants you to read this message for the camera. If you do good, if you make the government people believe it, and they listen to what Sarge has to say and not give us a hard time." Gitmo shrugged. "Then yep. That's it."

"Great," Frank said with a bitter chuckle. "I guess we're fucked then."

Colby swatted the back of Frank's head. "*Watch the cussin'.*"

CHAPTER 15

TURN OF THE SCREWDRIVER

"'My name is Linda Moffat.'"

She struggled to read the words Sarge had written for her, barely legible on the crumpled page. Gitmo held it up, the camera resting against his belly with the screen pointed up so he could watch.

Colby had dragged the broken metal chair over to the counter where Gitmo's tools still lay and watched her with a dark look. A single-barrel shotgun he'd brought in from the truck stood against the wall at his side.

"'My husband Frank and I are uh, being hos—*held* hostage by the Hell's Gate Posse. You have s-seen what these men are capable of. Please d-don't dismiss their demands out of hand or they will—'"

She stopped.

"Would you like me to hold it closer?" Gitmo said.

Frank gave her a look of concern. "Linda?"

"'They will kill us,'" she finished and turned to Frank.

He shook his head. The movement made him wince.

"'We demand...'" She swallowed, her mouth and throat dry. "'We demand that the hundred acres of land which was legally granted to the Hill family by President James Buchanan in 1860 and was il-illegally p-purchased from Leland Hill under duress in 1957 be immediately returned to the Hill family, including any current structures on said property and several acres currently occupied as national parkland.'"

She swallowed. Gitmo urged her on with a nod.

"'If these demands are not met by noon, Sunday, May 28th, we will be shot—'" She shook her head clear, blinking through tears. "'We will be shot in the back of the head at exactly twelve-o-one. Our blood will be on the hands of the American government. Please,'" she said, staring into the lens, trying to make whoever eventually saw this tape *feel* the words. "'Do not take their demands lightly.'"

She'd reached the end of the page. There were no more words left to say.

Gitmo pressed the record button, and the red light winked out. He lowered the camera and folded the crumpled page to his pocket.

"You did good." His smile showed through the mouth hole of his mask. "Very convincing. Let's just hope they take it seriously."

"They will," Colby said. "Nothin' tugs on people's heart-strings like a pretty, white lady in distress. It's just too bad they don't got kids. You don't have kids, do ya?"

"That's enough for today, Colby."

Colby clenched his jaw, eying the back of the torturer's head as Gitmo gathered his tools back into the box. The one-armed man returned his attention to Linda with a leering grin.

"Stop looking at her," Frank told him.

"Or what?"

"Leave them alone, Colby!" Gitmo turned with the open-end wrench held tight in a gloved fist.

Colby sneered up at his colleague. "What do you care about them, huh? After what you just did—"

"You heard what Sarge said. I'm in charge of this operation, and I say they've been through enough for today."

"Like heck." Colby stood and stomped halfway to where Frank hung. "This piece of crap *killed* Jackson! They *maimed* Biscuit! I had to put the poor girl down myself!"

Gitmo grabbed Colby by the shoulder stump and turned him around. Towering over the man, he lowered his head to Colby's level. "This camera is gonna record every goddamn thing you do." He pointed at it, the lens aimed at Frank and Linda, the red light on. "You move it, you turn it off, you even look at the fucking thing, and I will fuck your shit up."

"Watch the cuss—"

"*Fuck* your cussing. And fuck *you*, Colby. You stepped in this shit, and we're all stuck with the stink. You make this any goddamn worse, and I will personally make your life a living hell, you hear me?"

Colby jutted out his chin, refusing to back down. But he said nothing. Clearly Gitmo was not just the larger of the two men, he was also tougher.

Gitmo nodded and returned to the counter. He closed the lid on the tool box, latched it, and carried it past Linda to the door. Its hinges creaked on his way out.

"Go on, get the heck outta here," Colby grunted, kicking dust in Gitmo's direction.

Outside, the tool box clattered in the back of the truck. The driver door slammed, and the engine turned over. The trumpets from Johnny Cash's "Ring of Fire" blasted from the stereo, fading away to nothing as Gitmo drove off.

Colby grinned. "Now we got ourselves some privacy." He slipped his thumb into the waist of his pants and sauntered over.

"Don't forget the camera," Frank said.

"The camera makes it more fun." Colby's grin widened. "You two should know that."

"What's that supposed to mean?"

"Frank." Linda shook her head. "Don't."

"You know what it means," Colby said. "I seen the two of you on tape back at the lodge. Heck, I might just make a copy of that for myself for those *long*, lonely nights."

He ran the back of his hand down Linda's cheek. She cringed, twisting away from his rough knuckles.

"Leave her alone!"

"Tough words for a fella strung up like a buck, 'bout to be butchered."

Colby inhaled sharply through his nose and slapped Linda hard across the face. She winced but didn't cry out, knowing it would only fuel his brutality.

"Ooooh, she is a fiiine woman, Moffat. I bet she gives it just as hard as she takes too. The aggressive type." He winked. "Feisty."

Frank struggled against his chains, and Colby spun on the heels of his boots. "What are you gonna do, tough guy?"

"Let me out of these chains and I'll fucking show you."

Colby's fist struck Frank's eye before he could pull back. As the stars cleared, Frank wondered how his face must look. Bruised beyond recognition most likely.

Colby grabbed his jaw and squeezed. "Git ain't here no more, Moffat. This ain't a cussin free-for-all." He pushed Frank's face away and turned to Linda. "You ever done it with a man with one arm, princess? What I lack in limbs, I make up for in length, I guarandamntee ya."

Linda spat in his face.

He showed his too-white teeth. "Best save some of that for later. You'll need it for lubrication."

Linda tore away from him as he laughed uproariously. He turned to the camera and approached it in a jig, laughing like a malevolent clown.

"Oh, this is just like Christmas mornin'!" he said to the camera. "Let's see what Santa's got for us under the tree." He pinged something metallic against the counter and turned back to them with the screwdriver in his hand. "Gitmo ain't the only one who plays games. I like 'em too." He raised the screwdriver in front of Frank's face. "Which end, Moffat?"

"W-what?"

"Choose which end I shove up your wife's cooter."

Linda kicked out at the air in front of him. "Stay away from me!"

Frank pulled the chains taut. "Don't you touch her!"

The man watched her feet dance with a wide smile. "Moffat, if you don't let me play, I'm gon' get ornery. And ornery men should not be trusted with shotguns, if you get my meaning."

Frank settled against the chains.

"You know what? Let's save that game for later, shall we?" Colby slipped the screwdriver into his belt and skirted around Frank. He scooped up a hood from the floor, flicked it loose, and draped it over Frank's head a couple of times before finally managing to pull it down.

"Leave him alone!"

"Then do it! Cry for me, princess! This is America. You're either a victim or a victimizer, so *assert your goddamn victimhood*!"

She cringed away from the man, and he grinned. Turning back to Frank, he grabbed the cuffs and raised them off the hook. Frank let his arms fall immediately, glad for the breather.

"On your knees. You fight back an' I'll jam this Phillips into your lady's head."

Frank staggered onto the knee of his injured leg, then to the other, arms held out in front of him as if he were praying. If he had ever been a praying man, now would be the place and time for it.

He heard the man unzip his fly.

"If you touch her, I swear—"

"This ain't for *her*, Moffat. This Bud's for you."

"What—?"

Linda turned away as Colby pulled out his flaccid, uncircumcised penis and let loose with a stream of piss in Frank's face.

Frank shut his eyes, twisting away as hot urine drenched the fabric. The acrid smell stung his nostrils. His eyes burned. And suddenly he was drowning, choking on piss. Turning away hadn't helped. The hood had stuck to his face, and he couldn't inhale through his nose without sucking in sour piss, and he couldn't breathe through his mouth without tasting it.

He held his breath, trying to pretended it was just water. But water didn't burn unless it was boiling. Bile rose in his throat. He swallowed hard, and the stink seeped into his nostrils. The only thing keeping him from puking was the thought that he would choke on it and die.

Finally, the stream became a trickle and stopped entirely. Bubbles of piss stung his sinuses when he sucked in a desperate breath, but he didn't dare open his mouth again until the hood was off his face.

"Frank...?"

Colby tore off the mask and Frank gasped. Urine-damp hair hung in his face, dripping into his eyes and mouth. He spat, blinked piss from his eyes, and looked up at his captor, who had thankfully returned his filthy dick to his pants.

Frank doubled over and puked at the man's feet. It dribbled down his chin and he gagged and coughed while Colby laughed gleefully.

"Waterboarded the sucker!" Colby danced toward the camera. "Waterboarded 'im with piss!"

"You're a psychopath!" Linda cried.

"Best be quiet, princess, or you're next. Might take me a while to brew up some more though."

Frank coughed and wiped his mouth with a forearm. He spat a thick wad of phlegm and saliva, never so glad for the taste of vomit.

"What other toys did that big critter leave us? Not much, not much. I guess that leaves only one thing..." He dug the screwdriver out of his belt and approached.

"Please," Linda begged. "Please don't."

"I like it when you beg, sweetie pie." He twirled the tool around in his fingers. "Trust me, you gon' be beggin' me to keep goin' in a hot minute."

Frank staggered wearily to his feet, heavy from the weight of the chains.

Colby swung the screwdriver toward Linda, holding the

blade just shy of her throat. She flinched back, the tip of it pressing against her trachea.

"*Stick right there*, Moffat. Less you wanna see how quick I can jab this thing in her neck."

Frank stayed still. Colby returned to his side, slipped the screwdriver into his pocket, and grabbed Frank's cuffs. He yanked his arms up and settled the cuffs back on the hook.

"Haven't you humiliated us enough?" Frank snapped.

"I decide when we're done." Colby pointed at himself with a thumb. "*Me*. Not you. Not her. M-E. Y-O-U killed my battle buddy. Far as I'm concerned, Y-O-U deserve a whole helluva lot worse and *then some*."

"Fine," Frank said. "But leave her out of this. I'm the one that killed your friend. I'm the one that snapped the bear trap on your dog. Hurt me, not her."

Colby's eyes shone with glee. "Ohhh, but that's what I learned watchin' Gitmo go to town on you two. He hurt you more hurtin' her than he done hurtin' you. So I'm gon' hurt you, Moffat. But I ain't gon' touch another hair on your piss-stinkin head."

Movement in the window beyond Linda caught Frank's eye. He saw the man's shadow fall over the sill before he saw the man himself.

Impossible, he thought. *Beat me so hard I'm seeing ghosts.*

Neville Lumley stood outside the window, staring in, dressed in what looked like a hospital gown.

Frank tore his gaze from the sight, hoping his captor hadn't noticed his attention had drifted. When he dared another glance at the window, Neville—Jamal—was gone.

Linda gave him a curious look. He frowned, shook his head lightly.

"I'm still curious about one thing," Frank said. "Who were you trying to shoot when you killed Neville Lumley? Your friend Jackson said it was an accident, but Sarge seemed to think you were hunting somebody else. Someone from the government? A banker?"

"I don't question orders."

"So Sarge sent you after him."

"What difference does it make?"

Frank noticed the flash of anger in Colby's eyes and decided to dig. "You don't care about any of this? You're risking death, or prison for the rest of your life if you're lucky, for a plan you don't even care about?"

Colby seemed to consider it.

"You and Jackson fought for this country. Did Sarge?"

"Saw combat in 'Nam, I understand."

"And you see no problem with his ideas about the government? About this country whose ideals and freedoms you fought for?"

"I don't get mixed up in politics."

"Wake up, man. I mean he's clearly using you. You think he gives a sh—" He stopped short of cursing, watching Colby slowly back away from him. "You think he cares whether you live or die? He probably *wants* you all to die so you could be martyrs to his cause. Next thing you know, he'll be asking you to strap on a suicide vest and blow yourself up for a hundred acres of dirt in the middle of nowhere."

Colby startled as the back of his legs hit the chair, and he sank down hard in it.

"He's right," Linda said. "Sarge was *glad* Frank killed your friend."

"No." Colby shook his head, eyes on his boots. "No, that ain't true."

"He said he never liked him. He probably only tolerated him because he was some woman named Clara's son."

Colby's gaze snapped to her. "He *said* that? He said her name?"

"He said Clara's boy didn't even deserve a eulogy," Frank said. "He would have let us leave after I shot him *in self-defense*, if he thought we'd have kept our mouths shut and not gone to the cops."

"That mother—" The man stopped himself with a sneer. "That...*snake*."

"Let us go, Colby." Somehow, Linda managed to look

sympathetic, despite everything the man had done and had been prepared to do to her. "You can erase this tape. Burn it. Whatever. Anything happens, we'll leave your name out of it. I promise you. You were just following orders. Manipulated by a con man."

"No, that's—" Colby shook his head. "That's not how it is. I don't *get* manipulated. I ain't stupid."

"Colby," Frank said. "Dude. It's nothing new. It happens to everyone."

"I said *I ain't stupid!*" The man stood with a ferocious scowl and charged at Frank with the screwdriver held out before him.

Frank reared back, raising a leg in self-defense. The blade caught him in the thigh and penetrated to the hilt, tearing through meat and muscle and deflecting off the bone. Linda cried out, and Colby twisted the bit, his too-white teeth gritted, eyes fixed on Frank, feeding off his pain.

Frank struggled to remain conscious as the cabin went gray.

Colby let go of the screwdriver and staggered back. He dropped into the chair, breathing heavily, eyes downcast.

Frank gingerly lowered his leg to the floor. The screwdriver popped out of the wound and clattered on the tiles, glistening with his blood.

"Are you okay?" Linda asked.

He swallowed hard and tried to nod. His head drooped to his chest instead, chin striking the chains.

Colby drew the shotgun into his lap and held it in both hands. "I don't want to hear the two of you for a while." His focus remained on the floor. "Don't make a peep, or the next word any of ya'll say is gon' be the last, I guarandamntee it."

Frank kept his mouth shut. There was nothing left to say.

CHAPTER 16

END OF THE LINE

The cabin had been silent for so long Frank hadn't realized he'd drifted off until the sound of the truck woke him. The last light of day was fading. Both his legs prickled with pins and needles.

Linda watched him with a concerned look. When he caught her eye, she forced a smile.

Colby stared at the door, waiting.

The driver door slammed. Boots trudged toward the cabin.

Colby raised the shotgun.

Frank and Linda both shied away. But he was aiming between them, at the door.

Gitmo had promised to hurt him if he tortured them further. The evidence was on tape, and Colby clearly intended for Gitmo never to see it.

"Blaze of glory," Colby muttered under his breath.

As much as Frank didn't want to get shot warning Gitmo, he knew that if Colby shot the man, the two of them were next.

Frank wondered if Colby had intended to kill Gitmo the minute the man had left with the tape, or if they had driven him to it with their suggestion of mutiny.

Both Frank and Linda thought, *What now?*

The door creaked open behind them.

"What the—?"

Colby fired, silencing Gitmo's query. Behind them, the tall man grunted and fell against something solid.

Colby broke the shotgun between his knees. The shell exited with a hollow *thoomp* and clattered on the floor while Colby reached into a pocket for another. He got to his feet and inserted a fresh shell, snapped the lever closed over his knee, and strode toward Frank and Linda as the injured man behind them groaned.

Flesh slapped against tile.

"*Heh heh heh*," Gitmo said. He spat.

Frank and Linda wanted so badly to watch the men kill each other, but fear the next shot might be for them kept them from turning. They stood facing each other as another shotgun blast rattled the cans on the shelves. They said "I love you" as the red light on the video camera began to flash, the tape running out with a steady *beeeeep beeeeep beeeeep!*

The light winked out.

Feet shuffled behind them, squeaking on the tiles. Something heavy and metallic—the shotgun maybe—clattered to the floor. Then more footfalls, both men grunting.

Someone slammed into Frank, knocking him off his feet. Rotating on the hook as he swung outward, Frank saw Gitmo had his hands around Colby's neck, and Colby had his hunting knife thrust to the hilt between Gitmo's ribs.

The wound dripped, splashing gore at their feet.

The torturers staggered away. Colby fell against the counter, knocking the video camera to the floor. Linda saw the plastic cover smash, and Colby pulled out the knife, arcing a spray of blood across the floor. Gitmo held the man's head against the counter, squeezing the life out of him.

Colby jabbed him again. Blood rained down over their boots He stabbed Gitmo a third time, less forceful than the last, his face turning purple, cords standing out on his neck.

"Fuck...*you*," Gitmo grunted.

"Don't..." The word came out as a gasp. "...*cuss*."

Gitmo slumped over him. Both men slipped away from the counter and landed on the floor beside the broken camera.

"Are they dead?" Frank asked.

"I think so." The pool of blood grew under the two men, staining the floorboards. "I don't think they're breathing."

"How are we gonna get out of here?"

"I've got an idea. Can you hold my weight?"

"Christ...I mean normally, but *now*..." He nodded. "I can try."

"Okay. I'm gonna swing over and grab onto you with my legs."

"Hello," he said, forcing a grin.

She chuckled weakly. "When we get out of here, there'll be all the time in the world for that. Just tell me to let go if it hurts too much."

"Whenever you're ready."

She stepped as far back from him as the chain would reach, pulling it taut. Then she lifted her legs and swung. Her toes scraped across the floor, slowing her momentum.

"*Shit.*"

"Try again."

"I don't know how much longer I can hold myself up."

"Take your time."

The crotch of her shorts had long since dried, but her underwear was still damp, and her inner thighs itched like mad as she backed up for another try. Not that Frank had faired any better. His t-shirt still looked damp, and it wasn't even his own piss.

This time, she lifted her whole body while raising her legs off the floor. Her arm muscles strained beyond exertion, but she focused on the goal. On the upward arc, she kicked her legs out wide and upward like a little girl on a swing set, only with no urge to shout *Wheeee!*

Her inner thighs struck Frank's chest, and he reared back on his bad—*worse*—leg, but she locked her legs around his waist before he could fall, and she clung to him. The hook hung from her cuffs with enough slack that she thought she might be able to slip it off.

"Ready?"

Frank stabilized himself. The wounds on both legs wept blood. His face was a bloody, bruised mess, but determination looked good on him. "Ready."

"This is gonna hurt." She raised her arms. The hook pulled with the cuffs, chains rattling. She tried again, faster. The hook pulled along with them.

"Do it slowly," Frank grunted. His face had gone red. Veins and tendons stood out on his neck.

With her leg muscles overstrained, she couldn't hold on much longer. But Frank was right. Ever so slowly, she raised her hands. She heard the metal clink and grind together.

The cuffs slipped off the hook, and she found herself in free fall.

Instinct kept her legs taut around Frank's straining torso, but she let go as her spine bent backward, and she slammed down hard on her shoulder blades. The breath expunged from her lungs, and for a moment, she thought she might black out.

"You okay?"

She rolled over onto her side. "I'll survive. You?"

"I've definitely been better."

Linda got to her knees and crawled to the dead men on the floor. Her palms pressed down in Gitmo's sticky blood, and when she reached for the key ring on Colby's belt, her palms reminded her of when she was a kid and the teacher had made her dip her hands in red paint to make turkeys.

She tore the keys off his belt, opened the padlock linking her chains, and shrugged out of them. She used the other small key on both sets of cuffs.

Stretching out her limbs and twisting her wrists, she returned to Frank. She helped him raise his arms first and removed his cuffs from the hook. He stumbled forward, drained of energy. She hugged him to her, his head slumped in the crook of her neck.

"Let's get you out of those chains."

"I saw Neville," Frank said as Linda freed his hands. "He was standing outside the window dressed in a white gown."

"A gown? He's dead, Frank. I *saw* them kill him."

"I know." The shackles fell from his shoulders and he shook his head, neck joints popping. He rubbed his raw, bleeding wrists. "I guess I was seeing things."

She took his hand. "Let's get out of here."

"I wish we could burn this fucking place to the ground," Frank said as they reached the door. He hopped out on his less injured leg.

Linda followed behind him. "When this is all over," she told him, "we'll come back with bulldozers."

In the last of the sunlight, she hurried around the front of the truck. The keys hung from the ignition, and she was relieved not to have to return to the cabin and root through a dead man's pockets. "I'll drive."

Frank climbed in after her, pulling himself up to the cab with a pained groan. The engine started on the first try, and the radio came on full blast, Willie Nelson singing about always hurting the one you love.

He flicked it off.

She turned to him as she threw the transmission into reverse. "Good call."

The receding sun rippled on the surface of the pond in the rearview, all peach and pink above the slate-gray mountain peaks. There wasn't much gas left in the tank, but she was pretty sure it would be enough to get them at least as far as the main road. She put the truck into forward and headed away from the sunset.

They had almost reached the woods when headlights swished through the trees up ahead.

"What now?" she said.

Frank gripped the armrest as Linda slammed her foot on the brake, tearing up grass. "Too small to be truck lights. Could be the four-wheelers."

"With guns." She looked over her shoulder. "We have to go back."

Frank stared at her a moment, mouth agape. "We don't know if there's any road past the cabin, Lin. Even if there is, it could lead us straight into the mountains."

The headlights swung their way, beams narrowing the closer they got to the outer edge of the woods.

"If we keep going this way, we're dead for sure," Linda said frantically.

"*Not if it's the police.*"

Linda hesitated, hovering her foot over the accelerator. Any minute now, whatever vehicles were out in those woods would come roaring out. She couldn't chance it.

"If it's the police, we'll be fine either way. If it's them, we're dead."

"You're right." Frank nodded. "Let's go."

She threw the truck in reverse and backed up the low rise.

Frank saw the two quads emerge from the darkening pines, headlamps flashing through the windshield and catching the two of them in the front seats like prison yard spotlights. The ATVs bounded up and over the rocky terrain, and their lights fell away from the windshield.

Linda slammed the gearbox into forward, practically jumping on the gas.

The ATVs had halved the distance by the time she swung the truck around the front of the cabin and began heading toward the sparse aspen forest where they'd encountered the dog.

Frank tried to get a decent look in the side mirror, but the truck rocked so aggressively on its suspensions all he saw was a blur of dark green and brown. When the ground evened out, he glanced over his shoulder just as the first four-wheeler zipped out around the side of the cabin.

The rider wore camo. "It's them," he said.

Linda wheeled around a thick stump. The engine roared

as she floored the gas, all eight cylinders firing. A spray of black muck flecked the white aspens.

The road began to incline and she had to slow, unable to navigate as easily as the woods grew denser and larger stones littered their path. Soon it would be too dangerous for the truck to continue, and the four-wheelers would gain the upper hand.

Frank turned with a concerned look. "We have to get out of the truck."

She glanced at him and spun the wheel, narrowly avoiding collision with a massive moss-covered rock. "Are you *nuts*?"

"If we get stuck, they're gonna catch us. We get out now and start running, we'll at least have a head start on them."

"What? That doesn't make sense."

"*It makes sense.* Trust me, Lin."

Linda saw the determination in his eyes, and even though she wanted more than anything to stay safely inside the truck and keep driving farther and farther from the men at their heels, she knew he was right. The trees ahead were so dense she doubted the four-wheelers could navigate them, the hill craggier and mud slicked.

He was right. If they got stuck, they would be frustrated, angry, and careless. They wouldn't be ready to run. They would make stupid mistakes.

She slammed both feet on the brake.

The truck swerved on its front wheels as it tore to a halt, launching both of them forward. Without hesitation, they threw open their doors and leaped down into the mud-slicked leaves.

"Run!" Frank shouted, staggering ahead.

Linda bolted, slipping in the muck but gaining traction the farther she ascended.

Behind them, the ATVs buzzed, bounding over rocks and zipping around trees, maybe forty or fifty feet below, and gaining steadily.

How much farther would they have gotten in the truck?

The aspens she passed grew much closer together, and the earth was much rockier, with mudslides in places. The truck had been built to haul heavy equipment, not to drive all-terrain.

She glanced over her shoulder.

Frank wasn't behind her.

The four-wheelers had veered off, following him. When she'd turned to run, Frank had staggered through the bushes opposite the truck, leading them away. The men weren't far behind, but he had the advantage of being easily able to avoid the trees and climb over rocky terrain that could easily tip their vehicles.

"Dammit, Frank!"

She charged down after them, desperate to catch up before the men caught Frank or to distract them after they had. Either way, she was certain she and Frank had reached the end of the line.

She ran, leaping over roots and stones, grabbing tress and using them to slingshot herself forward. Her lungs burned. Every muscle ached. Her inner thighs chafed. She'd been hungry so long that her insides felt hollow.

At least I don't have to pee, she thought.

She looked ahead to where Frank was leading them and felt the first real burst of hope since they'd landed themselves in this hellhole.

Beyond the trees, a stretch of pavement twisted around the side of the mountain, about a hundred feet from where she ran, closing the distance. Just two lanes, not as wide or kept up as a highway. But she thought it could be a county road. Light traffic, with any stroke of luck.

The mountain shot straight up from the side of the road, bare slate save a few small trees clinging to its side. They might have been able to climb it if Frank's leg wasn't so badly injured. The men might not be able to follow, but they could easily shoot the two of them down.

Frank rushed out onto the road and started waving his hands.

Hill's men braked and climbed off the ATVs, grabbing shoulder-strapped rifles and pursuing.

Linda felt her limbs begin to plod, and she willed herself onward, determined not to let Frank die without her by his side.

As she neared the edge of the trees, she heard the men shouting. Frank shouted back, holding up his hands. The militiamen aimed their rifles, and Frank dropped to his knees, hands behind his head.

Please don't let this be the end.

As if in answer to her plea, a bloodred light swept along the gray face of the cliff. Blue and red again. The first police cruiser took the corner, and its sirens blared around the mountainside.

Linda might have fainted from relief if the adrenaline hadn't kept her moving. She pushed her way through the bushes along the side of the road, a second cruiser hot on the tail of the first. Both vehicles skidded to a halt about twenty feet from where Frank knelt in the middle of the road. Hill's men stood with their weapons raised.

Frank turned from the police to his pursuers and back, torn between sheer terror and relief, caught in the headlights in the middle of an impending shootout.

The driver doors of both cruisers opened, emblazoned with sheriff's department logos, and the officer in the first vehicle dropped to one knee behind it, drawing his sidearm. The one behind him did the same, a woman wearing a brown campaign hat like a forest ranger.

Frank flattened himself against the pavement.

"Drop your weapons!" the officer in lead shouted. Linda recognized him by his mustache. It was the sheriff, the man who'd pulled them over what couldn't possibly have only been a day ago, but clearly had been.

"I do not recognize your authority!" one of the militiamen shouted.

"Your fascist laws don't got no jurisdiction on this sovereign land!" the other man bellowed, gesturing angrily with his rifle.

Both cops fired through their open windows.

The militiamen shot back as their bodies erupted with bullet wounds, jerking wildly. None of their shots hit a target. Both men slumped down in the road dead or dying, rifles clattering away from their bodies.

The sheriff rose from behind the driver door, holstering his Glock. "Sir, are you injured?"

"I'm okay!" Frank called back, not daring to rise an inch from the asphalt.

"You can get off the ground now, sir. Hurry on back and get behind my vehicle. Deputy Miller'll take a look at those injuries."

Frank got up and hobbled toward the closest cruiser.

"Frank!" Linda called out.

"Linda?"

Both officers reached for their sidearms, calming when they saw she was unarmed.

"Ma'am, please stay where you are until we ascertain these individuals have been incapacitated," the Deputy Miller said as she approached the men in the road.

Linda stayed put. "Frank, you asshole! You nearly got yourself killed."

"We wouldn't have made it together," he said. "I had to give you a chance."

"You can't just make that decision for us. We're a *team*. We have to talk about these things, okay?"

"*Are* we a team, Linda?"

"After all we've been through, you still don't know? I would've *died* for you today, Frank. I don't want to lose you, not again. All of that other crap is in the past as far as I'm concerned."

"*They're dead*," the sheriff said, returning to his cruiser where Frank stood, holding the hood for support. "Ma'am, you can hug your husband now if you'd like."

Linda began to smile as she crossed the road. Frank returned the smile, limping to meet her. She worried it couldn't be true. They were finally free, but it didn't seem right. She looked both ways down the darkening stretch of road, looking for the truck that would run them down or the dogs charging out of the woods.

Nothing came between them. They met halfway in an embrace.

"I love you, Lin."

"I love you too, Frank." Her breath on his neck made his spine tingle. "Please don't ever do that again."

"I won't, I promise."

"You'd better not."

She kissed his stubbly cheek, and he leaned back. They looked at each other's faces, bruised, battered, and bloody, and saw the love in each other's eyes.

Frank laughed, happy to be alive, even happier to be holding his wife in his arms again. When their lips met, they felt full of broken glass, but it was a kiss they would remember for the rest of their lives, however long they had left.

CHAPTER 17

—————

THE DELUSION OF FREEDOM

Frank and Linda sat hand in hand in the backseat of Sheriff Stanton's cruiser, listening to him explain the situation as they drove the dark, winding road toward the station.

"So really you're just lucky Deputy Miller and I were aware of the back road to the Hill compound and came that way when we did." He glanced at them in the rearview with a tight smile. "Those militia folk like to think they live in the shadows, but we've been keeping tabs on all of them down at the station house, especially the two fellas who got you the worst."

"Have they been in trouble before?" Linda wondered.

The sheriff raised his eyebrows and chuckled to himself. "Colby Digsby? You could say that. He's been in and out of my cells fairly often since he came back crippled from his last tour in Afghanistan. I've got a feeling a lot of his anger issues come—*came*, I should say—from his frustration with how badly the government failed him and others like him when they got home."

"What about the other guy?" Frank said. "Gitmo."

"Michael Day Rider. Blackfoot Indian, I think. Not sure why they call him 'Gitmo,' seeing as I don't think he was ever at Guantanamo Bay. He was a Marine. Discharged in '08, according to his service records."

"What for?"

"You'd have to ask him." The sheriff glowered in the rearview. "Although I don't suppose you'll be able to if he's dead, as you say."

Linda looked out at the black woods. "Will we be long at the station?"

"I don't suspect we will. I'll just need to take your statements and then you'll be free to go back to...Seattle, was it?"

Frank nodded. "That's right."

"It's just that we could really use a change of clothes," Linda said.

"I didn't want to be the one to point it out." Sheriff Stanton gave her a grim smile. "I'll see what I can do about that back at the station, but the wife may end up having to pillage our wardrobe."

They drove the rest of the way in silence, to a small, single-story building at the foot of the mountains. It could have been a dentist's office or a liquor store if not for the "Danby Sheriff's Dept." sign out front.

Sheriff Stanton pulled the cruiser up to the front and got out. He opened Linda's door, and she climbed out, careful not to hit her head as she had getting in. Frank slid across the seat and got out behind her.

"I'll have Stephanie ring up Doc Ambers to swing by and take a look at those injuries while you run your story past me."

He held the door for them. Linda stepped in. Frank hobbled in after her.

The front room looked like they were in the process of moving either in or out, with boxes everywhere and only a few photos of medal ceremonies and previous sheriffs on the walls, along with a "Wanted" list and a "Community Postings" board.

The young brunette at the front desk looked up, and her large blue eyes popped at the sight of them. "Oh gosh!" She laid a hand between her heavy breasts. "I don't mean to gawk, but the two of you look like you've been through the wringer!"

"We've had better days," Linda admitted.

"Steph, ring up Johnny's and get them to bring by a couple of house specials with extra gravy." Sheriff Stanton scowled in their direction. "You two do eat meat, right?"

"Even if I was a vegetarian, I would eat a horse right now," Linda said.

The sheriff grinned amiably. "Doubt it'll come to that, though Johnny's takeout has been mistaken for worse. Give Doc Ambers a call too, will ya, Steph?"

"You got it, Chief."

"Stephanie, how many times do I have to ask you please to stop calling me 'Chief'?'"

The woman grinned. "Just about every day, Gus."

The man shook his head with a half smile and gestured for Frank and Linda to go on ahead. Frank shuffled after her.

"Take a left in that room up ahead."

She stepped into the dark room, and Frank followed. In the light from the hall she could make out a desk and three chairs, a water cooler, and a filing cabinet.

Sheriff Stanton flicked on the light.

The office looked even less lived in, with a family photo on the desk along with a pen jar and a scattering of papers, the sheriff's credentials on the wall behind the desk. Linda supposed they didn't do a lot of actual policing here aside from traffic tickets and the occasional late-night drunken brawl, but it still struck her as odd.

"Is this office new?"

"We're in the process of moving to a new location closer to town," Sheriff Stanton said. "Now if you don't mind, start from the beginning. How did you come to be in the company of Gary Hill and his thugs?"

The sheriff gestured for them to sit. They did so gladly, Frank wincing as he sank into the hard vinyl, and he pushed the chair out to give both legs a good stretch. Aside from the one that had popped earlier in the day, his stitches had held on through everything, by some miracle. They'd have to be removed and redone by a professional, but he hoped that by then, he'd be heavily medicated.

Linda began to tell the whole story for the sheriff, and Frank managed to remain focused enough to pipe up with details when she stumbled, misremembered, or simply forgot. Sheriff Stanton listened intently, jotted down details, and asked questions when something required clarification or just didn't sit right.

Stephanie interrupted on the intercom twice: once to confirm their food order, which the sheriff dismissed with slight aggravation, and a second time to update him on the situation at the lodge.

"Well, we can bring our men home in one piece at least," he said when told that the state police, ATF, and FBI had taken over the siege at Lone Loon Lodge.

Once Linda had told him all she could remember, the sheriff set his pen on the notebook and leaned back in his chair, drawing his hands behind his head. "That's quite a story, Mr. and Mrs. Moffat. You don't think this doctor fella has any involvement with the Hill family, do you?"

Linda turned to Frank, who shrugged. "Do you have reason to believe that, Gus?"

The sheriff lowered his arms and folded his hands on the desk. "Up until an hour ago, I was under the impression Lone Loon Lodge was a rehabilitation center. Now I hear they were treating their patients to intense psychological abuse, and an actor under their employ may have assaulted you."

"*Did* assault me."

"Seeing as the man is dead as you claim, I don't suppose you'll want to press charges against him. However if you do want to take these people to task, I'd be happy to fill out the paperwork—"

"Forget it." Frank shifted uncomfortably in the chair. He hated police stations because of how often his father had been called away to work when he was growing up, and he just wanted to get out of there as quickly as possible.

Linda agreed with a fervent nod. "I just want to forget this whole weekend ever happened."

"Probably a good idea," Sheriff Stanton said. "Those Hill boys will see the inside of a prison cell by dawn. With all the potential charges against them, I'm sure they'll be wishing they never met the two of you."

The intercom buzzed. Sheriff Stanton scowled at it like an annoying child. His chair groaned as he sat up to flick the button. "If that's the food, Stephanie, feel free to bring it on in."

"It's not. I really think you need to come out here, Gus."

"Stephanie, I'm in the middle of taking a statement here—"

"There's a Dr. Kaspar at the desk. He says he needs to speak with you urgently."

The sheriff scowled thoughtfully. "Send him on in." He sat back with a curious smile. "Well, this ought to be interesting."

Linda and Frank watched the door, eager to finally meet the man in the flesh and give him a piece of their minds. A moment later, a knock rattled the frosted glass.

"Come in."

The door opened.

Frank jerked upright, gripping the armrests of his chair. Linda nearly toppled hers, standing up to get as far away as she could.

Gary "Sarge" Hill stood in the doorway dressed in a neatly tailored three-piece suit, clean-shaven with no cowboy hat. He held a clipboard under an arm. Alex stood at his shoulder, dressed in white like a hospital orderly.

"*What the hell is this?*" Linda said, taking the words from Frank's mouth.

"Sheriff Stanton," Sarge said with a slight Austrian accent, "my name is Dr. Kaspar."

"What can I do for you, Doctor?"

"That's not Dr. Kaspar," Linda said. "That's *him*. That's Gary Hill. *Sarge*."

Sarge gave Linda a look of keen interest, like an entomologist studying a new behavior in an insect. "It's just as I feared, Sheriff Stanton. Their delusion has gotten worse."

"Wait wait wait." The sheriff stood. "Mrs. Moffat, this man is not Gary Hill."

"*That's* the man who held us hostage!"

The sheriff surveyed the papers on his desk, found a newspaper, and unfolded it to a page. He slid it across the desk and pointed to a black and white photograph of a mustached man a decade younger than the man calling himself Kaspar, wearing a familiar cowboy hat and duster. The headline said "Hell's Gate Posse Boss Files Lawsuit Against Montana BLM."

"No. That's not him." The ground beneath her feet felt unsteady. She pointed a trembling finger at the man calling himself Dr. Kaspar. "*That's* Sarge."

Sheriff Stanton regarded her queerly. "Ma'am, my people have lived in this county as long as the Hills have, and I assure you, *that's* Gary." He pointed to the man in the photo. "Doctor...Casper, was it?"

"Kaspar," the man posing as Dr. Kaspar said.

"Right. Maybe you could enlighten me as to what their alleged 'condition' is, as it seems to me their only visible condition is badly beaten and possibly confused."

"Thank you, Sheriff. Frank and Linda Moffat were remanded to my facility last week for possession of large quantities of marijuana with the attempt to sell to an undercover policeman."

"He's lying." Frank tried to rise from the chair, but his legs gave out under him. "This is bullshit—"

"*Sit*," Sheriff Stanton said.

Frank plopped back down in the chair.

"If you administer a drug test, you'll find Mr. Moffat positive for marijuana use."

Linda shook her head. "You can't possibly believe him, Gus."

The sheriff held up a hand. "*Sheriff*. Let me hear his side, Mrs. Moffat. You'll have a chance for rebuttal."

The man calling himself Dr. Kaspar gave him a pleasant smile. "Thank you, Sheriff Stanton. The Billings police department sent Mr. and Mrs. Moffat to my facility due to *erratic* behavior presented during their interrogation." He held up the clipboard. "The two of them managed to escape my facility this morning. My team has been looking everywhere for them. I have the Involuntary Commitment forms here, stating they are to remain at my facility until further notice, if you'd like to see them."

"Your *facility?*" Frank shook his head. "It's a couples retreat! Alex, tell him."

Alex folded his muscular arms across his chest.

"Come on!"

"*Frank*," Linda said.

He turned to her. All she did was shake her head.

They had beaten them again, and she knew it. The best she could hope for was a phone call. She thought her boss might be able to call in a favor and get them released, maybe put the screws on these pricks before things got even worse than they already were.

Sheriff Stanton came around the desk, holding out a hand toward the man in the doctor's coat. "Let me get a look at those forms."

Frank grabbed the man's arm as he passed. When the sheriff glowered down at him, he realized he'd likely just turned the sheriff's department against them with a single gesture, and he hastily retracted his hand.

Sheriff Stanton met Sarge at the door. He took the clipboard and scanned the document. "Hmm."

"*Well?*" Linda said.

"Well, it looks legitimate—"

"Goddamn it, Sheriff!" Frank cried. "Gus? Come on! I mean, this isn't right! You have to know that. You *pulled us over* yesterday! How could we have been at his bullshit facility since last week when we just got here yesterday?"

Linda looked at the sheriff expectantly.

Sheriff Stanton scrutinized them a moment. Then he handed the clipboard back and shook his head. "I pull over a lot of people, Mr. Moffat. Just that time of year."

Frank slammed his fists on the armrests. "This is *insane!*"

The man calling himself Dr. Kaspar tutted. "Now now, Mr. Moffat. You know we don't like to use that word—"

"FUCK YOU!"

"All right, that's enough!" Sheriff Stanton growled, slamming a fist on the desk. The jar of pens toppled. They rolled off the desk and fell to the floor at Frank's feet, one after another.

The man calling himself Dr. Kaspar eyed them shrewdly. Alex wouldn't look either of them in the eye.

Sheriff Stanton sat back down behind his desk, shaking his head. "I'm gonna get to the bottom of this. Everybody keep quiet." He thumbed the intercom. "Stephanie, can you ring Billings P.D.?"

"Will do, Gus."

The five of them didn't say a word or move a muscle until the desk phone rang. Sheriff Stanton picked it up on the second ring.

"Danby Sheriff's Department, Sheriff Stanton speaking." He paused and nodded. "That's right... oh, do you? Yep, Chipper's a good man, all right." He chuckled. "Well look, Captal—James, all right then. James, I've got a strange situation developing down here, and I could sure use your assistance. There's a Dr. Kaspar in my office with Involuntary Commitment papers signed by your office for two individuals involved in a kidnap—no sir, they were the ones who claim to have gotten kidnapped."

He straightened the pen jar and returned a single remaining pen to it. "It's a long story, James, but the gist of it is that this Dr. Kaspar character claims these people fled his facility despite being under involuntary commitment due to peculiar behavior they allegedly exhibited during a routine arrest for marijuana possession—"

Sheriff Stanton sat up, suddenly intrigued. "Oh, you do know them? Moffat, that's correct. Frank and Linda. Well, that is definitely interesting... all right then. Thank you kindly, James. I'll be sure and tell Chipper you said hello."

He cradled the phone.

Frank held out his hands. "Sheriff, please, you have to believe us—"

"The only thing I have to do is return you to the custody of these two gentlemen."

"We haven't done—"

"*Shut. The hell. Up,*" the sheriff snarled, and Linda startled, arms draped across her chest where she'd retreated in the farthest corner of the room.

Frank sat and quietly shook his head.

"I'd like to know a little about their condition, Dr. Kaspar, if you will."

Dr. Kaspar cleared his throat.

"Everything he's about to say is a lie."

"It's over, Frank."

He turned to Linda in desperation. "*You're just gonna give up?*"

"They beat us. No matter what we do, they twist it around on us."

"They'll *kill* us, Lin..."

"All I know for sure is I'm done fighting. I'm *done*, Frank."

"Dr. Kaspar?" Sheriff Stanton said. "If you will."

"Thank you, Sheriff Stanton. It is my contention that Frank and Linda Moffat suffer from a shared delusion of persecution. A *folie à deux* in which no one can be trusted but themselves."

"We're *paranoid?* Look at us!"

"Sit down."

Frank sat. "I got stabbed, Gus. They burned her with a barbeque lighter. Show him, Lin." She didn't move.

"A man pissed in my goddamn face, Jesus Christ, Gus! You *shot two men* with rifles in the road out there! Was that part of our so-called delusion?"

"That's a good point," the sheriff said, and turned his quizzical gaze to the men at the door.

Sarge remained unflappable, speaking hurriedly in his phony Austrian accent. "Merely a coincidence. We've had difficulties with the Hill family in the past. They claim to be the rightful owners of land which I purchased many years ago. The Moffats were, as they say, in the wrong place at the wrong time."

Frank shook his head. "This is fuckin' incredible. I don't believe this."

"Of course *you* don't believe it. Your *delusion* prevents you."

The chair toppled as Frank pushed out of it, grabbing for the man's throat. Alex stepped in between them, holding him back with a hand.

"I'm gonna fucking kill you! Both of you! I'm gonna cut you up and pin your fucked up brains to the wall so future generations can study them under a *fucking microscope!*"

"*That's egoddamnnough!*"

Sheriff Stanton grabbed him in an arm lock. Frank fought back with what little strength he had left, but couldn't get free.

"Frank!"

He tore his gaze away from the man playing Kaspar to look back over Stanton's shoulder.

Linda gave him a sad smile. "It's time to stop fighting. *Please.*"

He struggled a moment longer and gave up. As he went slack in Stanton's arms, a very satisfied smile crossed Dr. Kaspar's lips.

Chapter 18

Asylum

Frank and Linda sat in the backseat of a long, white van while Alex drove. Sarge, or Kaspar, or whoever he really was, sat opposite in the jumper seat. Neither Linda nor Frank struggled. It was pointless to fight against the straight-jackets.

Sheriff Stanton hadn't even allowed them to make a call before they were hustled out to the waiting van, claiming the Billings police would have already given them the opportunity.

They were truly alone.

Linda waited until the man in charge turned to her. "Who are you really? You're not Sarge. You're not Kaspar either, are you?"

Again, the man gave them that satisfied smile. Both the Austrian accent and his prior slight Southern twang were gone when he spoke, replaced with a flat tone, lacking any recognizable region. "I am merely a man with a great deal of money and resources at my disposal."

"Then why are you doing this? Why us?"

The man playing Kaspar gave it thoughtful consideration. Alex turned from watching the road ahead to glance at him, as if wondering the answer himself.

"Quite a long time ago, someone very close to me asked

the same thing, Linda. I'll answer you the way I answered her: *because I can.*"

Linda looked away in disgust. Frank had already stopped listening, watching the mountains pass by in the tinted windows.

The man in the passenger seat turned to look back at him with an amused smirk. "You're especially quiet, Mr. Moffat. Cat got your tongue?"

Frank eyed him a moment and said nothing, just returned his gaze to the passing scenery.

The man smirked. "I'm glad you've finally come to understand how futile it is to challenge me."

Frank bit his tongue.

"No smart aleck remarks? No scathing commentary?"

Frank narrowed his eyes at the man.

"All right then. Let's just enjoy the scenery, shall we?"

The man, whoever he truly was, looked out the window at the dark blur of mountains and trees, and Frank grinned to himself, satisfied to have gotten the upper hand, however slight.

ALEX LED the two of them into the foyer of Lone Loon Lodge. The maid, Maria Luisa, stood spritzing the front desk with a cleaning spray and wiping it down.

Frank wasn't surprised to see she wasn't dead, nor that there seemed to be no sign anywhere of the altercation that had occurred mere hours before, let alone a standoff with the FBI. Nothing surprised him anymore. Jesus could fly in on a chariot and he'd merely shrug it off.

Linda looked around herself. "I don't understand. Will somebody please tell me what's going on? Was *anything* real?"

"That's what we're here to find out," the man in charge said, turning to face them as he reached the desk. "How can the mind separate fantasy from reality when the facts are lies and the fiction is true?"

"That makes no goddamn sense," Frank grunted.

"Doesn't it? In point of fact I'd say it's the *only* thing that makes sense. *Look at the world around you.* The news is full of hyperbole and opinion. The government is a puppet show, our entire economy based on IOUs. How can we say for certain what is true and what is false *in a world that no longer recognizes the distinction*?"

Frank looked over his shoulder at Alex, who prodded him along with a finger. "Does this guy ever stop spewing bullshit?"

Alex remained unmoved, but the man in charge grinned. "Glad to have you back in the game, Moffat."

Frank turned to Linda. "He's literally fucking insane."

The man chuckled. He thumbed a button on the desk, and the cedar panels under the stairs slid back to reveal an elevator car. Noting their astonishment, he gave Frank a wink. "You asked before about that elevator?"

The man stepped in. Alex pushed Frank ahead, and Frank staggered into the car. Linda shuffled in behind him. The concierge/orderly entered the elevator and thumbed "B1." There were two other buttons: a second basement level and "G" for ground.

The elevator doors slid shut, and it began to move.

It seemed to drop for a very long time before "G" changed to "B1" on the floor indicator above their heads. The bell dinged, and the doors slid open on a large room with white walls, too-bright track lighting, and cafeteria-style tables. Three male orderlies stood huddled in one corner near an observation window where a woman studied security monitors. Linda couldn't make out who the woman was or the orderlies from the distance. Several people shuffled about aimlessly or played games at tables on their own, dressed in white hospital gowns.

Maybe they'll let us out of these straightjackets at least, Linda thought. The idea of being kept prisoner here for who knew how long wasn't appealing, straightjacket or not, but it would be a relief to get changed out of her soiled shorts and underwear at least.

The air down here smelled like recycled farts to Frank. He noted the TV on a mount beyond the games tables, where Jack Nicholson, playing rebel without a cause Randall McMurphy, strangled Nurse Ratched while the other patients gawked.

"Ha," Frank barked.

Linda raised an eyebrow in his direction.

"This whole goddamn place is insane," Frank said and laughed again.

She shook her head.

The pack of orderlies at the far end of the room broke up, and each of the men turned toward their new admissions.

"*No*," Linda breathed, terror twisting her insides. "That's not possible."

Frank saw the men's faces and staggered back a step in shock. Rebel, Colby, and Jackson gave them impassive looks from across the room. A man about the size and body type of Gitmo approached, weaving his way through the tables.

"*I shot him.*" Frank jabbed a finger toward Jackson. "We saw them die!"

The man in charge shrugged indifferently. "You saw what we wanted you to see, Mr. Moffat. Blanks and blood packs. Breakaway glass. Retractable knives. We can review the tapes after our first session if you like. Suffice to say it can all be explained in excruciating detail—" He waved a hand in a circle. "But I'm sure you'd find it all rather boring."

The large orderly who'd played the torturer nicknamed Gitmo stopped in front of them, acknowledging them with a nod.

"Take Mr. Moffat to his room please, Michael," the man in charge said. "Get him changed."

Gitmo, whose name apparently was Michael just as Sheriff Stanton had revealed, gripped Frank by the forearm and began to pull him away. Frank struggled, but the larger man pressed his fingers into the divot above his clavicle as he'd done back at the lodge, and Frank nearly went limp.

"No, wait! Linda!"

"*Frank!*"

Alex grabbed her by the shoulders as she reached for her husband.

"I have to speak with my wife." Gitmo took his other arm, dragging him farther toward the doorway. "I have to speak with *my wife*!"

"Don't make me hurt you, Mr. Moffat."

Staggering, grabbing at the wall, Linda watched Frank disappear around the corner. "Remember what I said about that shit storm, Alex?" she said over her shoulder. "It's coming for you, believe that."

Alex said nothing.

"And you, you fucking psycho." She turned her anger toward the man in charge. "What you're doing here is in violation our constitutional rights, not to mention the Geneva Convention against torture."

"Speaking of ineffectual documents," the man said with a smirk, "I do have the contracts you and your husband signed releasing my people from any and all liabilities, including accidental death."

"You can't consent to torture. That won't stand up in court."

The man shrugged. "It's true. But my team of very expensive lawyers is prepared to bury you in so much red tape you'll think you were a Christmas gift. Mrs. Moffat, I would love to go on sparring with you like this, but I really must prepare your husband for his first electroshock treatment."

He made a curtsy as he backed toward the doorway.

Linda leaped at him, but Alex kept her still. "If you touch him, I'll kill you, Kaspar! *If you touch him, I will fucking kill you!*"

"Until we meet again," the man said, and slipped around the corner.

Linda fell slack, defeated. "How can you work for that monster?" she growled.

Alex said nothing, merely pushed her forward and sat her at a table. "It's better if you don't resist, trust me."

She looked up at him balefully. "Liars say 'trust me.' I noticed you say it a lot."

He gave her a tight smile and walked away, heading for the observation window.

Once he'd gone, Linda scanned the room, looking at the other "patients." Mathias, the man who'd played the cook, ploddingly put together a puzzle at a table near the television, his large brow furrowed in concentration. A woman with long, straggly hair pulled the joker from the bottom of a house of cards, and the entire thing collapsed.

Linda spotted a man in the uncomfortable-looking sofa set up in front of the TV. She recognized him by the shape of his head and his broad shoulders.

It was Neville. *Jamal.*

She remembered Frank telling her he'd seen the man outside the cabin window while Colby tortured them, and the white gown he'd mentioned made sense now, but everything else she thought she knew had toppled like the straggly-haired woman's house of cards.

The chair screeched as she stood to head across the room.

In the far corner near the games shelf, Jackson and Colby sneered at her in unison as if they'd been rehearsing it, just waiting for her to look their way. She directed both of her middle fingers toward them and kept walking.

"Jamal," she said, standing over him now.

The dead man looked away from the television, his expression shifting from startled confusion to a weak smile. "You made it. I thought they'd killed you for sure."

"No thanks to you."

He directed her toward the off-white cushion at his side. "Have a seat."

"I'm not interested in sitting with you. I'm not here to break bread."

Jamal nodded grimly.

On the television, Jack Nicholson's character underwent electroshock treatment. Linda thought of Frank and channeled her fear and anger toward Jamal. "What you did, what you were a part of, I don't understand how anyone could do something so vile."

"Linda—"

"*Let me finish.*"

His perfect teeth clacked together.

"I don't know how big a part you played in this. I know you're just an actor. I don't know if they paid you to fuck with us or if you're being forced to do it, but I hope you're fucking ashamed of yourself."

When he saw she was finished, he spoke. "Linda, you have every right to want to hurt me. I'm sorry for what I did, and I know that's not enough. But you have to know I wouldn't have been party to this if they hadn't forced me. That's why they had my character killed. They were worried I was going to blow the whole thing. That's why they partnered me with Harriet this time, instead of Cherise." Jamal nodded toward the woman rebuilding her house of cards. "So she could keep me in line."

He glared at Jackson and Colby. "*They're always watching us*, Linda. Not just them. Her too."

He nodded toward the woman in the observation room. From this angle, Linda could see her face: it was Teri Lumley. *Harriet.* All of Linda's confusion and exhaustion caught up with her, and she flopped down on the sofa beside him.

Jamal kept his voice hushed. "The whole woods are filled with cameras. They made the ones in the room easy to spot, so you'd be looking for big ones. You'd miss the tiny ones everywhere else, even in the bathrooms. All of us are mic'd-up with earpieces the second The Method starts, so Control can steer us with script changes if things go wrong."

"What about the dogs? The bear trap?"

"They still don't know who set that trap. When Frank stepped on it, I thought they were sending Harriet and me out there to bring you back in, call it all off. Then it turns out those two were already there with the dogs." Jamal shuddered. "My acting coach always used to say never work with dogs or kids. I can't tell when those mutts of theirs are just *acting* pissed or when they're about tear out my throat."

"So everything is a lie," she said.

Jamal shook his head. "Don't get comfortable with that. *This place is real*, Linda. I've been stuck in this goddamn hellhole *three years*. It's the only real thing I know anymore." He sniffed and squinched up his face. "Did they piss on you too? That son of a bitch pissed in my face when I came here." He jabbed a finger toward Colby, who snickered along with Jackson. "I think he gets off on it."

"I think you're right," Linda said, her embarrassment long departed. "When I saw you and Alex in the hall last night, I heard you negotiating salary."

"That was part of it," Jamal said. "It starts out as minor psychological manipulation to disorient the subjects. You and Frank. Then they start in with the physical abuse." He raised the right arm of his gown, showing her a tight row of pale scars down his forearm. "It happened to me, and I've seen it happen again and again. But *this time...*" He shook his head. "I think Dr. Kaspar's drunk his own punch, if you ask me."

Linda saw the sincerity in his eyes and suddenly flashed on where she'd seen him before. "'I always use Allen's Rub on my meat,'" she said.

Jamal let out a surprised chuckle. "Excuse me?"

"That's you, isn't it? You're the Allen's Rub guy."

He feigned confusion a moment longer before sighing heavily. "Yeah, that was me. Nobody remembers me when I play Othello off-Broadway, but the Allen's Rub guy, I can't get away from."

Linda stood, separating herself from him. "The way you

sell that awful stuff like you really believe it..." She shook her head. "How can I trust you either, Jamal?"

He opened his mouth to speak but then closed it again. "I don't know how to make you trust me, Linda," he said finally. "I wouldn't trust me either if I were you."

Linda looked up at the TV screen, where the tall Native American man known throughout the film as "Chief" smashed a sink through the window of the asylum and reclaimed his freedom.

And the film faded out.

And the credits came up.

If only this was a movie, Linda thought.

Tears blurring her vision, she turned to a doorway leading to a long, dim hall lined with closed doors, wondering if she'd ever see Frank again.

If they'd ever see freedom.

If they'd ever get their happy ending.

CHAPTER 19

WE DO WHAT WE'RE TOLD

Frank sat on the edge of the uncomfortable single bed in his cell, staring at the camera above the door. He'd lost track of how long he'd been sitting there in his fresh, white hospital gown with nothing but his own anger to occupy him. It had to be at least an hour, maybe longer.

He'd heard the man called Michael lock the door behind him but had still checked it himself to be sure. He felt like a man unhinged. The orderly had told him nothing, merely pointed to the folded gown on the bed and locked him in. He didn't know what was real. Didn't know if he'd ever see Linda again.

One thing he knew beyond certainty was the reality of his injuries. Both legs burned and throbbed in steady waves, like a volcanic tide. His head felt like a thunderstorm. He focused on that pain, holding it like a life preserver. If he could retain what he knew they had done to him, they would never break his mind.

Thinking of pain, he gave his shorts on the floor a good, long look. He glanced up at the camera and knelt painfully to pick up his shorts. Blood had soaked through the fabric where Gitmo—*Michael*—had cut him with the utility knife. The cover of the green notebook still tucked inside the pocket was stained dark brown, along with splotches on several of the pages.

HK + JD = PAIN

He wasn't sure what he thought to do with it. It wasn't like he'd suddenly become fluent in German. But now that he knew the man in charge was probably not really German—let alone actually named Kaspar—Frank wondered if the contents of the notebook were code rather than language.

He flipped through the pages looking for words he might recognize, looking for a pattern.

Nothing caught his eyes immediately, aside from one name repeated over and over: Julia.

Could she be the J of HK + JD? Frank wondered.

As he looked deeper with this in mind, he found several words that were either the same in German as they were in English or had no translation:

Baby.
Student.
Trauma.
Argument.
Aggression.
Inspiration.
Experiment.
Opposition.
Rebellion.
Illusion.
Terror.
Chaos.

A story began to form in his mind. Julia was a student, pregnant with Kaspar's child. She'd suffered trauma during childbirth. Maybe she'd lost the baby. They'd argued. Arguing became aggression. Kaspar felt inspired to create his experiment. *Die Methode.* The Method. At first, this Julia woman opposed it. But Kaspar manipulated her with "illusions." (*Delusions?*) He terrorized her. She rebelled.

What happened then? Frank wondered. *What happened to Julia?*

A single word came to mind, one for which he had no German translation.

PAIN.

The lock unlatched, startling him. He slipped the notebook under the mattress as the door swung inward.

Alex stood in the hall with the set of keys in his hand. "It's time," was all he said.

Frank stayed seated.

"Please don't make me come and get you, Frank."

"Would hurting me disturb your delicate sensibilities, or are you just too tired?"

Alex's eyebrows twitched in a frown. "I'm not a sadist."

"No, you're just one of the merry pranksters. You're in it for the laughs."

"I came here to *help* people—"

"Spare me the bullshit. You're no better than Colby and Gitmo, or whatever the hell their real names are. Is *anything* you told me true?"

"Look, I didn't know what this place was when I signed up. They wanted someone with acting and stunt experience. There aren't many parts for Asian actors, so when I got a callback, I was excited. I thought this was gonna be my breakthrough role. When they told me what I'd be doing, they made it out to sound like a prank. An experiment. It hasn't exactly happened as advertised."

"So why did you stay? Why are you playing along with them if this wasn't what you signed up for?"

"Do you think I wouldn't leave if I could?" Alex gave him a look of sincerity. "Frank, they said they would *kill my mother* if I walked. They showed me *pictures* of her. *They knew her address.* If I don't play along..." He chuckled darkly. "There's no doubt in my mind they'll do what they say."

"So you're just another one of their puppets." Frank shook his head in disgust. "Who's the puppet master, really? Who is Dr. Kaspar?"

Alex peered down the hall and took a single step into the

room. He pressed a hand over his right ear and glanced up at the camera above his head, making sure he was out of sight.

"*There is no Dr. Kaspar*," he said in a hushed tone. "Sarge, Gary Hill, Dr. Kaspar—he's an actor too. I saw him at an audition once maybe five years ago, back in L.A. He doesn't remember me, I don't think..." Alex shrugged. "Maybe he does, I don't know. We haven't talked about it. I don't know if I can trust him."

Frank sank back against the wall. He wasn't sure he could trust Alex either. The man could be feeding him more bullshit, for all he knew. But keeping the man talking postponed whatever pain lay in store for him.

"How far down does this go?" he asked. "Do you have any idea who's in charge of this place?"

"It could be anyone. Harriet. Jamal. For all I know, it could be you or Linda." He seemed startled by his own thought. "This could be some *Undercover Boss* thing, keeping tabs on your employees."

"Don't be stupid. Would I step in a bear trap if I was in charge?"

Alex shrugged. "People get committed to their roles. When I first started working here, Billy—the guy who plays Colby—he swore he was a pacifist. Said being in the war had changed him. He lost his arm over there. Iraq, I think. I don't doubt something like that would mess a guy up. But violence is contagious. You experience it enough, you deal it out day after day, it just becomes a part of who you are. Now he's one of the worst of us. But that's what being here does: it *changes* you. This place . . . it screws you up and twists you around until you don't know up from down."

"*Then how do we stop this?*"

Alex blinked. "You *can't*," he said, as if it was obvious. "The Method *never ends*, Frank. It just changes shape. One day you're a prisoner, the next you're one of us. I don't even think anyone knows what this experiment is about anymore. The only thing we know for sure is that we're never getting out of here. Freedom is just a carrot on a stick. We all know that. And when you lose hope, Frank, you lose your connection to people. You lose your *humanity*. That's what happened to Billy, to Michael. It'll happen to me, and it'll happen to you too, once you've been here long enough."

"No," Frank said. "I won't give in. I won't ever be like you."

He gave Frank an ominous look. "That's what I thought too. But that was before the electroshock." Alex looked at his watch. "We'd better go before they send Michael."

"I'm not going anywhere."

"If you don't go, they'll just send Linda in your place. That's how it works, in case you haven't figured that out yet."

Given no other choice, Frank pushed himself off the bed.

Alex smiled thinly and ushered him into the hall. "The only advice I can give you is don't resist. The more you fight it, the worse it is."

Frank followed him down the hall to where Michael stood taking up an open doorway. He stepped inside, revealing the man playing Dr. Kaspar, who stood beside an exam table, fiddling with the dials and switches on several gray machines set up on a rolling cart beside the table.

"Bring him in please, Alex."

Frank shrugged Alex's hand from his shoulder and stepped in ahead of him. He noticed the restraints on the table and a mirror taking up much of the wall to his left.

"Strap him to the table."

Frank hobbled a step toward it before the men grabbed either arm and helped him along. They sat him on the table, and he lay back. The machines beeped with each of Kaspar's manipulations.

Michael strapped his right leg tightly to the table. Delicately, Alex dealt with his left, giving him a sympathetic smile that Kaspar seemed to notice and favor with a disapproving scowl.

They strapped down his hands and stepped away from the table.

Kaspar approached with a tube of lubricant and several electrodes connected by thin, gray wires to the topmost machine on the cart. He placed a liberal amount of lube on an electrode and made to attach it to Frank's head.

Frank turned away, facing the mirror.

"When will you learn your lesson, Mr. Moffat? The more you play along, the easier it will be for all of us. Your wife included."

Frank turned back, staring knife blades. "Is that what you said to Julia?"

Kaspar jerked, his eyes flashing with conflicted emotions. Then his expression hardened. "I don't know who you're talking about," he said with his jaw clenched, and placed the first cold, wet electrode on Frank's right temple. As Kaspar squirted jelly onto a second and placed it onto Frank's left temple, Frank wondered if he'd really gotten to the man or if the notebook was another manipulation.

Kaspar stepped back to admire his work. "Did you know electroconvulsive therapy, or ECT, is still used today to treat depression? Chronic pain and many other neurological ailments as well. It's quite effective, according to some data." Kaspar smiled. "Of course, during the treatment, patients are sedated, and the voltage I'll be using today far surpasses the recommended amount. But we'll start slow. Who knows? Maybe it will help you with your pain." He nodded toward Frank's legs and smiled pleasantly. "Before the treatment itself becomes intolerable."

He turned to the machine.

With his head against the dense pillow, Frank looked down his nose at Michael and Alex, who stood barring the door, muscular arms crossed over their chests.

He thought, *My body is my temple.* The random thought led to how old temples and churches once offered asylum from persecution, and he hoped the same shelter could be found inside his own head.

Kaspar twisted a dial.

Frank hadn't prepared for the jolt. He couldn't have prepared, even if he'd tried. White fire exploded at the center of his head, far more focused and a hundred times more painful than the cattle prod Michael and Colby had used on them at the cabin and worse than the electroshock obstacle that had caused them to drop out of the endurance event. His limbs seized, jerking against the restraints. His frantic mind conjured up a faint image of himself swallowing his own tongue, which obliterated in a violent, chaotic LSD trip of random memories and images and jumbled words that spilled over each other, competing for space inside his thundering head and winking out suddenly like an imploding star, when Kaspar moved the dial back, leaving him empty.

Kaspar turned to him. "Well? How was that, Mr. Moffat?"

Frank's limbs settled jerkily, and he tried to answer Kaspar's question with a sharp retort. His mouth simply opened, and a cracked breath escaped.

He turned to the mirror, thankful to at least recognize the face looking back at him as his own. But his words still wouldn't return.

The man in charge grinned. "And that was at a *low* voltage."

Frank managed to recover his thoughts. The tendons in his neck creaked as he turned to face the man playing Kaspar. "*You. Can't. Break me,*" he groaned.

"Oh no? Honestly, Mr. Moffat, you should be *thanking* me. You got exactly what you came here for. Your wife *loves you* again."

Frank looked up at the ceiling, where a florescent track light flickered and buzzed like his frantic mind. "She always loved me," he said. "She loved me so much the only choice she had was to push me away."

"Then *submit* yourself to us," Kaspar said through gritted teeth, "and Linda can go home."

His head felt like it was full of broken light bulbs when he shook it. *"I don't believe you."*

LINDA WATCHED as the woman Jamal had called Harriet stepped out from behind the observation window. Harriet's hard soles clacked as she crossed the room and approached Linda, who turned to look at the blank TV screen.

"Come with me please, Mrs. Moffat."

"Go fuck yourself, bitch."

"Do you want to see your husband or not?"

Linda looked up. The woman's black hair was pulled back in a tight bun. She held a clipboard snugly to her chest.

"Where is he?" Linda demanded.

"In the electroshock room. You can see him if you come with me."

Linda stood obediently and followed the woman to the doorway Alex had led Frank through an hour or so earlier. She briefly considered driving her fists into the back of Harriet's head like it was a volleyball, but Colby met them in the hall with a sadistic grin.

"Hey there, princess!"

Linda ignored him as they passed. He fell into step behind them.

"Have you heard of the Milgram experiment, Linda?" Harriet said over her shoulder.

"No."

The woman led Linda to a door, which she then unlocked. She stepped aside, gesturing for Linda to enter. "It was a fascinating social experiment conducted in the early '60s to test the effect authority figures had on *conscience*. Stanley Milgram wondered if the accomplices to the Holocaust could be held accountable for their actions, or if they were simply *preconditioned* by existing societal structures to follow orders regardless of consequences."

Linda moved past her into the dark room. Harriet and

Colby stepped in behind her. One of them switched on a dim light.

Colby closed the door and locked it.

To Linda's immediate right, a window took up most of the wall, under which stood a low table with a gray switchbox that had a single toggle. Beyond the window, Dr. Kaspar fiddled with dials on a machine. Alex and Gitmo stood sentry by the door.

Frank lay strapped to a hospital bed looking toward the window, electrodes on both temples. He looked beaten. Broken. His forehead and hair were sweat dampened.

Linda made a move toward the window, calling out his name.

"He won't hear you," Harriet said. "The glass is sound-proofed. He can't even *see* you in here."

Linda stepped back and watched the scene play out in the other room. Kaspar spoke, and fiddled with a dial on the gray machine. Frank turned to him, and said something that made Kaspar flinch.

Linda allowed herself a smile.

Frank wasn't broken yet. There was still a chance.

"In Milgram's experiment, participants were told to ask an unseen participant in the next room a series of questions. If he got them wrong, he would receive a shock administered by the participant. The participant was told to increase the voltage after each wrong answer. At a certain point, the man receiving the shocks would cry out in pain, warning the doctors—and the participant—about his heart condition. Most participants would hesitate at this point, but the doctor in charge would instruct them to continue. Very few refused to administer the highest voltage, despite knowing it was possible the man behind the wall would suffer a heart attack and *possibly die.*"

The woman set her clipboard on the table. "*Sixty-five percent* of participants administered four hundred and fifty volts to a man with a heart condition simply because a man with a clipboard posing as a doctor told them to."

"That was a long time ago," Linda said. "And I *know* you're not a doctor."

Harriet gave her a patient smile. "They recreated the experiment in 2009 under the same belief you've expressed, that people would be more skeptical today. More apt to question authority. *Sixty-three percent* continued to the highest voltage. Just two percent less than fifty years ago." She chuckled drily. "We do what we're told, Linda."

"I'm not going to shock my husband because you told me to."

"Of course not. We have no perceived authority to you aside from the fact that we hold the *keys to the cage*."

Linda looked at the switchbox on the table, the black cable snaking from it into the other room. "What are you saying? You'll let us go if I flick the switch?"

"Not you. Just Frank." The woman paused, letting it sink in. "Before you make your decision, I should tell you he'll receive the maximum voltage when you flick that switch. He may not survive. But if he does, he'll walk away a *free man*, believing you died to spare him."

Linda looked through the window at Frank. He spoke with Kaspar, but she couldn't hear what either of them was saying. They appeared to be arguing, but Frank didn't look like he had much fight left in him at all.

"What about me?" she asked.

"You?" Harriet's eyes twinkled with malevolent glee. "You'll become one of us, absorbed into The Method."

A LIGHT CAME on behind the mirror, and Frank saw Linda looking at the glass. Teri Lumley stood at her side, dressed in a lab coat. Colby barred the door. Frank tried to wave, forgetting his hands were strapped to the bed. He cried out her name with what little strength he had left. She was studying something on the table and didn't seem to hear.

"There's no use, Frank," Kaspar said. "She can't hear you or see you."

Frank relaxed into the springy pillow. "What do you want me to do?"

Kaspar approached the bed with a thin smile. "*Submit yourself.* Fully. Everything we ask of you, you'll do without question. Do what we say, and Linda walks away from here believing you died during the electroshock. Say no, and we'll make it so the two of you no longer exist. Believe me, Frank. We can do that."

Frank believed him. It was the only thing the man had ever said that Frank truly believed. He wasn't sure if they would let Linda go as promised. But he knew that if he refused, *the two of them would disappear.*

He turned to Linda, and for a moment, it seemed like she caught his eye. He supposed she must have been looking at something in the mirror as her gaze fell away, back to the small gray box on the table.

"Fine," he said. "I'll do whatever you want, just let Linda go."

"That's good, Frank. That's *very* good." His cold, blue eyes twinkled. "Here's what we want you to do."

"WILL YOU DO IT, Linda? Would you risk his life to save it?"

Linda hesitated only a moment.

Then she reached for the switchbox.

"ALL YOU HAVE to do is say you no longer love her." Kaspar's voice reached the point of ecstasy. "Say it while looking into her eyes... and she'll go free."

Frank turned to the one-way glass.

THEIR EYES MET through the window.

Almost like he can see me, she thought.

Frank thought the same.

So much pain and suffering. So much terror and exhaustion. All of it solved with one simple yet frightening act.

"I don't love her anymore," Frank said.

"*Do it now*, Linda," Harriet hissed at her side.

"To *her*, Frank," Kaspar demanded. "Not to me."

Frank's voice boomed over the intercom in the same moment Linda flicked the switch: "*I don't love you anymore!*"

Then his entire body began seizing on the bed, held in place by the straps at his wrists and ankles. His head rose from the pillow, tendons stretched, eyes squeezed shut in agony.

Frank saw her surprise and knew they'd let her hear him, that his last words to her before she left him behind were *I don't love you*. He had little more than a moment to process this before the electrical storm erupted in his head, and all of his guilt, fear, anger, everything vanished, replaced by a single sustained image of pure white agony.

Frank's torture chamber darkened. The glass between them became a mirror, and Linda stood looking at herself, immobilized by guilt, confusion, and fear. In what could have been the last seconds of Frank's life, he had seen her throw the switch on the machine that killed him. If he survived, he would leave her behind believing she'd tried to kill him because of what he'd said.

After everything they'd done to break them, she'd ended up breaking them both herself.

Linda dropped to her knees, laid her head in her hands, and wept.

CHAPTER 20

CLOSURE

They let her shower. The hot running water felt good on her skin, but she couldn't enjoy it knowing Frank was gone. She was glad they'd told her though, glad they hadn't hidden his death from her, leaving her to wonder if he was still alive, glad they hadn't told her he was out there in the world without her, only for her to find out later it had been a lie.

Hot water washed away layers of dirt, blood, and piss, but her tears kept flowing long after she'd gingerly toweled herself off, careful to avoid the angry burn above her breast, the slash on her arm, and the large lump over her eye. Her thigh muscles felt like she'd run a marathon without stretching. Her arms were so sore she could barely hold the towel above her head long enough to get her hair halfway dry.

They made him say that, she told herself. *Tricked him somehow. I know he loves me*—loved *me.*

Thinking about him in the past tense made her heart feel hollowed out. It would take time to heal. Physical injuries were the least of her worries. The psychic ones hurt far worse.

Once she'd changed back into the fresh shirt and loose-fitting pants they'd retrieved from her luggage, she sat on the uncomfortable bed in her sterile, otherwise empty room and stared at the camera above the door.

The lock unlatched. The door swung inward.

Alex stood in the hall with a tight smile. "I'm sorry for your loss, Linda. You might be glad to know that Control decided the least they could do was let you go, after what happened."

Linda barked a bitter laugh. "How magnanimous of them."

"I really am sorry."

"Sorry's not going to bring my husband back, is it?"

Alex hung his head.

She stood and looked around the small, featureless room with a sneer. "What makes 'Control' think I won't tell everyone what happened here? What makes them think they can keep this place a secret anymore?"

He gave her a sympathetic look. "You think you're the first person to ask that? You wrote your next of kin's addresses on your contracts, Mrs. Moffat. They'll be watching you out there. If you tell anything to anyone, they will not hesitate to murder your father, Frank's father, or any one of your friends or family. I know you don't talk to your mother anymore, but I'm sure you'd regret it if you found out they killed her because you couldn't keep a secret. Trust me: *you do not want to challenge these people.*"

Despite all of his lies, she had no reason to doubt the veracity of this. She'd seen what they were capable of and what they'd been able to cover up.

"Even if you did tell, what would be the point? Like you said, it won't bring Frank back."

Linda balled her hands into fists. "People would be *held accountable*. They'd burn this fucking awful place to the ground with all of you in it if we're lucky. And I wouldn't *piss* on it to put it out."

Alex lowered his head and stepped out of the room. "I'll take you upstairs when you're ready."

"Lead the fucking way," she said.

The games room stood empty when she entered behind him. No Harriet behind the observation window, all the monitors turned off. No one sitting on the sofa watching the blank TV on its mount. No one stacking up cards or piecing puzzles together.

The Method was finished.

At least for Linda and Frank.

She assumed sometime in the very near future, maybe as soon as next weekend, another couple would step in through the lodge's front doors brimming with hope, filled with thoughts of reigniting lost love.

The poor bastards, she thought.

In the elevator, Alex hummed something that made her skin crawl.

"What's that song? Why are you humming that?"

"Huh? Oh, um...I'm not sure. I guess I must have heard it somewhere."

She eyed him as the elevator dinged and the doors slid open. He waited for her to step out into the main foyer. The large room was equally as empty as below, everything in its right place.

Reset.

As though she and Frank had never been here.

A strange urge overcame her as she looked up the stairs toward the loft, and the cedar panels slid back into place. "I want Frank's luggage. I want to bring it home with me. Where it belongs."

"I'm afraid that's not possible. It's been incinerated."

"You people have everything covered, don't you? Well, how am I going to explain what happened to Frank? Or did you forget about that?"

"You were in a car crash. That's why you have so many injuries."

"A car crash. You've probably got the hospital records and police reports all ready to go." She chuckled bitterly, remembering Trevor and Dillon's motorcycle accident story. "I still don't understand why our friends would tell us to come here."

"You'd be surprised what a parent would do to protect their child."

Linda remembered the way Trevor's expression had darkened before he'd revealed what had brought them together, before Dillon had practically forced him to recommend coming here, to Lone Loon Lodge, to experience The Method for themselves. She wondered if she might have done the same under similar circumstances. If they'd threatened Frank's life, had he survived, would she recommend The Method to their friends?

"Anyway," Alex was saying. "I don't think they would have given your friends much of a choice."

"*They*." Linda spat the word. "You still act like you're not as guilty as the rest of them. You were just following orders. *We do what we're told*, right?"

"I'm protecting the people I love, just like you did."

"*By hurting others?* Does that make it sit right with you? For all you know, the family you're protecting is already dead."

His eyes went wide.

Linda's laugh was full of venom. "You've never even considered that, have you? That *they* could still be pulling the wool over your eyes after all these years?"

Alex opened his mouth to reply. Closed it.

She was surprised by how much satisfaction the look on his face gave her.

"I'll show myself out, thanks."

And she did.

FRANK AWOKE STRUGGLING against the straps and nearly ended up punching himself in the face. For a frantic few minutes, he couldn't remember where he was or how he'd come to be in this cramped room with white walls. Then he felt the dull aches in his left calf from the trap and right thigh from the screwdriver, the soreness in his face from multiple punches, the slash on his left thigh, his fingers crushed against the kitchen tile, the bruises and scratches on the sole of his left foot, the burns on his temples.

So much for electroshock pain therapy, he thought, and when he laughed, his head hurt.

Slowly, he rose from the uncomfortable bed and looked around his dismal cell. The walls blank, the mattress stripped down to a white sheet. They'd put a cast on his leg, bandages elsewhere, and dressed him in fresh clothes from his luggage, a clean t-shirt and shorts.

The camera above the door buzzed as it focused. He gave it the finger.

Linda was probably long gone by now. He still found it hard to believe she'd actually flicked the switch that caused the last burst of electroshock to knock him unconscious, but he supposed they'd somehow manipulated her into doing it. He hadn't seen malice in her eyes. She had looked terrified.

At least until she'd heard him say it.

I don't love you anymore.

After that, she'd looked surprised. He supposed hurt might have come next, but by then, the shock had already hit him, and everything that had happened since was lost.

The door unlocked and swung inward.

Alex pushed a folding wheelchair in. "Good news. Control has decided to let you go in light of what happened to Linda."

Frank sat up, wincing as a bolt of pain shot up his leg. "What happened to Linda?"

"Oh." Alex looked annoyed and sighed. "I thought someone would have told you by now."

"*Told me what, goddammit!*"

The man gave him a sympathetic smile. "Linda took her own life."

Frank fell against the wall. The back of his head struck the tile, and he cried out in pain. "Linda wouldn't do that," he said, rubbing his new injury.

"I am truly sorry, Frank. I don't know what to tell you."

"When?"

"What?"

"*When did it happen?*"

"Right after your electroshock session. Dr. Kaspar thinks she must have been racked with guilt after flicking the switch on you—"

"Oh *Dr. Kaspar* thinks that, does he? You mean after you *made* her flick the switch. Why would she feel guilty? What did you people *tell her*?"

"We told her you'd died." Alex seemed to think this was obvious. "Just like Kaspar said we would."

Frank ran his hands through his hair, fighting the urge to stagger out of bed and choke the man to death in front of the camera. It would certainly be a triumphant ending, bringing things around full circle, giving him a sense of closure.

"It wasn't supposed to happen," Alex was saying. "We take precautionary measures to prevent...things like this from happening. But I guess she found a loose screw on her bed and used it to slash her throat. By the time we saw her on the monitors—"

"*Please stop talking.*" Frank needed to think. Thinking required silence. He just couldn't take what this man said at face value when he'd lied to his face so often. "That doesn't make sense. Linda wouldn't *do* that."

"You never can know how people will react under extreme duress."

"I do. I *do* know. Linda wouldn't kill herself. If she really is dead, it's because you people killed her and you're trying to cover it up."

Alex's jaw tightened. "Regardless of what you believe, they've decided to let you leave."

"*Who* decided? Who's *they*?"

The man shook his head. "You know I don't know that," he said, and spread open the wheelchair.

Frank pushed himself to his feet. "I don't need your fucking wheelchair."

"I'm just trying to make your checkout as comfortable as possible."

Frank hobbled over to him. "I'll be sure to leave you a good review." He pushed the wheelchair aside angrily and limped out into the hall, one hand on the wall to help himself along.

Alex's shoes squeaked behind him. "There are a lot of support groups for grieving widowers—"

"You think I buy that bullshit *my husband's dead* story of yours? I'm starting to doubt if you really even are Asian."

Alex laughed awkwardly.

"How about you take your advice, and your stories, and shove those little factoids up your ass?"

Nobody was around in the games room. Everything looked neat and tidied. He thumbed the elevator button, but it did nothing. Alex sidled up to him and used his card key. The doors slid open and Frank stepped in.

They rose to the ground level in silence.

The lobby was just as dead as downstairs. It was still dark out, but the first orange rays of dawn glimmered through the large windows.

Frank hobbled to the front doors.

"I don't think I have to tell you it would be against your better judgment to talk about this place with anyone."

"No word-of-mouth marketing, huh?" Frank opened the door and leaned against it. "That's not a very good way to run a business, Alex."

"It's just that it would be very detrimental to your family and friends if you do."

Frank rolled his eyes. "Yeah, yeah. I get it. Shadowy organization watching my every move. If I hadn't figured that out by now, I'd have to be pretty damn dense."

He staggered out onto the porch and down the steps, out across the grass and around to the side of the building.

Their car was gone, but the Escalade was still parked where it had been.

Through the tinted windshield, he saw a woman hunched over in the driver's seat, obviously searching for something on the floor or in the glove box. She sat up suddenly, and Frank's heart literally skipped a beat.

It was Linda. She was *alive*.

Linda wore a similar look of astonishment and struggled to push the door open. "Frank?"

"Lin!"

He limped over to her, and she met him halfway. They hugged each other so tightly that their backs cracked, and she reared back to look at him, unable to believe her eyes.

"They told me you were dead," they both said, and laughed at the coincidence.

"What now?" they both said.

"Now?" Linda kissed him excitedly on the lips. Despite the pain, he kissed her back. "Let's go home," she said.

"Home." Frank nodded. "I think that plan's to die for."

Linda grinned and smacked his shoulder.

"Ow! Careful!" He winked. "I'm fragile."

"Oh, my fragile little flower." She kissed him on the cheek and headed for the car.

Frank wrenched the passenger seat back and hauled himself into it.

"I can't find the keys," Linda said. "I've checked everywhere."

Frank lowered the sun visor. The keys fell into her lap.

"Aha!" She turned them in the ignition, and the radio came on. As she turned the car around and headed for the road, she realized it was the same song Alex had hummed in the elevator, Willie Nelson's version of "You Always Hurt the Ones You Love."

Frank turned off the radio. "I hate that song."

"So do I."

A smile crept onto her face. She laid her hand palm up

on the transmission and glanced at her husband. Frank smiled back and slipped his hand into his wife's.

As the trees parted along the highway, Linda and Frank Moffat drove off hand in hand into the sunrise, the future uncertain, but it was *theirs*.

CHAPTER 21

THE METHOD

(ALTERNATE ENDING)

Frank and Linda sat alone in a bench seat at the back of the casual yet chic restaurant. It was several weeks later, and they still looked worse for wear. Like they'd been through hell and back. A cane leaned against the seat beside Frank.

They didn't speak, both of them somewhat nervous about the meeting ahead. They sipped their drinks, trying not to drink too fast or too much. When the server came by to ask if they were ready to order, both immediately shook their heads and thanked her, eager for her to leave. Their eyes never left the entrance.

After a moment, Frank spotted their friends and lifted the cane in greeting. Two casually dressed men, one in his thirties, the other just turned fifty, spotted them and waved back.

"You ready?" Frank said, patting Linda's hand.

She gave him a flat smile. "What happens if I'm not?"

Frank turned to her. He didn't need to tell her. They both knew what would happen. If they failed, they'd be trapped in The Method forever, like Alex and the others.

They had to do this right. This needed to work.

They both smiled and stood, Frank a little shakily on his healing leg, to greet their old friends.

HALF AN HOUR LATER, all four of them were a few drinks deep, and both couples had settled into the booth side by side. Frank draped an arm over Linda's shoulders. All four laughed at Frank's joke, which wasn't all that funny.

It was clear Glenn and Shawn weren't as comfortable as the last time they'd seen each other, when Frank and Linda weren't as close as they were now, shortly after she'd sprung back from chemo. Glenn had already told Linda over the phone he and Shawn had been having problems. Not terrible, but enough that it concerned him. Enough to make him worry it could grow into something worse. Frank could see it. It was noticeable in little things, like the way they smiled at each other's jokes instead of laughing, or drifted off as the other told a story they'd likely heard a dozen times before.

"No really," Frank said. "It was a life-changing experience. Wasn't it, Lin?"

Linda hesitated. Everyone looked at her expectantly. Frank, especially. Everything rode on this dinner.

Everything.

"It was," she agreed finally, with a genuine smile. "It really was."

"That's terrific," said Glenn, the younger of the couple. "The Method, huh?"

He shared a long look with Shawn, his husband of the past four years, considering it. Finally, Shawn placed his left hand on Glenn's, their rings clinking softly.

A silence drew out as the other couple looked at each other, each prodding the other with their eyes to ask the question that was obviously on their minds. "So I have to ask..." Shawn said finally. "Where did you guys get all those bruises?"

"Car accident," both Frank and Linda answered in unison, while under the table, they clasped hands.

"Well, we're glad you both survived," the younger man said. His husband agreed with an enthusiastic nod.

"So are we," Frank said. He picked up a piece of tuna from one of the many plates set before them. "This tapas is to die for, isn't it?"

Linda did the same, plopping it in her mouth. "It really is."

Everyone laughed amiably.

Afterword

With *The Method*, I set out to write a mindfuck of a thriller with a handful of shocking scenes of violence, and I feel like it turned out pretty much as I'd intended (aside from the entirely happy ending, which I'd decided while adapting it into a screenplay was a little too *nice* and *wrapped up*, considering all that The Method was—hence the "alternate ending" you find in this edition).

In the seventh grade, we had to read Richard Connell's short story, "The Most Dangerous Game," for an assignment, and I immediately became obsessed with the idea and all of its many possibilities. (I watched *Surviving the Game* a few years later, the action-thriller loosely based on the story, starring Ice-T, Rutger Hauer and Gary Busey, and while I enjoyed it, I felt like it didn't really add much to the original concept to make it all that noteworthy.) Add to that my interest in the Milgram and Stanford Prison experiments, my love of the David Fincher film *The Game*, as well as the notion that people often tend to come together in a crisis, and I felt like I had a pretty solid foundation for a book that would hold my attention for a little while. I sold it to myself as "The Most Dangerous Game" meets marriage counseling.

I'd always been skeptical when I heard the writer of *Forrest Gump* said he'd written the book in six weeks, but I burned through the first draft of *The Method* in a month, and the two books are about the same length. (I suppose you could make an argument that the quality differs. I haven't read *Gump*, only seen the film.) Not much changed from that first draft to the final, aside from some phrasings and typographical errors. What you've read is pretty much *as is*. I wrote it with the intention of entering it into the Kindle Scout contest at the end of the month, as a challenge to myself. Considering the fact that I ended up winning a contract, which included an advance for an amount unheard of for me at the time, I'd say I rose to that challenge.

This book was a ton of fun to write and I think I put just enough message in it to make it... not quite *important* but at least meaningful in some small way. Yet interestingly enough it's the only one of my books—at the time of this writing—to be optioned. The script—written by a psychologist/screenwriter—is terrific, and even though I know the movie business and Hollywood in general is notoriously fickle, I'm hopeful it will be greenlit in the near future.

I hope you've enjoyed reading it, and that someday soon you'll be able to enjoy a film adaptation as well.

I need to thank a bunch of people for their help and encouragement during the writing "process," the Kindle Scout campaign, and beyond. First, as always, thanks to my wife for her gentle nudges—which may or may not have involved "gentle" death threats—to get this bugger finished and out into the world. Thanks to my mom, who is always eager to read everything I write, even the stuff she probably shouldn't. Thanks to fellow writers, readers and others in the horror community. Special thanks to James Newman for reading the first physical copy and providing the 1st edition with an excellent blurb.

If you're inclined you can reach me directly on Facebook

and Instagram, and follow me on Amazon and Bookbub. And if you've enjoyed this book, you may also enjoy the pitch-black thriller *Where the Monsters Live*, available absolutely FREE with 9 other short stories when you sign up to my newsletter at www.DuncanRalston.com.

About the Author

Author of the cult smash-hit *Woom* and *Ghostland* and more than 15 other books that aren't the cult smash-hit *Woom* or *Ghostland*. His debut collection was blurbed positively by the legendary Jack Ketchum. His novel, *Pedo Island Bloodbath*, was nominated for a 2024 Splatterpunk Award for Best Novel.

For 10 *free* dark fiction short stories/novellas including the prequel to *GHOSTLAND*, "The Moving House," signed copies of Woom, bookplates and merch, please visit www.duncanralston.com.

For more delicious dark fiction, please visit
www.duncanralston.com and
www.shadowworkpublishing.com.